Fighting Fifty, Hot Flushes and Nose Hair

ELAINE NAYLOR

The Choir Press

This book is a work of fiction.
Names, characters, businesses, places and incidents are products of the
author's imagination or are used fictitiously. Any resemblance to actual
events or locals or persons, living or dead, is entirely coincidental.

ISBN 978-1-909300-12-5

First published in the United Kingdom in 2013
by The Choir Press

Contents

Acknowledgments

In school when the teacher would chalk up a topic on the blackboard and tell us to write a story, I would gaze out of the classroom window searching for inspiration to spark my young mind. When my imaginings were eventually unleashed I would scribble feverishly; my pen unable to capture fast enough the adventure that developed in my head.

It was fourteen years ago when I gave serious thought to writing a book. I didn't know where to start so I went to night school and studied creative writing. That was when I wrote my first Anita Richardson heartbreak tale. When the course ended I attempted to develop my stories but I never got that spark of inspiration so my book remained unfinished.

Six years ago as I mourned the death of my parents I struggled to cope with the surge of emotions that accompanied the loneliness. It was the solace I found in writing that helped me make sense of the depression and rekindled my aspiration to write a novel. I tinkered with a few ideas; but they ran out substance a few chapters along. It wasn't until my irrational fears of turning 50 were introduced to my premenopausal symptoms that it sparked a mid-life meltdown drama to form in my mind. Like watching the promotional trailer for a new TV show I could see the possibilities unfold. Excited and highly motivated it seemed only fitting to revive my Anita Richardson character and morph her into the middle aged woman I envisioned fighting fifty.

I took a number of workshops and as I honed my writing skills the pages quickly filled with words. I enjoyed testing random plots and scenarios to see how they played out. The year it took me to draft the story was the enjoyable part, the disheartenment came over the eighteen months that followed as I realised the enormity of work required to craft the story into a novel. When I spent weeks re-writing a chapter only to delete it and start over or when I read my opening chapter for what seemed like the millionth time because I couldn't figure out why it didn't feel right, I understood why so many people had unfinished manuscripts gathering dust in a cupboard. When my enthusiasm waned I looked set to join the many writers with an unfulfilled ambition and that is where the people I want to thank came in.

I am so lucky to be surrounded by friends and work colleagues who listened to me prattle on relentlessly when I needed a sounding board, especially my ten o'clock tea break companions whose reassuring words helped to keep me motivated and Melanie my writing buddy who is a constant source of encouragement.

I want to give individual thanks to four amazingly wonderful women, Trish, Jill, Cheryl and Lorraine who joined me on this journey as they repeatedly read early drafts of my first chapters and offered feedback. When I felt daunted by the task ahead and my confidence diminished each of these women offered praise, support, and endless hugs as they encouraged me to see it through.

Then there is my husband Kevin who never gets the credit or acknowledgement he deserves for supporting me in all my ventures over the last 30 years. I found Kevin an invaluable source of gambling knowledge as I developed my Casino Carl character and when he offer a man's perspective as I struggled with the mind-set of a male mid-life crisis.

Lastly I give thanks to my family. My brother David and the two most important people from my life who will never get to read my book, my late father Ray, who encouraged me to be independent and not conform to other people's ideas. His only insistence was that I should experience life outside of my home town and see the world; this ignited my wanderlust and has not only led to many wonderful holidays but brought me here into the lives of the people whose friendship I cherish. For these reasons and every selfless thing my father did because he loved me I thank him. And to my late mother and best friend Greta, whose exceptional flair and imagination showed me how to dream. Until recently I never truly appreciated what a unique and delightful woman she was. When she struggled through her own menopause I chastised her, I'd been too immature to understand. Well mother you got the last laugh because I certainly understand now.

Thank you all for your love and support, as without it I would not have found the courage to actually publish my work.

Prologue

Tucked up in bed with Tiny Tears and Teddy, Anita Richardson closed her eyes to concentrate as her mother's gentle voice narrated the story of Snow White from the oversized book of bedtime tales. As Anita drifted to sleep she feared the horrible queen, promised herself she wouldn't eat an apple, then dreamt of the day a prince would be so enchanted with her beauty, he'd fall in love with her. Had Anita's mother mentioned any of the seven menopausal dwarfs, Itchy, Bitchy, Bloaty, Sleepy, Sweaty, Forgetful or Psycho, then revised the tale to warn how they would sneak up to invade Anita's body with random attacks, to drive Anita to the brink of insanity or at the least into a perpetual state of mild oddness, Anita may never have slept again.

Like every good fairy tale this began once upon a time on a hot day in August, when Anita's father stood her on the window ledge to show her the Wendy house he'd spent hours building. She grabbed Teddy and Tiny Tears and ran into the garden chatting of the adventures they would have. The next day when she sat in her canvas bubble her restlessness stirred; she complained, 'I'm bored, Teddy, I want to fly away.'

The March winds echoed her personal howls of grief for the second chapter of Anita's tale. As a mature woman she held the hand of her father, who lay in a hospital bed, paralysed, blind and hooked up to a machine. Although her father showed no signs he could hear, Anita reminded him of the insurmountable reasons she loved him more than anyone else in the world. When she reminisced about the happy times they'd shared she recalled her father's fiftieth birthday.

'Do you remember, Dad? Mum waited until she heard you snoring, then we snuck down to hang a birthday banner across the chimney breast. I sellotaped the balloons above the door as our tiger was just a kitten and wanted to play with the ones on the floor.' The serenity of her father's face encouraged Anita to continue. 'Then we spread presents in front of your chair.'

Her father's age-withered body substituted for the man who'd been excited as a child as he shook each package to guess what hid inside. When he'd ripped open the wrapper, regardless of whether he unveiled a tub of sweets or a pair of socks, he'd smile as if his family had given him the one gift he wanted.

Anita giggled like she had that day. 'Do you remember Lassie licked the chocolate liquors when you left the lid off the box?'

When she thought her father smiled tears rolled from her eyes.

As Anita held her father's palm against her flushed cheek he exhaled his final breath. She wept with the realisation that at the end, only a soulless shell remained of the man she'd loved, admired and respected. Twenty-three years had passed since his fiftieth birthday and other than retirement she couldn't recall any further milestone in his life. The sadness turned to trepidation when she considered the possibility that her fifties could be a prelude to death. She blamed her irrational fears on the metric system that equated fifty with half; by that logic she calculated a life expectancy of a hundred. Gloom and doom overwhelmed her. Anita had enough money to survive until her mid-fifties; if her lifespan earned a telegram from the monarch, financially she'd be screwed.

Her mind scrolled through a rapid list of questions. Could she live on a state pension? Would a state pension exist? As her mental and physical health deteriorated, who'd take care of her? What standard of care could she expect from a diminished health service? (Anita recalled the vision of her father left on a gurney for two days in a hospital corridor because they had no beds available on the ward.) Had she left it too late to have children? What age would she die? What if she had one year left to live? Would she stay with Carl or divorce him? That night Anita initiated her 'fighting fifty' plans. She used the to-do list to face her own mortality or at the least maintain the illusion of control.

Anita mourned her father's death with self-indulgent material whims. She embraced her independence further. If Carl found himself too busy to join her on holiday, she went alone. Short of cash, she applied for a loan or charged the purchase to any one of her credit cards.

The penultimate chapter of Anita's story began six years later when the doctor diagnosed her mother's lung cancer as terminal.

For their last coherent conversation, her mother squeezed the hand of her only daughter. 'Oh lovie, I thought I had more time; don't let your dreams slip away.'

Anita recalled how her mother hadn't been the same person since the onset of an early menopause had changed her. Imprisoned by a nervous disposition, she had lost her fun outlook to depression despite the multitude of drugs the doctor had prescribed. When she had expressed regret for unfulfilled dreams or struggled to put into words how she yearned for something different, Anita, too immature to understand, had chastised her mother to instigate a change rather than grumble.

As she cradled her mother's frail listless body Anita assessed her own yearnings for something different. She wanted to be single but liked the security of a husband; she felt blessed to have married a good man. Although her heart ached to nurture she liked the freedom no children afforded her. Anita wanted financial security but spent without conscience. Her mother's four-month death sentence stirred up a restlessness to find the prince so captivated by her beauty he'd love her for eternity.

Although the cynic in Anita blamed TV, which brainwashed women like her with the romantic genre, her mother's words forced Anita to consider the possibility that her fifties could be a prelude to a happy ending. She took her to-do list to add the one experience her heart yearned for: to find the 'happily ever after' found on the last pages of a fairy tale.

The same year Anita buried her mother her optimism shone with the sun's warm glow as she headed to an interview with Mr Ryan Conner, executive manager of Western Elite Engineering Project Solutions, more commonly known as the WEEPS division. There she allowed herself to believe she'd met the prince, so captivated with her beauty he'd love her for eternity, the first time she looked into Elliot Parker's eyes. Although she couldn't have realised the scent of lime basil and mandarin masked the villain who'd assassinate her heart, at her age Anita should have realise how the pain of grief forces you down an emotional road you wouldn't normally travel.

Three years, seven months and eight days later, as they strolled back to the hotel at the end of a late business dinner, Elliot hustled Anita into an empty bus shelter to shield them from an unpredicted storm. Under the influence of alcohol, Elliot loosened his tie, unbuttoned his shirt, then offered her the use of his neck to explore the aroma of his skin and guess which body wash he'd used. As Anita leaned into his torso a television programme came to mind, in which the host, Dr Love, divulged the techniques to locate the male erogenous zones: guaranteed to create an instant arousal in your mate. Anita used the tip of her nose to skim the warm flesh of his neck. In between kisses from her moistened lips his shallow gasps synchronised with hers. That night outside her hotel bedroom, she understood the contradictions that wrestled her mother's conscience when a strict upbringing, the moral dilemma and fear of the consequences forced Anita to decline Elliot's invitation for an adulterous end to the night.

For the final chapter of Anita's tale almost forty-four years had passed since she had sat in her Wendy house, yet her restless spirit still yearned to fly away. A course in cognitive dissonance helped her accept the eccentricities passed down through her DNA. Months of therapy entwined with hours of self-analysis helped her summon the strength to embrace how her dreams, regardless of how impossible they seemed, nurtured the essence of her spirit. She accepted that without them, like a flower that hadn't been kissed by the sun, she would wither and die. Although had she recognised happiness was merely an illusion she may have guarded her heart against what the cruel hand of fate had in store for her.

Three weeks ahead of her fiftieth birthday, as Anita examined her reflection in the vanity mirror, she updated her to-do list to concentrate on her looks. She read her plan aloud to Teddy and Tiny Tears, her aged childhood friends, bound together in a protective sheet of dust-covered polythene on top of the wardrobe.

'Step up my anti-aging campaign. Book long weekends at the spa.' Anita checked her hairline in the mirror. 'Shorten the time between visits to the hairdresser's.' Anita took her tweezers to remove the coarse hairs that sprouted from her chin. She looked down at her short skirt. 'Buy sensible clothes but avoid the antwacky look.' Anita glanced down again. 'Nah, save that for your sixties.'

As she sellotaped the page to the side of the wardrobe, the to-do list no longer served as a catalogue of her fears. Each item became a part of her master plan in fighting fifty, hot flushes and nose hair.

Today, as she sat alone in her office, Anita's late father's words echoed in her mind. *'Just because you chase rainbows doesn't mean you'll find a pot of gold.'*

The Eruption

Rain splattered cat-paw images against the office window as Anita willed Elliot Parker to look in her direction; instead he pulled up the collar on his Ashby waxed jacket, plunged both hands deep into his trouser pockets and hurried across the gravel car park. Anguish oozed as apprehension of their meeting in eleven minutes kept her anxiety levels high. Instinct forced the fingers that massaged her temple to squeeze the flesh above her right eye. Stormy weather often provoked a headache. Trepidation generally prompted Anita to pinch her eyebrow, a 'tell' her husband Carl had come to recognise over the last thirty years. He often said 'the pinch' warned him to get the hell out of her way.

The pulse of the office clock that vibrated from the top of the large grey metal cabinet became louder to count down the seven minutes until her meeting. As Anita applied a second coat of the aptly named 'Keep Blushing' ColorStay lipstick she stepped into the mist of Gucci Envy perfume she'd sprayed into the air. She checked her reflection in the PC monitor; to remind Elliot of what he'd discarded with ease, she undid an extra button, not that her cleavage needed enhancement. With three minutes to spare Anita picked up the bright red contract file and left the office.

As Anita composed herself outside the ground floor of the weather-corroded modular office, the air chilled and the sky darkened. The openness of the sidings offered no shelter from the intense unpredictable winds that churned the swirls of grey clouds. Too short to see through the drizzle on the entrance door window, Anita teetered on her three-inch heels. She stretched to peer past the organogram display board. The prominent header incorporated the division's colours. Bold purple text labelled a colour headshot, framed within a thick turquoise border; listed against her photo for the upper tier of the annex opposite, *Anita Richardson, Senior Contract Manager*. Against the last desk within the lower tier of this building: *Elliot Parker, Decommissioning Projects Manager*.

As a gust blew wisps of recently-dyed auburn hair into her mouth Anita used one hand to keep her weather-ravaged tresses at bay. Her other hand slipped off the still-wet door handle as a second flurry forced the aluminium door to slam against the metal handrail. This contributed to a dramatic entrance. Everyone turned to look; everyone except him.

As Anita hurried inside the smell of burnt toast filled the air. Alan Turpin, the project planner, emerged from the back of the partitioned cabin. Steam rose from the coffee cup clutched in Alan's hand. He extracted the slice of toast wedged between his teeth, chewed, swallowed, then used his tongue to lick the big clump of butter from the corner of his mouth.

He nodded as he mumbled, 'I should have guessed it'd be you.'

Anita's eyes widened as they halted at the familiar sight of Elliot's torso, hidden beneath the crisp cotton shirt that had been her favourite. The colour brought to mind the sexy azure dress that hung unworn in her closet. As Anita stalked her prey, Pike, who hadn't been called by his real name since the guys in the office had recognised the college graduate's uncanny resemblance to the *Dad's Army* character, looked up from his PC and smiled. Henry Taylor, the office self-proclaimed relationship expert, glanced towards Elliot, then turned to face Anita and shook his head. Her fiery temper had been witnessed on more than one occasion; the severe look on her face as she homed in on her target brought smiles with occasional sniggers as the team waited for the showdown. Anita hesitated two feet short of Elliot's desk, dropped her contract file on the floor, then wheeled a chair from the empty desk behind him to sit at his side.

Conscious that anxiety or anger manifested a cringeworthy Scouse twang that, when mixed with her normal woollyback dialect, ladled her common accent with an aggressive tone, she spoke with a softer voice. 'Elliot! I've anticipated your response for days; we must re-evaluate the contractors' erroneous submissions. I need the bit you said you'd finished.'

With the gentle hum of the air conditioner for company Anita watched her adversary use one swift motion to wipe the toast crumbs off his desk and into the plastic bin at her feet. Stimulated by the scent of lime basil with mandarin, Anita snatched her file from the floor to suppress her desire to smell his neck and nibble his lobe. Months earlier, sitting this close, she'd have feared her lust-inflamed heart might explode from the cavity of her chest. As Anita raised her head the empty stare from Elliot's feral green eyes forced the thump of her heart to match the tempo of the tears that prickled her eyes. Perspiration tickled the top of her lip. As Anita faced the reality of what she'd lost her memory savoured the taste of his last kiss on her lips.

Anita pulled out the tissues she kept tucked inside her bra strap, a habit she'd inherited from her mother who hated clothes with sleeves.

Elliot's large hands rubbed his eyes immersed within an ashen complexion. He nodded towards a stack of papers on the desk. His eyes focused on her cleavage. 'That's it. What now?'

Anita absorbed the contours of Elliot's gaunt face. 'Let's review it.'

Elliot raised his half-drunk cup of tea to swallow the last dregs. As he sighed, his thick mop of tussled hair fell forward and the fluorescent celling light highlighted the colours of conkers nestled in a field of autumn leaves. As Anita reviewed each section of the 120-page tabbed, colour-coded document Elliot's body tightened. He surveyed her through the forefinger and thumb that arched against his forehead to massage his tension as her comprehensive explanation failed to convince him of the contractual vulnerability.

Anita pointed to a statement on the tenth page. 'They state a preference to provide a supervisor for each work face? This adds thirty thou, per person, per year.' Anita hated how her Scouse accent exaggerated a word that ended in K to sound like the static from a poorly tuned radio.

Elliot concentrated on the precision of the square he was doodling on his desk pad. 'I've told them we provide the super-vision.' He put legs on his box. It looked like a table.

'That's the point; if you accept their conditions here, they can charge us.'

Elliot forced the tip into the paper. The nib snapped off his propeller pencil. 'Take it out then.' He clicked the top. A fresh nib popped up.

Anita struck two lines through the section with a red marker.

'This one,' she said: 'if they can't get access by 7.30 delays will be reimbursed by us.'

Elliot's next doodle resembled a voodoo doll. 'They've sent their generic terms 'n' conditions. They know they can't access the site earlier than nine; anyway, I won't pay.'

'Yes, but why create ambiguity?'

Anita watched Elliot draw a spear through the heart of the figure.

'Come on, you know the "Big Contract" could see someone fired.'

A series of frowns hardened the forced smile Elliot reserved for their encounters these days.

Anita inhaled, then exhaled on the count of seven. 'We've worked hard on our contracts. Why d'you wanna include these willy-nilly conditions?' Finding him unresponsive to her logic, Anita changed tactic. 'I suggest a compromise because the contract ain't going out like this.'

His dimples indented as Elliot spoke through tightened lips. 'Well, the additions look fine to me. Anyway, when do we use the contract against a company?' His fingers strummed the desk. '*We* – rather *you* – put the effort in, and for what? Tell me, seein' you're so bloody clever.'

As Anita leaned towards Elliot she watched his nostrils flare when he inhaled. Her voice quivered. 'Oh, right, that's the way you see it.'

'Tell me how many times we've gone to arbitration. Well, how many? Aye, I'll tell you: none, that's how many.' Elliot bounced back into his chair.

'Do ye think that's because *we* or rather *I* produce carefully defined contracts, aye, clever dick?' Anita continued to fight her corner. 'OK, the "Big Contract" hasn't gone to arbitration, but—'

Elliot returned to his doodles. 'Whatever. Take it out.'

Anita bit her lip, then spun her chair. The exchange of glances from their office companions, accompanied by intrigued facial expressions, spoke louder than any words.

Anita swivelled back. 'You know the loss of profit on the 'Big Contract' will affect this year's bonus.'

Elliot stabbed his pencil into the paper. 'I've said take it out, haven't I?' He clicked the silver top; another lead popped up.

Anita looked at her watch. Twenty minutes had passed. Low murmurs superseded their audience's focus on work.

Common sense dictated they take a break. Anita elected poor judgement. 'I've told you once. I won't issue a subjective contract.' Her pitch increased.

Elliot jolted from his chair. His scent lingered in the air as the backs of his legs propelled his seat backwards. The tense situation fractured as the change in his pocket smashed against the seat's plastic arm. Elliot sidestepped as the chair ricocheted off the empty desk behind him. Caught unprepared, Anita felt fear constrict her chest too late to wheel her chair from his path; her knee banged the sharp edge of the desk. She rubbed the sore spot and swivelled her chair to watch her favourite blue shirt stretched tight across his toned broad shoulders as he strode towards the door. Unsure of what triggered her reaction; hormones or the build-up of hurt, Anita snatched the 120-page document from the desk. For the second time that morning she squeezed her eyebrow.

Anita stood to yell her scorn. 'Walk off, Elliot. I'll take this pile of crap home an' do your work for you.' Anita waved the document clenched in her fist. Her mouth appeared to have paused. The action proved deceptive and her heightened frustration accompanied the increased decibels as she shrilled, '*TOSSER!*'

The slow motion of Elliot as he took two steps towards her became the focus of everyone's attention. Anita watched his head wobble as the colour drained from his face. Anita felt scared, but she couldn't help but think of the giant Pillsbury Doughboy balloon she'd seen at the Macy's Thanksgiving parade.

Elliot's eyes locked with hers. 'Yep, you do that. I don't know why you bother to ask me anything. Do what you want, but as that's the original I suggest you photocopy it first.'

The sinister pitch in Anita's voice deepened as she exhaled. Breathless she strained the words, unable to release the pressure in her chest: 'Really, the original?'

Anita's intensified temper surfaced the way molten rock explodes from a volcano. The ream of papers erupted into the air. A large section dropped towards her right leg. Instinct prompted her to kick at the bundle of papers like a striker in front of goal. With a fierce vindictive expression etched on her face she concluded her Riverdance performance with three two-footed stomps at the same tempo she used for her rant of expletives. Aloof Anita flicked back her hair; the sternness of Elliot's facial expression failed to conceal his fury. The door slammed. Anita watched her nemesis stride towards the canteen. Raw anger stifled her emotional reaction as Henry the know-all smirked. Anita stormed from the office, the remnants of her tornado left in her wake.

Fuelled with anger, Anita snuffled her hello to three labourers, huddled beneath the smokers' shelter to perform the well-practised art of rolling tobacco from a battered Old Virginia tin into a Rizla. She hurried to find sanctuary at the far end of the depot behind four coupled freight wagons that would screen her from inquisitive eyes. She'd been at the sidings long enough to know the best places to hide. During the summer her work colleague and treasured friend Donna Francis joined her here to eat lunch as they pondered life and worked on their tans in seclusion.

Donna had waited until the second summer of their friendship to tell Anita she'd applied for her decree nisi. It took four Bend Over Shirleys, two Slippery Nipples and a Screaming Orgasm cocktail for Donna to share the painful story of how she had arrived home unexpected from a Christmas party, to find her husband in the passionate throes of sex with her closest friend. Donna confided how she'd stayed in bed for days, her personal hygiene kept to a minimum when she couldn't summon the energy to change into her nightclothes. As severe depression followed the devastation of the betrayal, she refused companionship and recoiled to a depth so low she scared herself when she considered suicide. She phoned the doctor, who prescribed anti-depressants and referred her to a counsellor. Six months later empowered Donna fought to gain control of her life and her self-respect. She changed her image with a visit to the salon. Once the stylist had breathed life into Donna's limp mousy brown hair with a Cleopatra cut and raven black dye, for a twist she added plum-coloured streaks. Donna looked stunning. To complete her recovery Donna had accepted a position at the sidings.

The smell of engine diesel thickened the saliva in Anita's throat as she paced like an expectant father. She tilted her head to allow gentle drops of light rain to kiss the evidence of her shame. Both hands cradled her head. Aloud she asked the usual round of rhetorical questions: 'What the hell's wrong with you, Nita? Why can't you forget him?' She ended with her current favourite: 'Why didn't Elliot love me enough?'

Anita plonked herself on top of two concrete sleepers positioned close enough to the spiked metal fence to be used as a seat. Her moistened eyes looked past remnants of a bygone era, represented by redundant lengths of steel, discarded clips, rotten wooden sleepers and wild purple flowers barely visible amongst the ballast built up to the side of the disused track. Anita fixated on the commuters across the railway lines who exited the 9.07 from Manchester Piccadilly when the train halted at the refurbished Edge Hill Station, the terminus at Liverpool Lime Street. She'd read that in the 1830s, trains stopped short of the entrance to the disused tunnel, so locomotives could be removed; brakemen would then use gravity to move the passenger carriages. This activity had spawned the local expression 'getting off at Edge Hill' as a euphemism for the withdrawal method of birth control.

Deflated, she blew her sore reddened nose with the same soggy tissue she'd used to dab dry her eyes, then ambled back to the office. If anyone commented she'd blame her recent condition. Anita had found the excuse no man dared challenge: the menopause. She entered the office to find the papers in the same jumbled mess she'd left them in. As she knelt on the floor bile rose in her throat when she realised that none of the document's pages had been numbered. Silent alarm bells rang in her head. Anita asked to nobody in particular, 'How on earth do I put this back into any kind of order?'

As she used her palms to straighten the creases an instinctive glance through the window rendered Anita rigid. She watched Elliot saunter towards the office. Her first cack-handed attempt to scoop the pile from the floor failed. She gripped the untidy bundle close to her chest. Anita declined to acknowledge Pike, Alan or Henry, who imitated the three wise monkeys, as she scurried from the office. As the cold air hit her face Anita tightened her grip in case a gust catapulted her papers on another journey into the air. She dashed to the safety of her desk, dumped the papers in her pending tray, snatched a handful of clean tissues and then hurried to the canteen to meet her coffee companion.

From their usual spot in the lounge area, Donna waved to Anita, who lingered at the chilled cabinet to revive her face that glowed from embarrassment, anger or another hot flush. Anita manoeuvred amongst the diners, who resembled inmates as they held their food trays waist-high and shuffled in single file to the next available one-piece moulded chair, and reached the opposite end of the canteen where two large coffees waited on the Formica coffee table. Donna pushed her glasses onto her head to give Anita a hug.

Donna cupped her mouth with her hand as she leaned forward. 'Pike said you kicked off at Elliot. I did a quick tour of the ladies'; where've you been?'

Anita took a sip of coffee to delay her reply.

'Have you been crying?' Donna rubbed the back of her friend's hand. 'You're freezing.' Donna emptied crisp crumbs into her mouth, grabbed her cappuccino and flopped back. 'Pike said he thought you might've nodded Elliot if you'd been a bit taller. What were you thinking, letting him get to you like that?'

'I want the answer to that question myself.'

Donna sat open-mouthed as Anita confided the details of her humiliation, furnished with facial expressions, animation and pauses to halt the onset of tears.

'Now I have to take his sodding contract document home and streamline the contents.'

When Donna interrupted, Anita prepared for a scolding.

'It's beyond me why you let that moron upset you so much.'

Anita hid behind her hands. 'Leave me alone. I'm frustrated, irritable, confused, sweaty, my feet are swollen and I'm fed up of bloody crying for no reason.'

A smile softened Donna's expression. 'Nita Richardson, you're a hopeless romantic, or should I say hormonal romantic?'

Spontaneous laughter relieved the tension. Anita picked at the edge of the corrugated paper cup as she murmured, 'What's the friendship motto? "Don't judge, support"?'

Given Donna's personal experience Anita understood why she launched into a lecture. 'Seriously, why can't you focus on your marriage? Carl's good to you.'

Anita held up her hands to surrender.

'Though I'd love to have seen Elliot's face when you tossed them papers. The guys in the office say Elliot's having a mid-life crisis.' Donna's private hurt surfaced. 'It's bad enough being the dumped wife without the humiliation of him flaunting a sloobag young enough to be his daughter.'

Anita watched Donna bite the edge of the paper cup as a substitute for her ex-husband's head. Donna slid her glasses onto the bridge of her nose, upturned her empty cup, placed it on the table, looked at Anita, then hammered the thin cardboard base with her fist.

As Donna wiped specks of coffee foam from her lenses Anita lightened the mood. 'I heard a good one the other day. A woman told her hubby, when he left her for a younger woman, "The grass might look greener on the other side of the fence but wait until you have to mow it."'

Donna concluded the conversation. 'Elliot's an arlarse.'

When Anita returned to her office she maintained a vow of silence as she pondered her dilemma of how to issue the contract and simultaneously avoid Elliot. She sent her friend Juliet Nash a blow-by-blow account of her standoff. Impatient for Juliet's reply, she rolled the mouse to refresh her inbox. A five-minute reminder for a get-together with Kylie Fisher, the procurement specialist for Elliot's troublesome contract, flashed across her monitor.

The office door closed behind her as Anita came face to face with Elliot, who'd taken the stairs two at a time. As they met on the top step Anita withdrew her smile when she realised he'd come to see Mark or Joey, his project engineers. Anita felt invisible as Elliot's large stature pushed past her. When he opened the door his facial expression changed. His words tailed off as the door slammed shut.

Strengthened in part by her friendship with Donna, Anita had established an alliance with the procurement team. As she waited for Kylie to arrive, Anita sat on the edge of Donna's desk and tuned in to the uncensored conversation, as Donna's work colleagues vented their combined animosity towards Kylie.

Betty the buyer, who always looked as if she wore someone else's hair, wobbled her head to nod towards Kylie's desk. 'How can she be fast tracked to Procurement Specialist ahead of her, who's actually qualified?' Betty nodded at Jill, her thirty-something office companion, crouched on the floor with a deep wire file basket stacked high. 'Or Lorraine?'

Head bowed, Lorraine concentrated on the stocktake figures as she shouted, 'Betty, I'll tell you once then I'll tell you no more: I like doing what I'm doing. I don't want a career at my age.'

In between each burst of comment Donna's head twisted towards the door. Anita kept her opinions to herself.

Jill lifted her head from the file cabinet drawer. 'Kylie doesn't care; she's got a brass neck and thick skin. Little madam.'

Anita took over the role of lookout when Donna answered the phone.

'She makes me cringe.' Betty screwed up her face. She mimicked Kylie's baby-talk voice. '"I fink I'm soooo important."' Betty's shoulders tightened as she clenched her fists.

Anita watched Kylie in the distance. Unlike the other ladies in the office, she dressed in a pair of hipster jeans that no doubt displayed the top of her G-string each time she bent forward. The crest of her brown vest top revealed small firm boobs that resembled eggs sitting in an eggcup.

Anita moved from the window. 'She's here.'

The distinctive sound of Kylie's brown strappy platform shoes scraping against the path prompted silence in the office. The woman exchanged glances; the men watched as Kylie paused in the doorway to remove her bronze glittery headband, toss back her ironed-straight burgundy hair, then slide the band back into position. She used her fingers to comb out her blonde-streaked fringe that fell to obscure one of her close-set titanium eyes.

'When d'ye fink you'll give me Elliot's contract? They've phoned twice already.'

'When it's ready.' Anita softened her tone. 'Friday, Monday at the latest.'

Kylie repeated the words she scribbled in her notepad, ripped off the page and stapled it to her file. 'What's the holdup? Elliot said as far as he's concerned he's done the additions.'

'I met with Elliot this—'

Kylie raised her hand, palm facing outwards. 'Talk to the hand; the face isn't interested in excuses. Don't fink I'm taking the flack. Elliot said—'

Anita took a step towards Kylie and lowered her voice. 'I don't care what Elliot said. I'm the contract manager. I say when it's ready.'

Kylie pouted. 'I never meant nofink. It's just I get moaned at if the contract goes out late.'

'An' I'm answerable when the contract's wrong.'

When Anita left the office to the echo of Kylie's false nails' hurried tap against the keyboard she guessed Kylie might be e-mailing Elliot.

The rain, which hadn't let up since late last night, pelted the office window to keep Anita's sorrow company as she sat at her desk and pleaded for the day to end. Startled when the phone rang, Anita snatched the receiver. Instead of Juliet she heard a man's voice.

'You free for a conference, two o'clock at head office?'

With contract issues a standard agenda item, Anita often accompanied her boss, Ryan Conner, to head office conferences.

'Nothing that can't wait,' Anita lied as she jotted a reminder on her to-do list to reschedule the two meetings she'd arranged.

Ryan's voice became distant. Anita heard the clips of his briefcase lock. 'I'm off now. I've got a pre-meet. Oh, and Mr M wants to see your draft report.'

Mr M, whose full title read Mr Charles Mason CEO, had made a modest fortune from the acquisition of a number of lucrative council contracts in the eighties. Some people called him a shrewd businessman; the proprietors of the smaller firms that Mr M's company had devoured called him a crook. When Mr M married his second wife he seized the opportunity to diversify and incorporated her late husband's moderately successful engineering company into his domain; as a result Mr M amassed a substantial fortune, a large part of which he'd speculated five years ago when the government had announced its lifetime plan to decommission aged power stations within the UK. Mr M had divided up his business acquisitions. He controlled his empire from head office at Manchester. One of his sons managed the logistics division from Chester; his other son ran a number of depots that supplied construction materials throughout the North.

To facilitate his plans Mr M had leased the disused railway sidings in Liverpool to create a business division with a proven reputation for the management of high-risk engineering projects, which would give him a competitive edge against the established companies when he bid for a slice of the anticipated new build work. With a lack of family members able or willing to manage this part of Mr M's portfolio, he had headhunted his lifelong friend Ryan Conner who'd gained an exceptional track record for project delivery in the UK and from his years of experience decommissioning power stations across the USA.

Mr M's stepson Gerry Tyndale, the one person in the family who'd shown a desire to follow in his stepfather's footsteps, managed the Chrystalmere division, which concentrated on construction work throughout the South. Mr M gloated when Gerry announced he'd outbid his major competitors to be one of four companies engaged under a framework agreement to undertake works associated with a lucrative project in Marsh Moore. Gerry pleased his stepfather further when the client announced the Chrystalmere division had won the contract to refurbish Seven Point Power Station, with a carrot of a five-year extension as principle contractor to decommission the site when generation ceased. However, over the last few months a series of issues had put the Seven Point project in jeopardy. Mr M spent weeks in negotiation with Raymond Philpott, the client's head honcho, and a host of senior managers. Eventually Raymond agreed that due to Ryan's impressive reputation, he'd give him an opportunity to present a recovery strategy to the client's project management board on the 29th of November. Acceptance of Ryan's proposal would initiate a six-month probationary period. If at any point the programme slipped, Raymond could terminate the contract, and recover damages. With the current recoverable charges estimated at three quarters of a million, Anita expected a savvy businessman like Mr M to cut his losses rather than speculate on Ryan's success.

With renewed urgency Anita hit the keyboard. She listened for the shared printer to whine into life. It churned out the twelve-page double-sided report, paused, then spat a brisk string of single-sided attachments; the printer waited ten seconds and switched to stand-by. Anita checked the contents of her report, then clicked the mouse to rouse the printer for two further copies.

Anita checked her watch: 11.55. She sent Juliet an e-mail to say she'd be in Manchester by one o'clock, then, resigned to being a spectator in Elliot's life, she peeked through the slats in the pleated window blinds. With an unobstructed view Anita felt a pang of sadness mixed with relief as she watched Elliot's size thirteen boots crunch the gravel; he was heading for the canteen. She shoved the damaged papers into a carrier bag she found stuffed at the back of her drawer, set her out-of-office message, then made her escape towards the M62 and into Manchester.

Sitting in the multi-storey car park, Anita double-checked the draft report Mr M had asked her to prepare to redress issues with the Big Contract. She sent a text to tell Juliet to get the kettle on.

The 'Big Contract'

A twist of fate in the form of two huge storms, which pummelled the UK and dislodged part of the building's roof to flood the top floor at Manchester head office, had forced Juliet and Anita to relocate and share an office with the malicious business support team.

Anita and Juliet's friendship had formed as they had joined forces from their mutual discomfort when the well-established woman from the finance section huddled like witches around a cauldron, bitching venomous comments directed against the person who'd been unfortunate enough to leave the pack. The extent of the character assassination depended on their target's length of absence. On the subject's return, the smiling assassins replaced their derogatory remarks with insincere greetings.

Anita became unpopular with the witches and the bitches in part because of her refusal to serve up a tirade of insults. The noticeable attention Juliet received from the department managers contributed to her friend's fall from favour; as Juliet's sweet tooth became legendary, the corporate guys often brought her chocolates as a thank-you. Anita teased each time Juliet demolished half the sweets and then announced, 'I need to lose weight, chuck. The diet stars tomorrow.'

During the year the company took to complete the refurbishment their friendship was cemented. Although Anita returned to her original office, Juliet opted to take a development opportunity for a business manager's role, which required her to monitor budget spend, ensure strict legal compliance and maintain meticulous financial records to withstand the scrutiny of an external audit. She still moaned how she loved the job but hated working in the same office as the vipers.

*

Anita gagged on the smell of aftershave as Ryan, with an arm full of photocopying balanced on a plastic file, stepped from behind Juliet's part-closed office door. 'Splash it all over, why don't yer?'

Ryan blamed his polyps; he insisted he couldn't smell anything.

Anita mused on how good Ryan looked for a man of sixty-one. The cut of the jacket complemented his athletic build. His salt-and-pepper close-cut hairstyle gave him the look of a fleet admiral in a made-for-TV movie. Anita watched Ryan's freshly dry-cleaned charcoal tailored suit disappear at the end of the corridor.

Puzzled, she mouthed to Juliet, *Why didn't he use the copier on the top floor?*

Juliet shrugged her shoulders. 'Right, chuck. Here's your coffee and a butty' – she rattled a paper bag – 'and a cake for afters.'

Juliet's smart clothes disguised her overweight figure. She styled her thick brunette hair in a loose bun with a few strands pulled to soften the appearance of her rounded cheeks. A mother of black ancestry combined with her father's Chinese origin gave Juliet the most characteristic almond-shaped eyes. Her flawless olive complexion gave her a Mediterranean look; her unmistakable northern accent left no doubt she'd been born a Yorkshire lass.

'Has Elliot said owt?'

Anita summarised the salient points of her tantrum.

'For the millionth time, chuck, he's a …' Juliet blew out her cheeks as she searched for an appropriate word. 'You're off on holiday in a fortnight.'

With her elbows on the desk Anita cupped her frown. 'I know you're right but I miss being his friend, his confidante, his work wife.'

'I'm your friend. Elliot's too wrapped up in himself to be anyone's friend. You'll have to get over him, chuck.' Juliet stuck a cream bun under her friend's nose. 'Did you know Elliot applied for a job on the top floor?' Juliet peeked in her paper bag, then pulled out a chocolate chip muffin the size of her head. In the way a crocodile might devour a small child she took a big bite.

'He came for the interview last week; he's that thin his kecks hung off his backside.'

Anita couldn't determine if a sugar rush from the cream cake, a menopause symptom or the misguided fear of the prospect that Elliot might leave caused her sudden flurry of palpitations.

'What's he done to his hair? It's darker and spiky up top; he looks like an aged rocker on a bloody comeback tour.'

Anita felt blessed to have friends like Juliet, who expressed their frank opinions with good intentions. On this occasion the honesty of Juliet's words hurt. She searched her bra strap for a tissue. 'I can't help but think one day …'

'Stop thinking like that, chuck. He's made his choice. He's separated from the wife and kids and thinks he's God's gift because of his "hot young girlfriend".' Juliet used air quotes for the latter part of her statement. 'As Carl's away let's meet up at the tapas bar later, or no doubt you'll be sat alone moping to sad country songs.'

'And it'll delay my review of Elliot's stuff. Meet you in our usual spot. Seven thirty.'

Juliet offered a handful of tissues. Anita tucked them in her bra strap.

'Oh, I know what I forgot to tell you,' Juliet exclaimed. 'I saw Nathan Mills when I called in the shops for my bits and bobs.'

'Better known as cake and wine.'

Juliet told how she'd recognised Nathan's brown corduroy jacket in the checkout line, then hid behind a stack of promotional offers. She digressed. 'I hate how supermarkets do that. Strategically place a display to tempt bored shoppers as they wait to pay.'

When Anita went to offer her views Juliet scowled. 'Shut up, it's my story. Anyway, I ducked into the pet food aisles so I could see what he had in his basket.'

'And you don't have a pet, subtle.'

Juliet had had the biggest crush on Nathan when he had worked with the finance section at head office. They'd both been surprised he had left the department without asking Juliet for a date. When Juliet stalked him on Facebook she decided he had a girlfriend. They agreed that the contents of his basket – a bottle of red wine, fruit, a large pizza and a pack of four toilet rolls – offered no clue to his dating status.

Anita checked her watch. 'Conference starts in ten. I better go the loo first.'

Juliet squeezed her friend's shoulder. 'If you'd left Carl …' Juliet hesitated. 'I know life's difficult at home but Elliot's not the answer.'

Anita stopped by the ladies', rinsed her face and touched up her makeup, then, satisfied that she looked better than she felt, she headed to the boardroom.

Anita passed pleasantries with the head office team, poured two large black coffees, then took her assigned seat next to Ryan. Mr M, the chairman, marched in, followed by 'Two Litre Rita' as the men from the top floor called her in recognition of her enormous assets. When Rita stretched to place a copy of the agenda in front of each of the attendees, seated around the oversized maple desk you could see your reflection in, even the women took a sneak peek at Rita's cleavage.

Mr M opened with the routine items as Two Litre Rita switched on the overhead projector. She sat at her laptop like a pianist, her fingers poised to access the electronic data allegretto. The first item related to the contract Anita had prepared the report for and the one she'd referred to during her rant at Elliot; her colleagues called it the 'Big Contract'.

'As you know, Ryan presents next week in an effort to salvage this atrocity. This project's a major embarrassment to the company.' Mr M nodded at Anita. 'Ryan's team have their work cut out but I'm confident they'll succeed.'

Each person who examined the hard copy of the financials recognised how Ryan's successful resurrection of the worrisome contract would be a healthy addition to the company portfolio given the current economic climate.

Although Mr M had spent a fortune on private elocution lessons to perfect his Manchester accent so as not to feel intimi-dated by the 'all brass an' no balls brigade' he met at high level at board meetings, when he got angry, as he was today, he slipped into his hard-knock persona. He directed his sarcastic remarks at his stepson Gerry, whose face reddened. Mr M corrected his tone to end with an eloquent 'The South West team need a kick up the derrière.'

The discussions ebbed and flowed with the time monopolised by technical issues. At 5.15, 'any other business' concluded the conference. Poised to leave, Anita checked her mobile phone for messages.

Two Litre Rita whispered in Ryan's ear: 'Mr Mason wants a word with you both.' Rita's curt tone sang the words that told Anita to get a move on.

Mr M stood behind his Chesterfield leather chair with a whisky glass in his hand. As they entered Mr M draped his tie on the antique coat hanger that held his trademark camel-hair overcoat. Ryan sat in the oversized burgundy leather chair in front of the desk. Anita sat at Ryan's side.

Mr M swirled the twenty-year-old malt, then tossed a legal-sized manila envelope stamped 'confidential' onto the desk. 'I've told Gerry to clear his desk at Chrystalmere and concentrate on the Marsh Moore project.'

Ryan lifted the gummed seal, then locked the envelope in his briefcase.

'I met with Raymond earlier. He's left me under no illusions; if we don't perform he will terminate this contract.' Mr M held a shot of whisky in his mouth, then swallowed. 'And you know how that will hurt us.'

Ryan updated his boss as they each skimmed Anita's draft report. 'I've completed an indicative recovery plan. Anita's reviewed the associated contracts. We present to Raymond's management board next Tuesday, then wait for the outcome.'

Mr M took a decanter from his globe drinks cabinet to pour a large scotch as Anita updated him on the subjective, ambiguous works information, but assured him they could mitigate the contentious issue.

'We've got a good handle on this; it's our bread and butter

work,' she said. 'The Chrystalmere team are primarily construction; they never had a chance from day one.'

Mr M sat down for the first time during the conversation. 'Whatever it takes, this project's our priority.'

Mr M downed the last of his drink, placed his thick-cut whiskey glass on the desk, then stood to shake their hands. 'Sounds like everything's in hand. I'll ask Rita to clear my schedule Tuesday afternoon; I want you to see you both in my office. There's a lot riding on this. And the other issue?'

Ryan tapped his briefcase.

As they left Ryan rubbed his forehead. He excused himself and explained he had someone to see. Anita bade him goodnight. A few seconds passed, then Ryan shouted, 'Sorry, goodnight and thanks for your help.'

From the roof of the multi-storey car park the illuminated city skyline offered a bright conclusion to Anita's turbulent day. The workforce who hurried home excited by the night's prospects mirrored her enthusiasm for the challenge ahead. Her optimism displaced her original fear that as she approached fifty she'd be written off for career development. Employers overlooked many of her middle-aged female friends for promotion, in favour of 'the fast track route' for a youngster. Donna gave Kylie's unexplainable promotion as a perfect example. Rather than letting Anita feel superfluous, Ryan had recruited her help to resurrect the high-profile Big Contract two months ahead of her fiftieth birthday. Ryan endorsed her involvement when he told Anita how he admired her tenacity and often directed his project managers to consult her on contractual issues; he'd tell them, 'If Anita can't find a way through the problem, she'll find a way around it, over it or under it, but she won't be defeated.'

Change motivated Anita. Carl would wait for the disenchantment to show, then remind her how she 'brought it on herself'. His cutting remark masked in a joke: 'At your age you should be home baking pies, not trying to live life like an episode of *Dallas*.' Maybe if she'd heeded Carl's words long ago she wouldn't be going home to an empty house.

Casino Carl

Anita opened the door to a house void of laughter or welcome. She picked up the post, which she no longer had to forage for in the various places where the dog used to bury it, thoroughly chewed, for her mistress to find sometimes days after delivery. Glossy leaflets were easier to locate; Anita suspected Tara liked to look at the pictures, as she used to find all shiny paper in the dog basket. As Anita rolled her bottom against the hall radiator she split the mail into four piles: letters for her, bills addressed to Carl that would eventually come to her to be paid, letter for Carl; she weeded out the junk mail special offers Carl might find of interest, then tossed the rest in the green recycle bin.

Over the last five years she'd grown accustomed to her husband's absence. Although five months had passed since the vet had euthanised Anita's seventeen-year-old crossbreed Tara Loo, she hadn't grown accustomed to the absence of a nudge from a wet nose to welcome her home, or the way Tara's black and tan Alsatian ears would prick up as the whippet in her little dog jittered around the hall, wagging her long tail, if Anita shook the lead or offered a treat. Like most childless women Anita bestowed the love for the baby she hadn't birthed on her pet, the canine companion Carl had brought home as a ten-week-old abandoned puppy from the RSPCA in Speke. The loss of her little dog had softened when Carl had brought Tara's ashes home from the vet's, in a little wooden coffin Anita now kept at the side of her bed.

Having placed her coffee and a handful of biscuits on the lounge table, she stood on the hearth to thaw her legs as she scooped the former contents of Carl's pockets from the mantelpiece. She plonked the mishmash of fluff, slummy and crumpled till receipts on the computer table. As she straightened her displaced authentic Navaho ornaments Anita looked at the 1985 limited edition Grand National print proudly displayed above the fireplace. Horseracing and the thrill of the wager had been Carl's first love, his passion and the mistress whose company he preferred for as long as she could recall.

Anita picked up their wedding picture, Carl's fine speckled blonde hair a sharp contrast to Anita's thick rich auburn. 'Salt and Pepper', that's what their friends nicknamed the couple whose wildly different tastes, like the condiments, complemented each other; now Anita and Carl mixed like oil and water.

With an hour to spare until she met Juliet, Anita rang Casino Carl, his user name amongst the online gaming community. Vanessa, the hospitality host for his betting provider, rewarded Carl's VIP status and her other high-end traders with expenses-paid packages, which included overnight accommodation and the use of a private box at premier race meetings. Anita suspected that as Carl's resolve to appease his wife diminished he welcomed the lure of four days in Newbury this week for the Hennessy Gold Cup, and his three-day escape weeks earlier to attend the Open meeting at Cheltenham, to engage in the enthused conversation he craved.

On the eighth ring Carl's voice crackled into her earpiece. 'I'm in the middle of something, whaddaya want?'

Thankfully Carl's deep Scouse accent was the only trait he shared with the stereotypical Liverpool scally portrayed on TV; if anything her husband shared the homely look of the father depicted in any American family show from the fifties.

'I've been at a conference today. Ryan's asked if I'll go on secondment to Chrystalmere for six months if this presentation goes well next Tuesday. What do you think?'

When Carl paused Anita strained to identify the background noise. She imagined his twisted expression at the sound of her voice.

'You should do. I take it they reimburse all your expenses or give you a pay rise? You should tell them you want more money.'

'I meant both of us going.'

Another pause. Anita checked the mobile phone display to see if he'd been disconnected.

'I've gotta go, there's a game about to start; can't we talk about it Sunday when I get home?'

Anita reminded her uninterested husband she'd be in Chrystalmere Monday to prepare for the Tuesday's presentation. Carl fobbed her off with a promise to mull it over, although for now his sports wager took precedence. Anita remained resilient to Carl's moods, which changed in line with his profit and loss statement. When Carl won big he upped his monthly contributions to a number of animal charities he supported. When Carl lost he became distracted; when Anita nagged his irritation manifested frustration and anger.

Carl's abruptness as he hung up the phone reminded her why she had allowed her affiliation with Elliot to supplement her marriage as he had unleashed the passion that had lain dormant for years. Unlike Carl Elliot showed patience if she waffled on as they discussed a concern. He showed attentiveness when Anita shared a personal story. She'd been flattered when Elliot remembered a minor detail she'd revealed.

Sitting in the conservatory, which doubled as her study, Anita stared at the carrier bag on her knee that contained the rage-ravaged contract papers. She reminded herself how easily Elliot had replaced her, something Carl would never do. She threw the papers on the table, then left to meet Juliet.

The barmaid with a personality as large as her oversized figure held a glass under the optic. 'Usual, ladies: two large Jack D's and a bottle of house white.'

Anita ordered without the menu. Juliet kicked off her shoes and curled up on the two-seater settee beside the fire, which crackled and spat as the embers crumbled to displace the logs. Anita settled in the reupholstered grey and navy striped fabric chair to rest her feet on the magazine shelf under the low pine wood table.

As they waited for their food Juliet asked whether her friend could shed light on the unscheduled audit of her accounts.

'Mr M, leveraged up to his eyeballs against the Marsh Moore

project; Raymond could bankrupt the South West division if he pulls the plug.'

The waitress interrupted to place six dishes from the three-for-£10 menu onto the table. Juliet tucked in to the mezze platter, oblivious to how the off-the-shoulder, bright red chiffon top that clung to her breasts then flowed to her thighs attracted male attention. Anita counted five men who'd sneaked a look as they passed by their table.

'I doubt Mr M will go hungry, with his off-shore accounts; however, my reputation could be damaged, chuck, what they call guilty by association.'

Preoccupied with thoughts of how Juliet would have a duck egg if she knew the precarious situation Mr M was putting the company in, Anita took a moment to realise that Juliet had changed the conversation.

'Talk of the devil, sure to appear. Guess who's just come in?' Juliet asked. 'Nathan.'

Nathan waved when he spotted them. As he walked towards them he couldn't take his eyes off Juliet. He scrunched up next to her as he explained how he'd moved back to Manchester to do some off-the-books work for Mr M. He touched her arm. His eyes fixed on her lips when she spoke. When Juliet chuckled, longer than one of his lame jokes deserved, he told her she had an enchanting laugh and a beautiful smile. Juliet beamed at Anita above the rim of her wine glass. Anita excused herself.

A quarter of an hour later Juliet sent Anita a text to 'get back now!'

As Anita rushed towards Juliet she looked around for Nathan. ''Ave you frightened him off?'

Juliet's crimson face shot her one of her looks. She took a gulp of wine. 'Oh, chuck, I'm mortified!' She squealed the last word, topped up her wine glass and took another swig.

'Surely it can't be that bad; he couldn't keep his hands off you. I almost asked the barmaid to pass me a bucket.'

Juliet interrupted each episode of their encounter to take a mouthful of wine, followed by an 'Oh my God, Nita, I'm mortified.'

Juliet set the scene: how Nathan had enquired of her divorce, where she lived and drank, how often she came to the tapas, the usual chat-up lines. Ten minutes later he excused himself. He explained he'd have stayed longer but had a business appointment with Mr M. He gave Juliet a peck on the cheek.

Juliet paused. 'What do you think happened next?' Juliet buried her head in her hands.

Anita had one question.

Juliet's claret-coloured face suggested she might die of embarrassment as she continued her tale. Apparently Nathan had taken a few steps, then taken out his mobile phone and turned back towards her.

She drained her wine glass. 'I asked Nathan if he wanted my phone number, you know, nodding towards his mobile? If he'd done that to you, you'd think he wanted to type your phone number into his bloody phone, wouldn't ye?'

'Get to the point.' Anita topped up Juliet's wine glass.

'You should have seen the look on his face; he says, "No, I'm checking the time." 'Ave you heard the likes? Checking the time; why doesn't he wear a bloody watch like everyone else? Who gets their mobile out to check the time?' The faded fire cackled at Juliet's saga.

'What did he say as he ran for his life?'

Juliet took two tissues from her bag and handed one to Anita. 'Funny woman; nowt except cheerio, then he left.'

The glass collector stoked the fresh logs he'd thrown into the fireplace as their hysteria-driven laughter, helped by the free-flowing alcohol, became infectious. Juliet's encounter with Nathan was a perfect illustration of the mystery they could spend the rest of their lives trying to solve: how they could continue to misread men.

The night concluded when Juliet gave Anita an extra-long hug. 'Are we still on for Saturday?'

She'd been so caught up in the day's events Anita had forgotten she'd arranged to host this month's ladies' lunch. 'Yes, of course; I think Donna'll be at mine for two.'

Anita, Donna and Juliet took turns to host a get-together

once a month. Although November was Anita's turn to play hostess, Donna took charge and circulated the invite to include former work colleagues Merlot and Libby. Each invitee replied to Donna's e-mail with a note of what goodies they would fetch. Juliet agreed to stop en route to pick up a selection of shop-bought cream cakes. Donna offered to contribute a salad with a homemade pasta dish. For this occasion Merlot and Libby, who added a positive dimension to the usual trio, having both found contentment with their second husbands, offered to pool together for cheese and wine. Anita offered to replenish her stock of wine for the ladies, Jack Daniel's for her and Baileys for coffee.

At home Anita sauntered into the kitchen. As she waited for the percolator to fill up with fresh coffee she switched on the wall-mounted flat-screen TV to catch up with the day's events on the ten o'clock news. Bored with severe weather warnings, she hit the 'random play' button on the CD player, then shrugged at the irony when it selected Alison Krauss and Union Station's *Deeper than Crying*.

Armed with her coffee pot, she settled in the conservatory to sift through the jumbled mess of contractors' submissions that summarised two months of technical dialogue. The contract had been initiated six months ago when Elliot had phoned her from Ryan's office: 'Hi, titch, we have to put together the biggest contract of my career. Eyes'll be on us, major turbine hall refurbishment, at the power plant outside of Runcorn, usual stuff: replacement of bearings and other moving parts.'

With the prospect of a new challenge, they had fallen into their routine of endless development meetings. She'd work late into the night to amend the contract data. The next day, like a child who runs home with a picture they've painted in school clutched in their hand, she'd present her revisions to Elliot. Poised with a red pen, he'd make the tedious fun by adding daft comments or funny remarks to highlight the corrections he'd marked up.

Anita extracted enough acceptable information to fill fifteen sheets. She logged on to her laptop. With the near side of the moon visible against the midnight sky she opened up Elliot's last e-mail to her, the one he'd signed, *hugs and kisses, Elliot x*.

She hit the reply button.

> *Elliot, I love you. I have from the first moment I looked into your eyes. I cared too much to take advantage of your situation. I wish I'd known your marriage was over. If I*

Like a coward, she deleted her words, then the e-mail history. She attached her review with the suggestion he mull over her comments. Anita proposed a 10.30 get-together to finalise the contract. As she hit the send button relief drained from her neck. Unfortunately her sense of calm would be short-lived, as today's dance with Elliot proved far from over.

An hour later, for a second consecutive night, the furnace that stoked hot sweats disturbed her slumber. Anita punched the pillow, then tossed it on the floor as she reached for the dry one she kept at the side of the bed for these occasions. As the temperature of her naked body soared she battled it from beneath the quilt. Agitated she rolled from side to side. Unable to relax, Anita switched on the table fan, then searched her nightstand for her emergency supply of sleep aid tablets.

Streams of light from the headlights of the car that drove over the stoop seeped through a gap in the curtains. Anita bolted upright when she realised she'd hit 'dismiss' instead of 'snooze'; a glance at the luminous digits concurred, she'd overslept. With fifteen minutes to make herself beautiful she dragged herself into the bathroom to refresh her dehydrated mouth, then spend five of those minutes in the shower. As the force of the warm water soothed her sleep-deprived head she drew frowning faces in the condensation, trying to unravel the tangled memories of Elliot with a logical explanation; each event only raised contradictions that confused her conscious thoughts further. As she rushed her facial her irritability confronted the previous night's confidence. This unexplained darkened mood might have contributed to her menopausal meltdown episode on her way to work.

Road Rage

Anita jammed her elbow onto the horn as she slammed her foot on the brake pedal to avoid a collision with the cobalt blue car that darted from a side road straight into her path.

She indicated, then pulled alongside to mouth an insult. *Moron.* She accelerated. The idiot sped up. *Wanker.*

Anita eased her foot off the accelerator to pull in behind his Nissan Micra, which slowed to block her attempt. Unaware he'd picked the wrong day to mess with her, the idiot grinned. Anita, trapped on the wrong side of the road, felt her anger intensify when she spotted a bollard ahead. With her foot flat to the floor Anita avoided the bollard to pull in ahead of him. She slammed on the brakes and flung open her car door. With one foot on the road Anita realised this Sterling Moss wannabe intended to race on. Traffic on both sides of the road stopped as he swerved to pass her. Anita shouted a further insult as the smell of burnt rubber wafted through the air. Fate intervened when a bin wagon pulled out to foil her tormentor's escape. Anita took off behind him. She pulled up close enough to read his bumper sticker, which said 'if you're reading this you're too close'. She glared into his eyes reflected through his rear-view mirror.

His indicator flashed in time with his failed attempts to overtake the big grey refuse wagon that decelerated to retrieve the black bin bags from the roadside. For the next two miles a stream of oncoming traffic made his attempts to flee futile. As Anita's intention to follow him to his final destination became apparent he indicated to pull onto the motorway, then darted back onto the main road. A mile later, as they approached her turn-off, Anita relented. However fate still loved her. Without caution the idiot pulled up in the middle of the road, then got out. Oblivious to the line of drivers he'd blocked at the turn-off, he expanded his puny chest, then pushed his black-rimmed glasses against the bridge of his nose. Anita scowled, though she wanted to sneer; a few yards further she'd have resigned herself to defeat and continued her journey to work.

'Are you following me? If you are I'm calling the bizzies.' He held up his thumb and finger to the side of his face.

'You pulled out, no wave or sorry.' Anita delivered her summation of the incident.

'I'm in a hurry. So do I call the bizzies or what?'

She'd had her fill of ultimatums from men. Anita directed her venom mercilessly towards this idiot driver.

The idiot stepped back. Anita took a step forward. 'Call the police, go on, call 'em, then I can tell 'em how your idiotic actions could have killed someone!'

As hysteria engulfed Anita she stumbled forward. Her tormentor took a large stride back. His face displayed the fear that Anita might haunt him for the rest of his life.

'Get in your car and go, before I really lose my temper.'

He didn't need to be told twice.

Anita waved an adrenaline-enriched apology to the queue of spectators. She cringed at the sight of Ryan, who shook his head as he raised his forearm to exaggerate the motion of tapping his watch.

In the car park Ryan showed concern with his question: 'What on earth got you riled up?'

Anita trembled with guilt at how her loss of self-control had resulted in another misguided tantrum. 'I suppose in hindsight I may have overreacted. I lost it big time when he pulled out in front of me, then …' Anita reported the rest of her story.

'It looked like you'd been in an accident; I went to get out and help you. Though from the expression on his face, I felt it might be more fitting to help him. For a little 'un you're scary when you're mad.'

'Everyone's a bloody comedian; have you finished?'

Ryan laughed. 'There were at least four staff members who had a ringside seat.'

*

As her meltdown occupied Anita's thoughts she remained oblivious to Donna, who hollered Anita's name louder the second time. 'Did you forget our get-together to go over the delegation actions?'

As Donna would deputise for Anita when she joined Ryan to present to the client's project management board, and from next Friday when Anita swanned off to Vegas for two weeks with Carl for her birthday, Donna had arranged a handover meeting.

As they entered the office Anita's fatigue-fogged mind struggled to comprehend Donna's words. 'I hate Fridays. I need caffeine.'

When Mark greeted her with, 'Elliot's phoned, he's off till Monday,' Anita flung the contract on the desk. 'Why do I bother?'

Mark looked up and shrugged.

Donna made an 'oh-oh' noise, looked at Anita's face, then murmured, 'I'll get the coffees.'

Anita e-mailed Carl with a summary of her journey to work, then rescheduled her face-off with Elliot for Wednesday.

As Donna appeared with two vending machine cappuccinos the phone rang.

Carl delivered his usual sermon down the line. 'Get to the doctor's, you need HRT or Prozac. What if he'd been a nutter or given you a smack?'

'Stop telling me I need a doctor.'

Anita glared at Mark, who announced to the office, 'She's off.'

Anita lowered her voice. 'You know I don't want to take drugs, you know what my mother went through. Anyway, why couldn't you talk last night?'

'Studying form; it's how I make my living, remember?'

Carl went to speak again but changed his mind when Anita ambushed his pause. 'We need to talk. I need to know what to say if I get offered the secondments. It'll be a good opportunity for me; I don't want to be torn between my job and my marriage. And you know what you're like, left to your own devices, the house'll be a tip and you won't drag yourself from the sport to put a wash on, and—'

'I'm going; I can't listen to your whiny voice any longer. I'll see you Sunday or Wednesday or whenever you're back.'

The dead phone line confirmed Carl had hung up.

Donna sucked on the arm of her glasses as she sat with her notepad balanced on her knee.

'I had a road rage episode on the way to work,' Anita muttered. 'All I get from him is HRT or sodding drugs. Oh, Donna, what if I end up like my mother?

Anita had witnessed the onset of an early menopause inflicting the most noticeable change on her mother already shackled by a nervous disposition. Her mother had confided in her twenty-eight-year-old daughter how she felt on the verge of a mental breakdown and added how she understood why in Victorian times they locked menopausal woman in madhouses.

'And of course Elliot's off so the contract's pending. I won't get back from Seven Point till Wednesday.'

'He's a moron.'

Donna's matter-of-fact logic failed to defuse Anita's fretful mood. 'This contract's high-value, tight profit margin and brimming with issues associated with a timeworn chemical plant. This contract of Elliot's leads a number of subcontracts. The client's adamant he wants mobilisation early January. At this rate they'll be at least a month behind schedule.' Anita took a breath. 'So the shit hits the fan if we delay past next week.'

'Who gets the blame?'

'Probably me; Elliot'll say it's my job to get a contract issued.'

Donna bit the arm of her glasses. 'And you still cover his arse, so you'll take the backlash.'

Donna knew Anita would defend her actions. Anita knew Donna would scold her misplaced loyalty.

Donna hugged her friend. 'OK, what can I do to help?'

Donna's smile dissolved as Anita slammed the contract into the photocopier tray and banged the green button with her fist. Anita's day went from bad to worse as the office photocopier fought back to snatch and mangle the contract pages. It took three efforts by Anita, who squashed her fingers into hot parts to free the jammed papers. Her third attempt at clearing the various faults illuminated on the Perspex display with a bold red X, employing the time-honoured 'opening plastic bits and then banging them closed' strategy, failed. Anita switched the beast on and off twice, then figured two slams of the lid should clear it. Anita inserted the papers into the tray again; on her second attempt she yelled 'Walla!' as her two copies shot into the stacker tray.

Anita thrust a copy at Donna. 'That's it; we can't wait any longer. I'll double-check the contents. You can peer review each section.'

As Mark and his comic counterpart Joey formed a double act to mock Anita with every woman driver joke they found on the Internet, Anita and Donna painstakingly checked the contract contents. Anita signed as contract manager. Donna signed as checker.

'I'll send Elliot an e-mail to tell him Kylie has the final version of the contract for him to sign, when he decides to grace us with his presence. We'll give this copy to Madam on our way for lunch.'

Anita and Donna stood in the doorway of the procurement office and exchanged a glance as eight pair of eyes watched Kylie walk the full length of the office towards the bank of file cabinets. Her petite five-foot frame looked trim in skinny jeans.

Kylie held a stack of papers like they might explode at any minute. 'Can one of yews gizza hand please?'

Her damsel in distress role deserved a standing ovation. As she completed her SOS one of the industrial placement lads in the office tripped over his own feet in his rush to beat the others to be crowned the damsel's knight in shining armour.

Kylie left her helper to file her documents. 'That ready to go?'

Anita passed Kylie a copy of the contract. 'Can you get Elliot to initial it when he's in work next, then issue the contract?'

Kylie checked the cover for the appropriate signatures, then flicked through the pages to check it adhered to the strict procurement review process. 'Ell's back in Monday, he's got private stuff going on. You know …' Her words tailed off as she emphasised the gesture of clasping her mouth with her hand.

'Why he's off isn't my concern, just tell him to sign the damn paperwork.'

As they left the office Anita whispered to Donna, 'I hate how envy consumes me.' Donna shook her head.

Anita hankered more to be thirty-two than to be twenty-two, although her ego had been bruised when the guys in the office had paused mid-sentence to watch Kylie strut past. With intakes of breath they'd focused on Kylie's arse firmly imprisoned within a pair of size-eight jeans. Anita brooded on the memory of how she'd been a young woman with a firm bum and perky oversized boobs. She'd asked Carl how men could be so fickle to judge a woman's physical attributes rather than her soul.

Carl had glibly replied, 'It's down to the lure of the beaver.'

At the end of the day with the handover complete Donna gave her friend a hug. 'Don't forget I'll be at yours tomorrow for two at the earliest, so find your cheery face and wear it.'

Ladies Who Lunch

Anita completed her robotic procedure to check a second time that she'd locked the doors and windows. They hadn't been opened, but last time she'd driven halfway into town then returned home when she couldn't shake off the fear she'd forgotten to lock the back door.

With the contents of her bag laid out on the hall table she checked each item as she dropped it back into the bag: keys, purse, cash, credit cards and change for the pay and display. She locked the front door, then peeped through the letterbox to check she'd retrieved the contents from the table. The postman waited for the odd woman from number eleven to rattle the door handle a third time, then handed her a package of mail: a combination of bills and birthday cards secured with an elastic band. Anita pushed the bundle through the letterbox. Satisfied she hadn't left anything behind, she rattled the door handle a final time, then made her way to the salon.

The heightened activity from the OAPs who took advantage of the blue rinse special added to the bustle. Anita sat in the cubicle opposite a twenty-something image-conscious girl who flicked through a six-month out-of-date celebrity magazine as flesh-eating fish, for her piranha pedicure, nibbled the dead skin from her feet.

The not-so-pretty beautician closed the partition curtain. Anita updated her with a diluted version of her upcoming holiday as she shaped and tinted Anita's eyebrows before whisking her into the treatment room for her facial and half-price massage. The therapists kneaded Anita's body to melt the tension knots from the previous weeks' fiasco.

The beautician handed Anita off to Margie, her regular hair-dresser. Since Carl had taken to calling her 'snowy' she asked the stylist to pay extra attention to the recent growth of grey hair around her temples. As Margie plastered the thick auburn dye paste to the grey roots Anita laughed out loud.

Anita shared her childhood memory of her father, who dozed in the armchair unaware that his wife had snuck up to squirt Grecian 2000 on his grey sideburns. Halfway through her father shot from his chair and demanded an explanation. Mother told him he looked old; she wanted the young man with the raven black hair she'd married. Father called her vain, then reminded her to judge people by their actions rather than their looks.

Mission accomplished, Anita drove home rejuvenated. She flashed her deep red painted fingernails against the contrast of the steering wheel. With a positive frame of mind she looked forward to an afternoon with her friends.

Anita passed Juliet's empty car parked in the street. She rang Juliet's mobile; it went to voicemail. As Anita entered the house she bent to pick up her cards; she patted the empty mat. She took a moment to ponder if she'd experienced a senior moment. Anita mentally retraced her earlier encounter with the postman. She shouted hello; although it was unlikely, she thought Carl might have come home.

As Anita followed the smell of warmed pastry into the lounge an assemblage of women she called friends greeted her. Party poppers exploded streamers into the air. 'Surprise!'

Donna rushed forward to garnish Anita with a silk pink sash that announced in bold silver letters *Fifty and Fabulous*. 'Happy birthday, our lovely special friend.'

Anita stepped back to compose herself. Bewildered she digested the effort of her friends, who'd decorated her lounge in a red and gold colour scheme. Birthday banners hung on each wall and across the front of a borrowed foldaway table packed with an array of party food. On a silver stand sat the centrepiece, a birthday cake the shape of a handbag in bronze and gold, with a Gucci clasp made of icing. The girls were aware the 'genuine' article topped her birthday wish list from Carl, along with a pair of Jimmy Choo's.

Balloons had been blu-tacked to the stationary objects with a few loose ones being hand-patted across the room. Birthday-themed tablecloths covered the nest of occasional tables, the pattern obscured by the stack of presents, the contents hidden beneath shimmering gold, silver or red gift wrap, secured with exaggerated bows. Anita guessed the gift bags that leaned against the legs of the table contained alcohol.

Anita caught Donna exchanging a glance with Juliet, who whispered in Anita's ear, 'You sure you're OK? We couldn't cancel; we've been planning your party for weeks.'

The warmth of her friends' concern thawed her frozen smile. 'I thought I'd lost my soddin' marbles earlier when I couldn't see my birthday cards on the mat. I actually thought I'd dreamt it.'

'Come on, Nita, speech!'

Anita stammered her tongue-tied words as her mind raced ahead. She looked at her sash. 'Oh, ladies, I'm gobsmacked. How did you manage to pull this off?'

Donna popped a second champagne cork to top up the glasses as the froth diffused. 'That's a first; she's stuck for words.'

'Carl gave me the spare key.' Juliet raised her glass in a victory salute as she passed Anita a glass of her own with a colourful napkin wrapped around the stem. 'He booked you the pamper package to keep you out the way, chuck, to give us lot time to prepare your surprise party.'

'Thank you; I'm lucky to be able to call each of you my friend. You've no idea how much this means to me; it's gorra be the nicest present anyone could give me.'

The girls gave a rapturous round of applause.

Anita watched Juliet put her plate on a chair to free her hands. 'Though might I suggest you grab a plate of food before Juliet devours the lot?'

Donna remained in her regular role as barmaid and poured generous measures of alcohol into long-stemmed glasses. Juliet dished out the pasta, as a cluster of friends demanded Anita's attention. She greeted each of her guests with a hug, appreciative of their presence.

Once she'd completed her rounds Anita stopped to catch up

with Nicky, who she'd known forever, as their mums had been friends since their teens. Like the big sister she had begged her mother for, Nicky had been Anita's role model throughout her turbulent teens, then into womanhood. Nicky had served tea with sympathy to ease the torment of a stupid mistake Anita couldn't take back. She had been her confidante when Anita had experienced a succession of crushes on boys, and her comforter for a number of subsequent failed romances. Anita had matured into her thirties before she truly valued her oldest friend's wisdom. Although Nicky rang on alternate weekends, Anita hadn't seen her since she had moved to Cumbria eight years ago when she had suffered the fate of a husband tempted by another woman to end twenty-five years of marriage. Since then her life had revolved around her youngest daughter who wanted to continue her career despite an unplanned pregnancy. As Nicky peered above the rim of her 1980s big red glasses, once referred to as her Deirdre Barlows, Anita thought how her friend hadn't changed in thirty years.

Nicky took a hairband from her wrist to snatch back her straight brown hair. 'You're spoilt. There's Carl and you off to Vegas for your fiftieth; what did I get? A wet weekend in Whitehaven. Even that minge bag I married only took me to Blackpool for our honeymoon.'

Merlot, who'd been given the affectionate nickname for consuming copious amounts of red wine at a works conference, brought a silver tray full of crispy garlic bread from the kitchen. She looked like the Pied Piper as she led a chorus line of woman impatient for a slice. They called her, aged fifty-nine, 'the wise one'.

Merlot raised her large glass of red wine in salute. 'I think your fifties are a time for reflection. Enough people from your past have died that you question your own mortality. This of course prompts the life-changing considerations.' She rested her hand on Anita's shoulder. 'A few years pass until God's final joke, the menopause stifles your reproductive use. Then what?' Merlot bagged the armchair, reached down and pulled the leaver to release the footrest. 'When hormones no longer run wild to manipulate your mood, you realise time doesn't evaporate any quicker than ten, twenty or thirty years ago. I know as a mature woman I recognise my accomplishments. I've gained wisdom and forgiven myself for my mistakes; fact is I've come to realise it's those mistakes that have made me the wonderful woman I am today. I mightn't know what I want from the future but I sure as hell know what I don't want.'

Libby placed a well-stocked silver tray on the pouf between the recliners. 'What did Mark Twain say: he gets his daily paper, looks at the obituaries page and if he's not there he carries on as usual?'

Merlot called the menopausal years 'puberty in reverse'. Libby concluded as they picked at the food remnants that by the time they reached sixty they'd revert back to the stroppy attitude of their teens.

Parked on the leather two-seater under the window, Juliet shared her tale with Ali and Sue, the sisters from the top of the road. 'It took me ten years to muster the courage to leave my hubby. The long bitter divorce and the two years to finalise the dissolution of the marriage took their toll.'

Ali asked if Juliet had regrets. As Anita listened to Juliet's reply she wondered if, despite her original objections, the affair Juliet preferred not to mention in public had supported her emotional pitfalls through those dark days.

Libby joined Juliet to debate the potential downfalls when you make life-changing decisions during your pre-menopause years. The topic expanded to the fear of getting back into the dating game with the joys and disappointment that change entailed.

'Oh, chucks, I've had a few corkers, I can tell yer. Though Ernest, now that's a tale an' a half.'

Juliet's fan club listened to the tale of the distinguished gentleman she'd dated. She described Ernest as an older gent she'd met at the baths. Juliet recalled the fun she'd had at first when he'd leave a note on her windscreen. Or she'd open the front door to find flowers or chocolates on her doormat.

Juliet held the plate of cakes as if reading a book. 'I couldn't put him off so I agreed to go to dinner at Angelo's in town. He looked OK under a dim light. I laughed at his embellished tales of life as a CEO for a big corporation. I fantasised how like Jock Ewing he sounded. Anyway, we had a few more dates, but once he told the same bloody story for a third time. I told him bye bye.' Juliet gave a limp wave to highlight the point.

As Donna replenished the drinks, out of the blue she announced, 'I'd have celebrated my twenty-seventh wedding anniversary Monday. If that two-timing cheating pig of a husband had kept his knob in his pants.'

She often told the girls she could understand her husband but the real hurt came from the dishonesty of her best friend, who she referred to as 'that two-faced tart'.

'Quite the cunning cow she turned into.' Donna looked at the glass of alcohol that had been her friend through her turbulence. 'She befriended me, then stabbed me in the back when she seduced my husband.'

'She'd blend in with that horrible finance team at head office,' Juliet added.

As women they shared the agony of their feelings and understood how easily you could get involved with the wrong man, but they couldn't comprehend how you could betray a friend's trust. Treachery couldn't be forgiven.

Anita wrinkled her forehead as she added a well-pondered remark. 'Do you realise Carl's the one constant in my life?' She looked out of the window. She spoke more to herself than anyone in the room. 'My taste in music has changed over the last thirty years. My hair's been a multitude of colours. I'd have gone mad looking at the same wallpaper for years, but I look at the same man day after dreary day.'

'That's true, chuck. Imagine wearing the same style of clothes you did at twenty.'

Anita downed her drink. 'Although I'd love to still have them dusty pink hot pants Nicky gave me.'

Nicky came from the kitchen with a plate of vol au vents. 'You didn't do them justice; they didn't get anywhere near the action they got when I wore them.'

*

By 5.30 her neighbours, the woman from the local book club and a few friends from work had gone home. Discounting Sue and Ali, the two sisters from the top of the road who'd rested their drunken heads on the kitchen table and fallen asleep, six of them remained.

Feeling overstuffed from the lavish concoction of food prompted the ladies to discuss post-Christmas diets. Libby offered the first excuse for failure.

'Did you know excess weight's a recognised symptom of the menopause which becomes harder to shift at our age?'

Merlot chipped in. 'Clothes can disguise my body but I can't hide my failing memory. I walk upstairs, then I forget what I've gone for until I reach the bottom step. I'm fed up with it.' She gave an exhausted sigh.

Anita shared how she'd watched an episode of the conspiracy thriller *Rubicon* on TV with Carl. One scene included a woman who slept with her boss for money. Carl jokingly asked Anita if she'd sleep with her boss for a few bob; Anita had a complete mental block when she couldn't remember her boss or where she worked. The ladies sympathised with how unnerving these experiences could be, sadly aware their memory loss would worsen with age.

Libby told a similar story: 'When I saunter around the super-market I mutter through the alphabet in a desperate attempt to jog my mind to remember what I went in for. I've got that many toilet rolls I could build an igloo.'

Donna, who'd been unusually quiet, gave a wriggle. 'Actually, we've been talking.' The room fell silent. 'Instead of going on your own next year, Nita, how d'you fancy arranging a girls week in Vegas for my birthday? It could be our fighting-your-fifties tour.'

Donna's announcement excited the ladies.

'I've been no further than Spain,' Libby added. 'You can count me in.'

'I'm fighting my sixties but I'm up for Vegas.' Merlot and Libby high-fived.

'With my big pay rise I can actually afford to go.' Donna laughed as she filled Juliet's wine glass. 'You up for it?'

'You bet, chuck; we can each get "fighting your fifties" sashes made.'

Anita's irrational fear of her age emerged. 'How old are you lot? I'll arrange a holiday but I won't advertise my age. And FYI in the States over-fifties qualify for senior discounts.'

'Speaking of which …' Nicky pulled the magazine she'd taken from the doctor's waiting room from her handbag. She shrilled as she pointed at the title: '*For seniors aged fifty plus*? When did you become a senior at fifty? Given the increase to the retirement age they shouldn't label you a senior until you're seventy.'

Anita liked Nicky's logic.

'That's settled then,' Donna squealed. 'We have to agree on an age if anyone asks.' She looked at her face in the vanity mirror she kept in her purse. 'I reckon we can pass for forty-two easy.'

Anita promised to e-mail the girls Sunday with a holiday proposal.

As the darkness of the night shrouded the sky the party came to a close. As her friends dispersed Anita promised Donna again that she would e-mail the Vegas holiday options. Merlot and Libby woke the sisters, who hung onto each other's arm to stagger up the road. Nicky gave Anita a long hug, then headed to her brother's house.

When it became obvious Juliet had no intentions of going home, Anita left clean towels and a nightdress in the spare room.

A dishevelled Juliet vowed to cut back on the booze when she dipped her fingers in the half-drunk pint of water to flatten down her surfer boy quiff. She looked at her car keys, then phoned a taxi. As the black cab reversed off the drive Anita headed back to bed, where she stayed until Carl announced his arrival with a slam of the front door.

Anita held her head in place as she made her way downstairs.

Carl laughed. 'What's the hairdresser done to your hair? You look like a troll.'

In the kitchen, which looked like the aftermath of the breakfast rush at an American diner, Anita took two tablets as she answered Carl's questions: why Juliet had left her car parked outside, who would clean the mess in the lounge, and yes, she did want him to book Sunday lunch at the local carvery.

Anita guessed Donna had put the glasses in the dishwasher to clear space for Libby and Merlot to pile plates and dishes. Next door's dogs answered Anita's question of where the girls had left the bin bags of discarded food remnants by clearing the garden of birds to gobble the food they'd ripped from the black sacks. Anita knocked on the window. The black and tan mongrel scurried through the privets with a sausage roll; the older collie dog lay down to chew on its meat-filled crusty baguette.

Anita grabbed a bin bag to clear the remnants of her friends' party efforts. Carl handed her a dozen or more party poppers wrapped in a paper tablecloth as she picked up streamers entangled with the obliterated balloons from a mad moment. Inspired by the thriller *Stranger on a Train*, they had drawn a face on a balloon to resemble a man they wanted to inflict pain upon. They had given the balloon a kick, then swapped with a friend who stabbed it to death with a pin.

When Anita told Carl of Nicky's surprise appearance he sent Nicky a text that told her to get her arse in gear and help his wife clean up. Her reply told him to stick a brush up his arse; that way he could do it himself as he watched the racing.

Five minutes later, armed with her marigolds, Nicky rang the doorbell. Anita made a drink as Nicky updated Carl on life in Cumbria and the trials and tribulations of the children. When Carl assumed his position at the PC he became oblivious to their presence.

Anita followed Nicky into the kitchen. 'You've seen me grow up. Do you think people find me odd?'

Nicky put a sisterly arm around Anita's shoulder as she declared, 'No, honey. Being an oddball, it's why your friends love you.'

'I'm serious; am I losing my sense of perspective? Am I turning into my mother?'

'Listen to me. You've spent your life, no different than your mam did, refusing to conform to the stereotypical image of a woman. I'll say this slowly so it sinks in. When you do stuff that's a bit out there, or pushes the boundaries of convention, it surprises me. What doesn't surprise me is that it's you.'

Anita made a mental note to remind herself of Nicky's kind words when she felt this way again.

Peckish, Nicky opened the fridge crammed with plastic containers. 'I've told you a hundred times, men have a dickometer that leads them to anyone who offers sex.'

Anita shut the kitchen door. 'But why does having my heart broken at forty-nine hurt as much as it did at nineteen?'

'That's one too many serious questions,' Nicky said, glasses balanced on the rim of her nose. 'I'll think about it and get back to you.' She laughed and pointed to the sink. 'I'll wash, you dry, but first put the kettle on.'

With a clean kitchen and a tidy lounge, Anita said goodbye to Nicky and her well-worn marigolds.

Drained from the previous day's excitement, Anita engaged in mundane conversation with Carl as they walked to the carvery.

In between mouthfuls of food Anita tentatively broached the subject of their future. 'If I relocate will you come with me or do you want to stay here?'

She waited as Carl chewed his meat for an exceptionally long period of time. 'Let's see how it goes.'

Anita took a sip of water to wash down two more tablets. 'My work could take six months or more. You need to let me know.'

Carl's curt tone told her everything she needed to know. 'Give it a rest. Why do I need to let you know now? Frightened I might arrive unannounced?'

Anita sat puzzled at Carl's comment. His frown told her not to push the subject.

They finished their meal with another round of mundane conversation until Carl grabbed his keys off the table. 'Get your coat. I'll pay the bill.'

When they arrived back at the house Juliet's car had gone.

Carl severed the opportunity for further conversation when he adopted his predictable position to watch American football. As he busied himself at his workstation Anita said goodnight twice. On her way upstairs she heard Carl scream home a close finish from one of the obscure American horseracing tracks he watched in between time-outs in the Washing Redskins' game against the Vikings.

As the rain tap-danced a rendition of 1930s Broadway show tunes against her bedroom window Anita logged on to her laptop and e-mailed the girls options for their fighting-your-fifties tour of Vegas. She suggested August for low price and high temperatures. As she waited for the rain's next performance she pondered what dismay Tuesday's presentation to the client's board might offer.

The Presentation

Monday afternoon Anita checked into the Grange Hotel, which displayed all the rustic charm of a seventeenth-century Tudor period hotel. She unpacked, then followed the route along half-timbered hallways and through narrow doorways to the meeting room, where care had been taken to make the state-of-the-art conference equipment blend in with the hotel's Tudor style of bar code walls, low ceilings and thick wooden beams.

She hooked up her laptop and sent Carl an e-mail to let him know she'd arrived safe, giving him her room number in case of an emergency. She read the e-mail from Ryan telling her he'd been summoned to head office for a last-minute meeting with Mr M and Nathan. Juliet had sent a detailed message with a number of attachments Ryan had asked her to include. Within the confines of the makeshift office Anita rehearsed her draft presentation before an invisible audience. She ran through her 'to do' list and ticked off the completion of the design programme.

When the noises from her tummy demanded food she double-checked the finer points of her detailed report. Satisfied she'd answered the questions posed by the client, she packed away her paperwork and headed to the restaurant.

The waiter frogmarched her to the far end of the dining room. Once she had declined the wine menu and selected soup to start one waiter removed the excess dinnerware as the waitress delivered a basket of fresh baked bread. To give her mind respite from contracts Anita absorbed the Hollywood gossip in the *National Enquirer*. As she slathered butter to each corner of a thick slice of warm bread she studied the front-page headlines of celebrity mishaps. Still chewing the first she buttered a second slice and flicked the pages to read the supermarket tabloid's gossip section.

In true nouveau cuisine style the waitress placed an oversized soup bowl on the table. Anita used the last of her bread to soak up the consommé and accepted the waitress's offer to replenish the empty bread basket. Convinced fame and fortune didn't equal happiness, she folded her magazine and turned her attention to the real-life action of the two middle-aged women at the next table. On the second glance Anita realised she'd seen the lady with the straight limp grey hair earlier in reception. Her dark-haired dining companion, who looked a few years younger, squinted around the room, then took a pair of spectacles from her bag to read the menu she held at arm's length. Anita stifled the urge to laugh when she passed the glasses to her friend who stuffed them under her napkin when the waiter arrived to replenish their wine glasses.

Anita thought of Merlot's comment that once she had hit fifty her eyesight had deteriorated overnight. Vanity forced a number of her friends to keep a secret pair of glasses in their handbag, to read a menu or small-print magazine article or to check if a blurry man looked less attractive with perfect vision. Alas, with enough horror stories on the Internet to put her friends off, Anita had been the only one from the group brave, stupid or conceited enough, depending on your viewpoint, to have her eyesight corrected. No matter which event she recalled from her past Carl played a major role; on this occasion he'd supported her decision to go ahead with the Lasik surgery despite the surgeon disclaimer that the procedure would be ineffective against the natural deterioration of her eyesight brought on by age.

When they day for the surgery had come Carl had wished her good luck as Nigel the nurse had taken her to the preparation room. With Anita's hair in a net Nigel had put Vaseline above Anita's eyes. Alarmed she'd asked, 'Are you shaving my eyebrows?' He'd laughed and reassured her that the thick jelly would stop stray hair contaminating the procedure. The doctor had completed the Lasik surgery in minutes.

Although Nigel had given her prescription painkillers, the

remedy for everything life threw at her started with a good night's sleep. Carl had closed the bedroom curtains and replaced the bulb with a low-wattage one. On her bedside cabinet he had lined up a torch, eye mask, eye drops and tissues at arm's length with the projection alarm clock set to illuminate the wall if she hit the button. When Carl had gone for a take-away Anita had shut her eyes tight, then secured the plastic guards with four large pieces of duct tape. She had swallowed two sleeping tablets and rested on the bed.

Carl had roused her from her semi-consciousness with the aromas of fish, chips and curry from the tray of food he placed on her legs. He had guided her hand to the four halves of bread and butter that balanced on the side of the plate, slid a knife and folk into her hands, then left for the start of the night racing.

Anita had soon realised Carl had forgotten to lock Tara from the bedroom when she had nudged her hand with her wet nose. If the food fell off her fork or Anita missed her mouth she'd hear the dog gobble bits of fish. When Anita had tried to make a chip butty she had counted three pieces of bread and butter. She hoped Tara had eaten the fourth; more likely she'd awake with the buttered side stuck to her face.

When her eyes had felt like sandpaper and released a stream of tears that tightened the skin on her face, Anita had wished she'd taken the painkillers. She had used the heel of her slipper to bang on the floor for Carl to remove the empty plate and the dog. Anita had fallen asleep before they'd left the room. She had awoken pain-free with perfect vision to see a beautiful day.

Anita's attention returned to the dining companions, who looked like a pair of secret agents; the dark-haired lady scanned the immediate area as the other spied above the plastic rim of her own spectacles, to check her cover as a glasses-wearing fifty-something-year-old female wasn't blown.

Consumed by the ladies, Anita jumped when Ryan bellowed over her shoulder: 'Sorry I'm late, we have a problem.'

A waiter hurried to the table, sensing the urgency as Ryan beckoned him to take his order. Anita dispensed with the pleasantries to concentrate on Ryan's tale.

'Today's meeting at head office: talk about one step forward.' Ryan paused as the waiter scurried to set the table for the imminent arrival of his food.

Ryan tucked into sausage and mash as he updated Anita on the notice Mr M had received from the Inland Revenue to advise on the UK government's decision to sever the double taxation loophole treaty with the Isle of Man. As a result Mr M had joined a number of other prominent businessmen to take legal action.

Ryan lowered his voice. 'He's in effect suing the government. We won't know the outcome until a court ruling.'

'No pressure then.'

They ordered liquor coffees. Anita watched Ryan's mouth twitch as the waitress placed the drinks on the table before the cream sank.

'There are allegations that Gerry's dealings for the framework agreement may be unscrupulous. It's speculation at the moment but we need to be prepared.'

When Ryan briefed Anita on the details not included in the report, Juliet's comment about the unscheduled audit made sense. Anita pushed Ryan for more information. He understated the full extent of Mr M's relationship with Raymond and how the three of them had been friends a lifetime ago, although she did glean from Ryan that they had no room for error.

Six miles out the distinctive blue and silver cooling towers of Seven Point Power Station glistened as the fortress structure commanded attention against a backdrop of snow-covered hills beyond the estuary. Half a mile from the entrance they joined the queue of traffic halted at the security lodge. Pass holders continued to the staff car park; visitors were re-directed to the visitors' car park.

Armed with their presentation and ready for battle they announced themselves to their security escort Trish Ireland, the only member of the six-person security team who didn't proudly display a moustache for the Movember charity drives to raise awareness for prostate cancer.

As they waited for Trish to check the pre-completed security form and confirm their clearance Ryan whispered, 'Don't be fooled by Raymond's kind face; he's no fool.' The tone of Ryan's odd comment hinted of a warning, which possibly explained why Mr M had brought Nathan back to complete a background check on Raymond.

Normally blasé in the face of expensive boardroom furniture, Anita marvelled at the care taken to space the twelve beige upholstered timber-frame chairs at equal distances around the boardroom table which dominated the executive office. She recognised the effort made to strategically place the twelve water glasses in a position that drew focus to the company logo that had been etched into the centre of the frosted glass panel.

Raymond acknowledged Ryan. Anita watched Raymond, tall and slender, take a black plastic comb from the top pocket of his charcoal suit and smooth his Brylcreemed hair. As he approached he used his hand to push his side part into a quiff. The web of lines on his face congregated around his Paul Newman eyes. Anita amused herself as she realised she'd inherited another of her mother's habits: comparing people to movie stars to describe them. Raymond shook their hands, as his secretary, Miss Fowler, a tall lady with a grey pallor that matched her wispy hair, hovered at his side with her notepad and pen at the ready. Introductions complete, Miss Fowler straightened the pile of scattered reports Anita had dropped on the desk. When she pointed to the refreshments table in the far corner of the room, Anita went for coffee. Ryan unloaded the contents of his briefcase onto his side of the desk; Miss Fowler clutched her notepad to restrain herself from tidying the mess.

The six executive board attendees walked in and sat at the far end of the table. Miss Fowler took them a hot drink, then spoiled the impressive layout to place a glass of flavoured water on a coaster that depicted the same logo as the table.

Anita watched Raymond and Ryan engage in a guarded conversation as she helped herself to a second cup of coffee. She couldn't lip-read but she could distinguish the words that related to Mr M and Gerry. Anita moved closer.

Ryan pulled the sleeve of Raymond's jacket. 'I hope this isn't personal.'

Raymond whispered into Ryan's ear, then walked off. He spoke to Miss Fowler, who scribbled in her notebook.

Raymond sat at the head of the table. At one side sat the commercial manager, a tubby man with a bad toupee. He introduced himself as Donald Turner. On the other side was Robert Bull, the senior project manager. Anita recorded each person's name and position against a seating chart as the other four nondescript members of the board introduced themselves as representatives of engineering, industrial safety, strategic programmes and finance.

The stern faces remained unchanged as Ryan explained his proposal to rebuild the team's reputation and ensure a continued working relationship to deliver this project.

Donald set the tone of the meeting. 'Thank you for your candour; frankly we've had promises from your predecessor. You've earned one shot to avoid termination of this contract. We expected you to bring an army of people.'

Ryan's tone complemented the strength reflected in his natural posture. 'We're here because we have the expertise within our division to meet your objectives.'

Raymond interrupted Donald, who was about to speak. 'OK, Mr Conner, you have our attention. Begin.'

Anita stood to introduce herself as Ryan distributed the information pack. The front cover stated in bold font the three areas of concern for the client. Anita gave her audience a minute to peruse the content as she explained the logic for her colour-coded report.

'The green section shows design progress. Red font highlights a number of outstanding reservations.'

Anita looked into each of the seven pairs of eyes that peered at her as she briefed the board on her report.

'To date no instructions have been issued, although dialogue suggest otherwise. I've summarised our responses and included the potential effect on cost and programme. They require closing before the design can be frozen.'

Two of the attendees discussed the content amongst themselves as they reviewed the matrix. Anita looked at Ryan, who gave her a nod to continue.

'The amber section meets your installation deadlines. Again your project manager has given verbal instructions that can't be implemented until we receive a written PM's instruction. Appendix B lists your proposed changes.'

This section prompted the most questions. Ryan served his answers and won game, set and match as the disproportionate assignation of blame towards his company became evident. Robert Bull asked more probing questions of his project team than of Ryan.

Anita paused. Raymond told her to continue. She wondered why nobody around the table referred to him as Raymond.

'Red section affects critical activities. Appendix C identifies a strategy to incorporate your proposals, with an acceleration plan to meet key dates and progress milestones should you instruct the changes.' Anita wanted to imitate ripping the pin from a hand grenade with her teeth and lobbing the device into the middle of the desk's logo. Instead she threw a verbal curve ball. 'I have noted how six of the nine potential changes impact your critical path activities.'

Anita wondered if Donald had worked with the New Engineering and Construction contracts when her suggestion for a telephone conference to double as a risk reduction meeting required an explanation. At Raymond's request Miss Fowler made a note for the minutes.

A knock on the door interrupted her flow. Two plump ladies in hairnets wheeled in a trolley filled with sandwiches and pastries and two pitchers of orange juice, covered with cling film and secured by an elastic band.

Raymond ordered a twenty-minute recess. Miss Fowler invited them to help themselves. Anita declined the juice and replenished her cup with steaming black liquid from the insulated coffee pot.

Break time over, Ryan concluded their presentation with a proposal for a formal presentation in two months' time, to give the client's project team time to review the proposals, hold the risk reduction meeting, resolve design reservations and issue the outstanding instructions within the contract timescales. Raymond instructed Miss Fowler to schedule a meeting for early February.

Ryan invited questions under 'any other business'. They directed the first question to Anita.

'Tell us, what went wrong?'

Concerned she'd weaken the effort they'd put into their presentation, Anita paused to give careful thought to her reply. She spoke slowly to dilute her Scouse accent as she shared her opinion

'The Chrystalmere team's forte is construction whereas the North West division are routinely involved in decommissioning power plants, chemical plants and other risk-averse industries. It's my understanding that the tender scoring showed our competitive price outweighed the risk associated with lack of site experience. When you consent to a project of this size you have to allow time to build a connection; trust doesn't happen overnight.'

The room fell silent when Donald Turner sniped, 'It's interesting you mention the tender scoring, given the allegations of improper conduct by your predecessor.'

Raymond looked up from his report, scowled at Donald, then nodded at Anita to continue.

Her defensive tone sharpened. 'Your company awarded us this contract based on our proficiency and proven track record. This form of contract works best when you commit to a collaborative approach.'

Robert Bull raised his voice. 'What's your involvement going forward? I can see you persuading us to work with you, then us getting left with the original team.'

The executive groaned like members of the House of Commons. Ryan stood at the front of their table. Anita remained at his side.

'I'm responsible for delivery,' Ryan said. 'Anita will be seconded to the South West to undertake sole contract management.'

The grilling over, Anita took her pen and pocket-sized to-do pad and listed a number of actions before she forgot. Miss Fowler told Ryan that Raymond wanted a quick word. Relieved she could leave, Anita arranged to meet Ryan at head office, then headed back up the M5.

At six in the afternoon, Anita sat alongside Ryan to update Mr M on the presentation. Ryan explained how their frankness had impressed Raymond, who'd expected stall tactics. Anita wondered why Ryan didn't mention the private conversation with Raymond or the snide remark about Gerry.

'His caveat, we deliver a full project recovery presentation early February.'

Anita responded to Mr M's request for an overview. 'I've concluded my initial evaluation; I'll issue a formal report end of this week. I'm on leave from the fifth, back in twentieth of December. I'll report to the Chrystalmere office third of Jan.'

'I want you at the top of your game for this one. Consider the relocation package.'

Ryan continued where Anita left off. 'I'll poach Alan to put the plan together. Pike can run point on design; he's fresh from college and keen. Any future resource I'll take on secondment when I need them; Elliot can deputise until you appoint my replacement.'

Mr M expressed his concern for the North West contracts in Anita's absence. One step ahead of the question, Ryan reassured him, 'I've asked Donna, who's agreed to undertake contract management responsibilities, under Anita's direction of course. It's a good development opportunity and it'll free up Anita.'

At home Anita gave a long sigh of relief. Carl welcomed his wife as if she'd been to the shops rather than away for two days involved in a career-enhancing project.

'The secondment's a definite; I start in Chrystalmere third of Jan.' Anita waited for Carl to answer. 'Have you had a chance to think about it? Will you come with me or what?'

'Don't pressure me; I'm not one of your contract lackeys.'

Anita protested, 'January's four weeks away. I have to give Two Litre Rita my accommodation arrangements.'

Carl took a deep breath, then exhaled. 'Take it you're going alone at first. We'll talk on holiday. Not now, I've got stuff on my mind; can we please have a night that doesn't end in a row?'

Anita went to reason with Carl, then changed her mind. She wasn't sure why she pushed Carl so hard for an answer when if she told the truth she would prefer to go alone. They already lived separate lives, slept in separate rooms. Anita spent time with her ensemble of friends. Carl spent time with his cyber buddies. Other than holidays she couldn't name an interest they shared, so why would he want to be a part of her working life?

Using the excuse that she needed to pack and an early night, Anita made two nightcaps. Carl said a sheepish goodnight as Anita took her drink upstairs.

With her vanity case packed with her artillery of travel-size skincare products she unzipped two large suitcases. Unlike when she'd gone to Vegas August and the hotel thermometer had hit 120°F the December weather would be a pleasant sixty-six degrees. She packed her case with daytime summer clothes and a selection of woollen cardigans, then tossed in a bikini for spa days, ten evening outfits and three pairs of shoes. In Carl's case she packed two pairs of trousers, then counted out fourteen T-shirts, underpants and pairs of socks: one for each day. Anita looked at both suitcases side-by-side on the landing and realised they even had separate luggage to match their separate lives.

Replaced

Anita entered the office as Joey slapped Mark's back in admiration of his ingenuity in finding a poster on Google Images that depicted the seven menopausal dwarfs. Anita focused on the words scribed at the bottom of the colour poster stuck on the wall above her computer: Guess Who?

She took a tissue from her bra strap.

'You OK? This your random weeping?'

A few months earlier, when Anita had wept without warning, she'd embarrassed the guys in the office. So at the team brief under 'any other business' Anita had declared, 'I'm menopausal and keep bursting into tears. If I sense upset coming on I will issue the random weeping alert; unfortunately for you the emotional symptoms will be difficult, but you are the chosen ones to take the menopause journey with me. One day you will thank me as it will put you in good stead for when your wives hit fifty.'

Donna arrived at 8 am with two large coffees and a contract. 'Did you get the message? Elliot's off till tomorrow, something to do with the kids. So Kylie's given you this back.'

'The mere mention of his name infuriates me these days.' Anita riffled through the pages of the contract she'd given Kylie on Friday and marked up the pages Elliot needed to sign.

Donna squealed, 'What have they done to your wall?' She read off the names of the seven menopausal caricatures: 'Itchy, Bitchy, Bloaty, Sweaty, Sleepy, Forgetful and Psycho.'

As Anita schedule a 10.30 showdown for Elliot's return she huffed, 'It'd be funny if it wasn't true.'

Donna's face searched for inspiration. 'You'll be on leave after Friday. What do I do? This is a great development opportunity for me; I don't want to blow it.' Donna's posture slumped.

Anita's vacant expression instructed Donna to repeat her question. 'How do I handle Elliot and his contract?'

'When I first worked with him he'd invite me to every meeting. That allowed me to mitigate any potential problems.'

Donna put her glasses on to take notes.

'Now he doesn't invite me to his meetings or want me in his life.'

Donna used the toe of her shoe to kick Anita's shin. 'He's a moron, I know. Get back to the contract.'

Anita dissected Elliot's contract to highlight the pitfalls. 'The client's adamant he wants mobilisation early January. At this rate they'll be at least a month behind schedule.' She took a breath.

Donna ran through the details of her development objectives for transition into Anita's role. 'I know it's a great opportunity. Are you sure I'm up to this? You would say if you thought I couldn't handle this job.'

'Of course I'd say. Not to your face. But I'd say it.'

Donna reacted with a hard kick to Anita's already bruised shin. 'You're not funny.' They both burst out laughing. 'You're gonna have time to help me with this contract stuff, aren't you? I'm panicking; you'll be snowed under with your new work; what if everything goes tits up?'

Anita shouted to be heard as the copier churned out the subcontract list. 'The tricky bit comes when we engage the interface contractors. It's good practice to flow the works information to the subbies.'

Donna clipped her pen to the printout. 'I get it. Elliot's contract needs to be signed or I can't finalise the next lot.'

''Ey, you're brighter than you look.'

'Cheeky bitch.' Donna looked at her watch. 'What else before you swan off to the States with Carl?'

'As Elliot arranges his meetings through Kylie, e-mail her, cc Ryan. Tell her it's mandatory for you to attend Elliot's meetings.' Anita took a large mouthful of cold coffee.

A timely interruption suspended their conversation when Anita answered a phone call from her electrical contractor.

'Hi, it's Jon; sorry you couldn't make lunch. I wanted to say thanks to you and Elliot for last year's business. I've sent a bottle back for you with the supervisor.'

'Thanks, he's here now dropping it off.'

Jon's supervisor plonked a shiny gift bag on the desk. Aware of the improved anti-bribery and corruption laws, Donna peeped inside and recorded a large bottle of Jack Daniel's in the gift log.

Anita considered asking Jon 'what lunch?' Instead she thanked him for her gift.

'By the way, Jon, you'll be getting a new contract manager. She'll manage Elliot's contract whilst I'm on secondment.'

'Oh, yes, I met her today at lunch; Elliot brought her. Kylie; she's adorable. I look forward to working with her.'

Anita rose abruptly. The phone skidded across the desk. Donna leaned forward to catch it as it dropped off the edge.

'He said you're off down south; I assumed. Have I put my foot in it?'

Anita barked down the phone. 'Kylie's the procurement clerk; did Elliot introduce her as the contract manager?' She twisted her torso to look at Donna, who still had hold of the phone. 'You'll be dealing with Donna Francis. I'll ask her to drop you an e-mail, then you'll have her contact information. Speak to Donna directly for contract issues.'

Anita hung up and kicked the wall. 'Can you believe he took her for lunch instead of me?'

'Who's Jon?'

'He thought she was my replacement?'

'Who's Jon and who took who? Although by the way you're ranting I assume Elliot's one of the "who"s.'

'Jon owns Sparks Inc. He's been my best electrical contractor for the last four years.' Anita stood up, then dropped back into her chair.

'Is that who you want me to e-mail? What did he say?'

'He must think I'm a bloody idiot.' Anita banged her forehead on the desk.

'Jon?'

'No, Elliot.' Anita lifted her head and pinched her eyebrow. 'What did Jon say?'

'He thought the adorable Kylie that Elliot took to lunch instead of me was the new contract manager. What's wrong with me, Donna?'

Donna stalled her reply until the familiar script played out.

'I thought Elliot and I …' Bored of delivering the sermon, Anita let her words tail off.

Anita counted her options like a recorded message: *For heartbreak support because you're a bloody idiot, press one. For repeating the same story hoping the outcome will be different, press two. For a list of untraceable poisons, press three. For advice on how to compete with a twenty-two-year-old bimbo, press four. For other options press the hash key.*

The first time Elliot's attentiveness had waned had been when he had enthusiastically suggested Kylie should attend their meetings. Given her role as procurement specialist the request had appeared reasonable, although onlookers would fail to recognise the significance when he sat opposite Kylie; during the early days of their friendship, Elliot had told Anita he preferred the view when he sat across from her. Four months ago, when Anita had asked him what she'd done to warrant his change towards her, he'd massaged her shoulders and accused her of an overactive imagination. Anita had told him that if their relationship had changed he'd have to spell it out. He'd certainly spelt it out now.

'Stop it. Stop torturing yourself. Nobody understands what you see in him. It's his loss.' Donna's rant stalled Anita's attempt to interrupt. 'He's bragging to his mates he's got this hotty. A mid-life quick-fix bonk won't last; he's an idiot. You're worth more than that; you should thank Chantelle for saving you from having to listen to his stupid self-centred stories and making the biggest mistake of your life.'

Anita wanted to wallow in misery rather than accept Donna's words. 'There's no fool like an old fool. I joked with him how he'd replaced me with a younger model. I meant the way he'd encouraged Kylie to be more active in our contract. Now I'm truly replaced.'

Donna secured the contract files in the lockable cupboard, then left Anita to type her to-do list. 'Try and rest, and push thoughts of that idiot from your mind.'

A reminder flashed in the corner of the screen, as if she'd forget her next-day meeting with Elliot. Like the dripping tap of torture, each reference to the man she'd believed to be her destiny drove her further insane. Anita consoled herself with the thought that it would be tomorrow before they duelled again and, as her mother liked to say, 'life looks better on a good night's sleep.'

How misguided that thought proved to be when a hot flush or hormonal reaction to another confrontation with Elliot infused an erratic night's sleep. Normally a heavy sleeper, she'd no sooner dozed than she woke to retrieve the covers she'd flung off moments earlier. When the sound of the central heating's hot water expanding in the metal pipes woke her, Anita lay in bed to mull over how she'd deal with Elliot. Had she known the pain he'd inflict today she'd have stayed in bed.

Ding Dong, Round Two

As the time neared twenty past ten, Anita couldn't concentrate on the conversation.

Donna snapped, 'Is your head on a spring? Stop watching for him coming back from tea break. Turn your chair around. Face away from the window.' She used the same pitch as a police officer on TV who uses a megaphone to tell the crowd, '*Go home, there's nothing to see here.*'

As they talked Anita used the tip of her finger to apply gel to the dark puffy circles under her eyes. 'I know he's pushed me away but he knows I'm good at my job.' Anita held up her crossed fingers. 'He should listen to sense.' She hoped her words sounded convincing.

Break time over, Donna took Mark and Joey's return to the office as her cue to depart. She mouthed a silent *good luck* as she left.

Anita stood with her back to the open window as perspiration trickled down her neck. 'Have you set the temperature control to tropical?'

The fact that the guys wore a fleece in the office answered her question. Anita applied a spray of Gucci, then reapplied deodorant as the sudden rise in her body temperature rendered the short-sleeved grey jersey knit dress inappropriate.

'Jeez, Nita, I'd sooner you stink of sweat.' Mark turned on his desk fan.

'Let me get this right: sweating tops the poll of the menopausal symptoms you lot can't tolerate. Not even sweating: trying to *mitigate* it. You'd sooner I stink than camouflage my perspiration with deodorant.'

'Yep; can't you go outside to spray?' Joey wafted the scent with his hands as he dramatised the need for an inhaler.

They reached a compromise. Anita agreed to stand in the doorway if the need to further refresh arose.

Unable to delay the inevitable she dialled Elliot's extension; he picked up on the third ring. The rapidness of her words permitted no juncture for Elliot to interrupt. As she attempted to disguise her nervousness with humour her common accent became magnified. 'I'm on the way. Don't run off, I'll only 'ave to hunt yer down.' She hung up, then wiped the handset with a tissue to absorb the sweat residue. Blowing her palms she left the office for round two of the battle to commence.

The shocked expression on Elliot's face as he read an e-mail spiked Anita's curiosity. She stretched to look over his shoulder. The sender's box listed Elliot's wife. Anita pulled up a chair. Elliot hit the forward button; the e-mail disappeared from the screen. His familiar sombre face half-turned towards her. Anita went to speak as his phone rang; from his deep low voice, combined with the 'hello you', Anita deduced his hot new girlfriend Chantelle might be the recipient of the forwarded e-mail. He replied in code. Bile rose from the pit of her stomach. To suppress the onset of tears Anita swivelled her chair to face Henry.

When Elliot whispered, 'OK, later babe,' Anita swivelled back; she failed to conjure up a fake smile as the sight of his self-gratified grin caused sickness to burn in her throat.

Elliot tilted his chair. As he reclined he clasped both hands behind his head and cracked his fingers. 'You called this meeting.'

Her disposition called for a direct approach. 'You have to understand the logic for my proposals. You know I can't flow the details to the subbies until we finalise this. I want the problems resolved today. I'm on holiday from tomorrow and not back till the twentieth, so Santa will be delivering the contract at this rate.'

'If you're repeating what you said the other day, save your breath; I've given you my proposal.'

Anita's sense of calm, it became apparent when she pinched

her eyebrow, was short-lived. 'What's your problem? I've explained my reasons.'

She'd underestimated Elliot's preparation for this meeting. 'Who makes the final decision of what goes in the contract?'

The controlled way Elliot answered irritated her. She played his game. 'You do. But consider my perspective.'

'Why do you keep arguing?'

Anita rebelled. 'I'm giving you my professional advice.' Saliva dried up in her mouth to constrict her throat. 'That's what I'm paid for.'

'Let's get one thing straight. I'm the project manager. I'm responsible for delivery of the work. Your job's to complete the paperwork, isn't that right?' Elliot leaned further back in his chair.

'What's it like to be important?' Anita tugged her forelock. 'I'll remember my place in future, squire.'

Elliot unclasped his hands. His distinct tone enhanced his elevated superiority. 'Stop trying to take over.'

When Anita took a break from her discourse she found her finger unconsciously moving towards her eyebrow. 'I'm trying to get through that thick skull of yours by explaining what's wrong with the contract.'

Anita felt sticky. She looked to see large wet patches had formed under each arm.

'No, you're patronising me. There's a difference.'

Embarrassment revived her anxiety. With her elbows tucked to her waist Anita fanned herself with her notepad, though she did consider doing what Halle Berry had done on an American chat show and lifting her arms to proudly display her perspiration rings. Though unlike Halle's, Anita's damp rings had spread to her belt. Elliot's eyes fixed on the secretion. His egotism taunted her attempts for a professional resolution. Elliot won; Anita chose to ignore the humiliation of the underarm evidence of her hot flush. If her interference in this contract annoyed him, imagine his displeasure if she dared to use deodorant. If the guys upstairs found it a punishable offence, Elliot might banish her from existence.

Anita stretched to poke her finger at random paragraphs. 'Let's look at your version. Crap, crap, oh yes, even more crap.'

Elliot's voice quivered. 'Change your attitude.'

Her tolerance level exceeded, Anita repeated her finger-poke action a number of times as she tossed sheets from Elliot's document to one side. Anita squeezed her eyebrow hard, then tucked her thumb into her palm. With her index finger jutting from her clenched fist she pointed at his flushed face. 'I'm really angry with you. Your contribution has been diminutive.'

Elliot jerked his head. The office wall impeded his attempt to preserve distance. Anita projected her frustration with a wiggle of her finger an inch from the bridge of his nose. She continued to point indiscriminately.

Elliot's nostrils flared as he fiddled with the stapler on his desk. 'Have you finished?'

Venom etched her face. As she salivated, spit sprayed between each word. 'If you'd done what we agreed, we'd have avoided this effin' argument 'cause it'd be done right and on time. It has to go today!' Anita snatched the stapler and slammed it on the desk. 'You were adamant you'd do it. Weren't ye, aye?' Her melodramatic tirade failed to get a response. Instead of a retreat Anita chose to mimic Elliot. She forced a deep voice that sounded nothing like him. '"Don't worry, Nita, I'm on top of it."' The pink tinge on Elliot's cheeks darkened. Anita moved closer. 'Have it your own way, you smug-faced arrogant tosser, I'm done and this time I mean it.'

Her hands trembled to fluster her attempt to collect the contract from his desk. An involuntary nervous smile raised the tension.

Elliot closed his eyes. His exhale preceded an outburst to release a tension that had built up in him for far longer than this conversation. Unsure which of her actions had triggered his onslaught, Anita stood bewildered, unable to protest. She turned to leave but found herself snared by the position of his chair.

Elliot incorporated a pause prior to each clearly pronounced word. 'Don't ever point your fuckin' finger at me again.'

Anita slammed the papers on the desk and donned the old

fishwife pose as her anger exploded to eject an aggressive retort. 'Last week at the meeting you swore you'd finished, but noooo, yer too busy acting like an overgrown schoolboy to give a rat's arse about work.'

Elliot's expression froze.

'Like an idiot I took this home, did your job for you. What'd I get in return: not a thanks, kiss me arse, nowt, and if you ever swear at me like that again Elliot Parker I'll knock your block off.' Anita barked the last statement at a rhythm to coincide with three points from her finger, an inch from his face.

A final twirl of her index finger indicated she'd finished. She thought of Oliver Hardy prodding his finger into Stanley's chest; under lighter circumstances Anita might have found it fitting to have finished with, '*And that's another fine mess you've gotten me into.*'

Elliot's rage-fuelled eyes pierced Anita as he swiped her finger from his face. His distorted features intensified her sense of fear. The adrenaline-enriched blood pumped around her body forced her heart to beat faster.

Elliot suspended his mouth close to hers. She smelt the faint odour of minty fresh toothpaste. He raised his voice to a booming level to deliver his knockout blow. 'And now you know why I replaced you with a younger, prettier model!' His eyes looked at Kylie, whose presence Anita hadn't been aware of.

Elliot moved his chair to permit her escape. The emphasis on the 'younger' portion of the statement had provoked a hurt Anita hadn't experienced in a long time. A stunned silence enhanced the uncomfortable atmosphere. Like an innocent man browbeaten and sentenced to the gallows Anita accepted defeat. She hung her head, each person's empathy visible through her tears as she staggered towards the door.

At the door Anita turned to watch Kylie's arse distract the guys' attention when she bent to look at the papers on Elliot's desk. Anita hurried to the canteen where the refuge of the ladies' bathroom awaited.

*

Coiled on the cold tiled toilet floor, she slumped against the fibreboard door, ripped lengths of single-ply tissue, blew her nose then tossed the soggy ball in the hope it would land in the white porcelain bowl. When the outer door opened Anita held the vapour of industrial-strength toilet cleaner within her nostrils until her attempt to remain concealed failed. She released the gurgled sigh of an injured animal.

'You OK? Can I help or get someone?'

Anita declined the offer between sniffs, nose-blowing and sticking loo roll under her eyes to catch the rolling tears. The noise from the hand dryer stopped. Instead of the thud of the door closing she heard the familiar sound of shoes scraping the floor. Anita counted the steps, one two three, then prayed for the ground to open up and swallow either one of them.

'Nita, you in 'ere?'

Anita reminded herself that Kylie didn't deserve to be the target of her anger. 'I'm fine. Please, leave me alone.' She listened for the sound of footsteps.

A hand came under the toilet door. 'Erm, I fought you might like this. I'll get Donna.'

Anita took the plastic cup of cold water. Each mouthful lubricated the rawness of her throat. The next sound came from Kylie's oversized heels. The door shut. Anita cried.

Donna arrived a few minutes later. She placed a wodge of towel roll on her shoulder, 'for the snot,' she explained; 'new blouse.'

Donna stifled her snorts of amusement as Anita's mascara-stained face rose from Donna's shoulder to give her the misguided impression she'd composed herself. 'He'll be sorry when he comes to his senses. Tell him to stick his contract up his arse; to hell with him. On second thought maybe not as they're now my contracts.'

Anita swilled her face with cold water.

'Your eyes look like emeralds when you cry.'

'Oh goodie, I'll get my heart broke more often then.'

For her next act of friendship Donna retrieved Anita's coat, bag and car keys, then accompanied her to the car park singing the theme tune from *The Bodyguard* as she pretended to shield Anita against any surprise attack Elliot might launch.

Anita arrived home with sore eyes and a deflated ego. She deflected Carl's concern as to why she'd come home early with the excuse that she needed to sleep off a migraine. As she waited for two sleeping tablets to kick in she permitted herself one more thought of Elliot and the night he'd whispered, 'I love you, titch.' As her heavy eyes closed Anita thought how she had taken his murmured words as a response to his arousal rather than a declaration.

Despondent about what lay ahead, Anita resigned herself to the possibility this might be as good as her life got. When she thought of the price she'd paid for her indecision, she buried her head in the pillow. She wept for the state of her marriage, and the guilt that consumed her for the hurt she'd caused Carl as his suspicion that his wife craved more than friendship from Elliot had impacted her marriage more than she'd anticipated. Her tears weren't confined to events of the heart; she cried for the loss of her youth, regret that she'd missed the opportunity to become a mother, the void in her life since the death of her parents and her dog. Anita sobbed for the demise of her love, friendship and the misguided respect she'd gained for Elliot and for the expired opportunity to find the true happiness that had eluded her for so long.

The Procurement Lunch

As Anita's was the only office on site that lacked a display of Christmas cheer, Lorraine from procurement called in to the office with a box full of leftover decorations she'd found in the stock room. With a lack of enthused participants Lorraine sellotaped odd lengths of silver, red and gold tinsel to the cupboards, then blu-tacked a plastic Santa to the door.

Anita arrived as Lorraine placed a foot-high, pre-decorated Christmas tree on Anita's desk, then parted with the words, 'Bah humbug, you miserable lot.'

Donna smiled as she busied herself at the spare desk, preparing the list of tasks she needed Anita's help with before they left at noon for the procurement Christmas lunch. Everyone else sat like zombies in front of their computer monitors compartmentalised by the half-height desk dividers personalised with photos of luxury cars, holiday snaps and children or, in Anita's case, a wall of death with pictures that kept alive the presence of her parents and dog.

Mark cradled the phone. 'Oi, when will Elliot's contract be issued?'

Anita disrobed from her thick winter coat, hat, gloves, scarf and leg warmers as she replied. 'Hopefully this week; tell them to call Elliot.'

Mark looked at Anita. 'You do know he's off today?'

Anita should have known better than to expose her raw feeling in an e-mail but it burnt inside. She didn't care; she needed to tell him exactly what she thought.

Elliot
I don't know why you're being so horrible but it hurts. I have tried to put out the best contract for you but all you do is reject my comments. I don't know what else to do. I'm leaving on a six month secondment from January. I care about you too much to end things like this. I know you've moved on but surely we can still be friends or at the least civil.

I hope you and the kids have a great Christmas.
Love A.x

At one o'clock Anita set her out-of-office message to say she'd be on leave until the twentieth of December and to contact Donna for commercial issues, then headed to the procurement office to meet the procurement team for the Christmas lunch Betty had arranged at the Old Schoolhouse Coffee Shop. She handed the same three bound copies of the contract to Kylie with the same request for Elliot's signature.

If you wanted a cosy place to get together, the designer coffee houses in town couldn't compete with the local village café. At two o'clock eight of them arrived at the venue, which had emerged from renovation with its original wooden beam features restored. The combination of chocolate brown and deep mauve furnishing gave a cosy feel to the deceptively large room.

When Anita's mother had brought her here for an ice cream on their way to Sunday school they had called it Joyce's. During Anita's teenage years the name had changed to Laurel's; she remembered how the village busybodies had caused quite a kerfuffle when she had installed a jukebox. Three owners later a local man had renamed it the Euro Zone. He'd made a notice-able change by mounting flat-screen TVs on each wall that played every Eurovision Song Contest from 1956.

As an avid coffee drinker Anita savoured the aroma blends from the industrial-sized percolator.

'OMG, did you hear my stomach growl? It's the smell of them paninis,' Kylie giggled as she rubbed her tummy.

Tempted by the selection warming on the sandwich press they placed their order then followed the server, who took the 'reserved' sign from the festively decorated dining table besides the traditionally dressed Christmas tree. The first to the table positioned themselves as far away from Kylie as possible, leaving Donna and Anita to sit either side of her. As she fidgeted to get comfortable, Kylie asked Anita if she'd heard from Elliot. She didn't reply when Anita asked why she wanted to know.

The waitress balanced the round maroon tray on the edge of the table, the lattes she placed in front of them a replica of the steaming coffee cup motif on the bib of her pristine apron. The girls pulled their Christmas crackers, then tossed the cheap plastic prizes into the middle of the table as the conversation turned to talk of Christmas. The nattering stopped in favour of watching a young Cliff Richards on the TV singing of congratulations and jubilations.

Betty pointed to the group of ladies in the corner. 'Someone's enjoying themselves.'

They all laughed at the seniors who sang the odd word as they swayed to a quick succession of songs from Lulu and Dana.

Donna quipped, 'That'll be us soon, batty old folk the kids make fun of.'

A second server wearing a grease-stained apron delivered their food and a stack of mistletoe-patterned napkins. Betty asked Anita of her birthday plans as the ladies broke open the piping hot food. Anita explained how their stay in Vegas coincided with the ten-day National Final Rodeo.

'I love the zest generated from the 200,000 rodeo enthusiasts who swamp Vegas. With the concentration of country bands that headlined at the best hotels I get to see loads of bands live.'

Anita went on to explain how Carl had pre-ordered tickets for the five concerts through Dylan Faulkner, the events coordinator at the hotel, who had ensured Anita a front row seat.

'Who you going to see? I've been line dancing with our sister and Jill here at the old village hall a few times.'

Betty surprised Anita when she recognised three of the five

artists: Brooks and Dunn, Clay Walker and Garth Brooks, but not Lonestar or Dierks Bentley.

Betty shook her head when Kylie squealed, 'Vegas for your birthday and cowboys; I'm soooooo jealous!'

Anita understood why the woman quipped but stopped short of a full-blown conversation with Kylie, whose immaturity and undeserved promotion rankled the ladies in the team. Donna, who normally remained impartial, disliked how, as Kylie had grown in confidence, her spoilt nature had emerged. It had become obvious to the department that Kylie had grown accustomed to getting her own way, especially when they contradicted or challenged her suggestions; Kylie would go into the manager's office, shut the door, then emerge with the look of victory on her face.

Anita's father wouldn't tolerate vindictive behaviour from either of his children. He had instilled the value of consideration for other people's feelings. Although over the years Anita had experienced disappointment when friends or close work colleagues had failed to return the same thoughtfulness she showed them, she liked the person she'd matured into.

Kylie tapped the edge of her plate with her spoon. 'What ya finking?'

The hot air from the middle of the panini tickled Anita's nose. She answered quickly, expecting to sneeze. 'Feeling old.'

Kylie looked at Betty. 'You're hardly an auld biddie.' She smiled at Anita. 'You could pass for forty easy.'

Anita contemplated the speed in which the years passed, then changed the subject to ask Kylie of her dreams.

'I want a good job. Marry a man with ambition, one that doesn't spend his time in the pub wiv his mates. I wanna buy a house near me mum, then pop out a couple of kids.' She made a popping sound to indicate three kids, then turned the question back on Anita: 'What do you want for right now?'

'Honestly, I don't know. I change my mind with the wind, as my mother used to say.'

'You do my head in sometimes. I thought you and Elliot had something going on.'

At the procurement meetings Anita had witnessed how Kylie's bluntness backed people into a corner. Like a child who continues to ask 'why' to each explanation you offer.

The words fell from Anita's mouth. 'We did but …' Anita cringed as the women fell silent to tune in to this snippet of gossip. 'We were friends, nothing more. You know how he's changed towards me.'

Kylie placed her hands on her hips and glared. 'Yes, well, you've changed towards 'im. Elli finks you're happy with Carl an' you'll never leave 'im.' Kylie arched her eyebrows.

Anita held her breath and silently counted to ten.

Donna chipped in with 'How do you know what Elliot thinks?', emphasising his name in full.

Dreading what Kylie might say next, Anita rushed through the last six numbers in her head like the seeker in the child's game who gets impatient waiting for the other kids to hide.

'We talk, you know. He's having a tough time. Everyone knows she has a fing for him.' Kylie nodded in Anita's direction. 'Though I told him the other day rumour has it you're separating from Carl.'

Kylie's comments escalated Anita's insecurities into a blunt response. 'Elli's also found a hot new girlfriend. Kinda makes me redundant as his potential love interest. Don't yer think?'

Betty banged the table with her cup. 'And you're still a married woman.'

Kylie mumbled under her breath, 'Old bag.'

Betty glared.

Jill, the woman in the team who deserved the promotion Kylie had received, broke the standoff. 'Rumour mill says Elliot's the new boss of the sidings when Ryan goes.'

Before Anita could answer Kylie chirped, 'Yes, he's taking over until Mr M brings someone else in. Elli said Mr M offered him the job permanent but he doesn't want it.'

'She'll be after Elli next,' Betty muttered. If Kylie heard the snide remark she never flinched.

Donna nudged her elbow into Kylie's arm. 'I heard you make dinner plans for the weekend.'

'Oh, going into town with a friend who's having a bad time.'

'Male or female friend?' Betty sniped.

Kylie waved to the waitress to order another round of drinks. Donna continued. 'Are you courting now?'

'Courting, what's that?'

'Going out with, dating a young single man,' Betty added with a sharper tone.

Kylie explained her no-strings-attached relationship with a friend's older brother. She bragged how he often made dinner reservations at a fancy restaurant then took her to the trendy new wine bar in Bold Street, with an overnight stay at a five-star hotel. Anita wondered if he'd spend that much money if sex weren't on the agenda. When Kylie went to the toilet Donna asked if Kylie had mentioned the lunch with Elliot and Jon. Anita said no.

By 5.30 the afternoon concluded. The ladies asked Anita to bring them back a cowboy. They each gave her a hug, wishing her a safe journey and a happy birthday. In the car park Anita spent a few moments reassuring Donna she'd be fine and telling her to text or e-mail if she had a problem.

Although she rebelled against the thought of turning fifty Anita couldn't wait to get to Vegas. Everything checked and packed, she prepared for an early night with a relaxing bath and a mini-facial. The cluttered dressing table displayed such a wide pro-collagen, rejuvenating and regenerating anti-aging arsenal for her fighting fifty crusades that Anita could open a spa. Each must-have product designed for women of her age came in a quality dispenser.

Anita's routine to maintain a youthful look included the need to pluck the group of coarse grey hairs that sprouted from the two moles on her face. She no longer used tweezers for her eyebrows since she'd alarmed herself one night when she'd pulled out a clump of hairs that left a bald spot. Instead Anita brushed brown powder on the noticeable grey hair that sprouted from her eyebrows.

She skimmed the tip of her finger across her jawline to locate the coarse stubble, invisible to the human eye. As her dressing table mirror was less effective than the Hubble telescope she pulled the vanity mirror closer to her face. The fear that Anita might one day find a small cactus bush growing from the side of her face came from the *Aladdin* pantomime her mother had taken her to see. When Widow Twankey had stomped the stage with an exaggerated mole sprouting long dark hairs you could sweep the theatre with, Anita's mother had warned her young daughter, 'That's what happens when you don't wash your face.'

Anita still felt the scars from the way her mother had inflicted her unique brand of humour, relying on ridiculous threats to impose parental control over her daughter's naughtiness.

During the ten minutes her anti-wrinkle mask took to penetrate, Anita scrutinised her face in the mirror that reflected the look of her mother. Applying a fine smear of rejuvenating serum, Anita recalled how throughout her tween years she'd watched her mother apply her favourite skincare products, paint her nails and colour her hair. She'd underestimated the significance of her mother's actions until she watched herself coat her own face with a layer of night collagen moisturiser.

Anita turned the mirror to the side when she recalled her mother's favourite: 'If you keep looking in the mirror, lady, one day you'll see the devil stood behind you.'

As Anita applied a generous amount of firming cream to her bust, which since she'd gained weight now came with mini boobs that hung over her double D cup, the presence of her mother's spirit kept her company. As a teenager Anita had dreaded the thought she might turn into her mother; she hadn't appreciated how proud she should have felt. Cupping her hands to inhale the bust cream residue that smelt like the lemon curd tarts she'd baked as a child, Anita looked at the night sky and whispered, 'I'm sorry, Mum.' As a woman in her mid-twenties she had become her mother's confidante. When her mother had complained of unfulfilled dreams or struggled to put into words how she yearned for something different, Anita had chastised her. She'd been too immature to understand. She understood now.

Viva Las Vegas

The agent from the kerbside airport valet desk at Manchester airport inspected the car, then issued Carl with a receipt. Although they lived thirty-five miles from Manchester, they preferred to spend the eve of their holiday at an airport hotel, especially since the time they'd been held up on the M56 for three hours and stressed they'd miss their flight.

In the hotel room Anita lined up her travel-size anti-aging products, then relaxed in the oversized bathtub of water infused with skin-nourishing milk bath. Carl logged on to his laptop. Due to the strict gaming laws in the USA, Carl wouldn't be able to access his online betting account until they returned from holiday, so he checked the early odds to place his weekend football bets.

Carl confirmed approval of his wife's black, low-cut figure-hugging dress with sheer silk tights and leather stilettos that had been buffed by the hotel shoeshine: 'Wow, what a doozie.' He pulled Anita close and kissed her. 'You look great.'

Anita licked her lips; Carl's kiss tasted like chocolate chip cookies.

In the lift to the skylight restaurant Carl frowned. Anita waited for his remark as the lift doors closed.

'Have you seen your nose?'

Anita inspected her face in the tinted glass; she couldn't see anything.

'You've got nose hair.' Carl tried to grab the long strand.

As the lift door opened Anita hurried to the ladies' powder room. She looked in the mirror and would rather have seen the devil standing behind her than the long black nose hair that protruded at least half an inch from her nostril.

Throughout dinner Anita twirled the strand between her

thumb and finger like the fiendish villain who's tied the damsel to the track and plays with his moustache as the train edges closer.

'Stop fiddling.' Carl pulled her hand from her face. 'It's hardly noticeable.'

Carl's tetchiness extended past visual imperfections. He'd contradict people who made incorrect statements or mispronounced a word. If Anita complained when he embarrassed her as a result of a faux pas in company he'd ask, 'Do you want to look stupid?'

She'd question what it mattered, why he couldn't overlook it.

He'd retort, 'How will people know they're wrong if nobody tells them?'

Anita couldn't argue with his logic.

Upstairs she rummaged through the vanity case for her nail scissors, stuck them as far up her nostril as possible and snipped the long dark strand.

Carl checked out of the hotel as Anita rummaged in her flight bag to double check she'd picked up their passports, the tickets and her purse. As they made their way to the departure desk, Anita unzipped her bag and checked again. Carl offloaded their cases to the cheerful airline agent at the first-class check-in desk. As she'd once dared to put her tweezers and nail clippers in her carry-on bag, then had them confiscated by airport security, Anita retrieved her vanity case to check she'd repacked her scissors.

Luggage-free they headed to the first-class lounge. Carl declared the official start to the holiday when he ordered breakfast for two as Anita scanned the brochure to choose their complimentary pre-flight treatment at the spa; Anita selected a manicure for herself with the Indian head massage for Carl. Two hours later the gate agent announced upper-class boarding, then escorted his elite passengers past the four hundred impatient travellers unable to afford the elevated fares.

Appreciative of the attentive service and the pods that allowed her the luxury of sleeping flat to cross the Atlantic,

Anita had insisted on flying first-class. Mindful of how, as airlines struggled to survive the economic challenges of the time, first-class no longer offered an on-board beauty therapist, greeted you by name or presented you with a hallmarked welcome gift from a famous London store, Carl responded to the diminished niceties by labelling this form of travel as 'cattle class with a civilised dining experience and a bed'.

Three hours into the flight Anita changed into her sleep suit and accepted the air hostess's offer to prepare the bed. With a press of the button the cushioned seat reversed. She laid the thin mattress, shook out the quilt and fluffed up the pillow. Anita contorted her body to get comfortable; she snuggled into her oversized pillow, then pushed in her earplugs, which diminished the sound of Carl explaining the principle of the casino's reward system to a group of Vegas virgins at the bar.

'Vegas casinos want your money, but they make the experience fun.'

Carl had the guys hooked as his pupils became aware they might miss freebies.

'Sign up for a player's card; it's the size of a credit card. Go to the slot club booth at the casino you're going to gamble in.'

Curious as to why Carl repeated elements of his conversation, Anita lifted her eye mask. She could see a man tapping notes into his PalmPilot. She fell asleep listening to the end of Carl's bedtime story.

'When you gamble on either slots or the poker machines, make sure you insert your card in the slot, wait for the display to show your name, then hit the play button. Throw your card on the table when you change cash for chips. The pit boss will monitor your action. I often get comped show tickets or vouchers for the steakhouse.'

The aroma of food warming in the galley wafted through the upper-class cabin to awaken Anita from her five-hour nap. Groggy, she changed out of her sleep suit as the air hostess returned the bed to a chair and shook out a crisp white table-cloth to prepare for afternoon tea. When Carl clipped the seat belt for the pod's visitor seat the air hostess decorated the table with a set of condiments in a minute jumbo jet and arranged two cups and saucers to match the side plates, with the silver cutlery positioned on top of a thick linen napkin; her assistant delivered an assortment of sandwiches.

Carl, an aeroplane enthusiast, read his wife's thoughts when she looked at her watch. 'Fifteen hundred miles, just under three hours to go.'

An animated Elvis with a microphone flashed on the TV monitor framed within the pod's partition to indicate the ground beneath the troposphere's weather clouds was Memphis. For the last six years any reference to Elvis had sparked the memory of Anita's mother.

'Thinking about your mum?' Carl took hold of Anita's hand, which fit into his palm. He was aware that it had been during the last mother and daughter trip to Vegas that his mother-in-law had fallen ill. On their return when she had spent three weeks in bed they had all passed it off as flu until Anita had called out the locum doctor, who had called an ambulance. The hospital had diagnosed a collapsed lung. Inflating the lung, they had found a tumour the size of an orange; four months later, she was dead. 'Go on, tell me again; I like to remember her full of life.'

Carl referred to his mother-in-law's first trip to Vegas, which had come about as she had complained, whenever Carl had asked her to mind Tara Loo for a holiday, how she'd not travelled further than Blackpool and the only time she'd been on a plane had been with her father during the war when they had gone to the Isle of Man. So for her sixty-fifth birthday Carl had treated his wife and mother-in-law to a holiday to Vegas.

Anita told snippets of the story he'd heard a thousand times. How her mother had complained for the entire ten-and-a-half-hour flight that she needed a proper cup of tea and a cigarette and how she had been wide-eyed as a child on Christmas morning as they'd passed rows of slot machines in the airport. 'It's a bit different than New Brighton,' she'd said every day of the trip.

'The look on her face when we arrived at the hotel and I pulled open the glass door to the casino was priceless.'

Carl used his thumb to stroke the back of his wife's hands. Anita found it hard to explain to people the excitement of the neon enticements or the shared energy from punters who whooped and hollered at the tables or how energised you felt from the pure oxygen they pumped into the casino, especially on your first visit, but Carl understood the exhilaration of Vegas.

They freed their hands to scoop jam and clotted cream from the small ceramic ramekin to smother on the oven-fresh scones.

Anita used the napkin to wipe melted cream from her chin. 'I'll never forget coaxing her to get a good night's sleep. Four hours later I hear, "You awake yet, lovie?"'

Carl laughed; he knew off by heart how as Anita had guided her mother through the casino en route to breakfast, her mother had stopped in awe of six Elvis impersonators standing around the craps table, each with a jet black quiff and white sequinned jumpsuit, and how when the dealer paid a winning roll they'd say 'thank you very much' with a deep southern drawl.

Carl returned to his seat when unexpected turbulence prompted the pilot to illuminate the 'fasten seat belt' sign. Anita peered through the drizzle on the plastic window as the ice that had formed at -65°F melted in the afternoon sun which shimmered golden rays across the vast desert landscape. Anita plotted the final part of the journey as they dropped a few thousand feet to prepare for landing. She traced the rugged 2,000-million-year-old Grand Canyon to the carved rim a mere 5 or 6 million years old. As they passed over Lake Mead they dropped close enough to see the civilisation that sprawled across the Nevada landscape to accommodate the influx of people who had fled to the area at the height of the state's economic prosperity. A stark contrast to today when the business pages reported how Nevada not only led the nation with the highest unemployment figures but for eighteen months straight had topped the poll for housing foreclosures.

The flight landed on time. They cleared immigration in less than an hour and made their way past eager gamblers in the airport lounge transfixed to a slot machine, a small flight bag trapped between their ankles and a Styrofoam cup of coffee and a vending machine snack clutched in each hand as they willed a big win. Anita wondered if any of them lost their holiday spend before they'd left the airport.

In the arrivals hall a chauffeur the hotel had sent held a sign with 'Carl Richardson' printed in large letters. With the frequency with which Carl and Anita visited Vegas they found the strip enticements too familiar to be fascinated, but they smiled their appreciation as the driver packed their bags into the back of the black limo and gave them the guided tour.

Anita and Carl frequented a hotel situated a few miles outside the heart of the strip, as a result of the loyalty reward enticements Carl held from his gaming turnover. The casino offered popular slot machines, which with the enhanced graphics resembled state-of-the-art video games. They offered roulette, craps and various types of card table games. The VIP poker room had been remodelled in preparation for the well-advertised poker tournament Carl would play in. With ten restaurants, a multi-screen cinema and a first-class spa you could enjoy your entire vacation without leaving the hotel.

Mid-afternoon they arrived at the hotel to find that casino gaming host Kerry Anne had upgraded Carl to a top-floor, strip-view suite. As they waited for the bellboy to deliver the luggage, Anita brewed a pot of coffee from the generous selection of blends in the welcome basket that sat on the breakfast bar beside a bottle of champagne in a cooler and a tray of chocolate-covered strawberries. She passed Carl the envelope propped between the champagne flute glasses; it contained the details of the 'seat' he'd been assigned in the poker tournament.

Carl pulled back the heavy drapes to unveil the floor-to-ceiling windows so they could watch the strip hotels' neon illuminations light Las Vegas Boulevard like a runway as the bellboy unloaded their bags into the bedroom.

Anita frowned at how her attempt to pay back her mother for the scary tales she'd tormented her with as a child had backfired as she watched Carl wheel the two suitcases into the bathroom and place the vanity case in the oval bathtub. The suite, like the rest of the hotel, was spotless, but Anita had been haunted by unease in hotels ever since she had read her mother an article about hotel bug infestations across America. The report gave a skin-crawling in-depth explanation of how bugs lived in the nooks and crevices of hotel rooms – beds, head-boards, carpets, furnishings and, especially as the pests liked to live in wood, clothes drawers – and tips for how to avoid picking up bed bugs when you're on vacation and taking them on a vacation of their own when you bring them back home in your unprotected luggage. Anita didn't go as far as to bring an LED light to inspect the room, avoid hanging her clothes in the closet or pack her clothes in sealable plastic bags; however, she always unpacked her luggage in the bathtub, placed her suitcase on a metal bag stand and used the wooden drawers for Carl's clothes.

Anita unpacked the toiletries each side of the 'his and hers' wash basins.

Carl issued his orders like a drill sergeant – 'toothbrush and toothpaste' – then updated her on the complexities of the poker tournament. 'Starts day after tomorrow at noon; the buy-in gets you 10,000 in chips. The ante and the blinds look fair. Can you put your hand on my shaver?'

Anita pushed the plastic toiletries bag into the middle of the van-ity unit. 'What's the ante and the blinds when they're at home?'

'The compulsory stake you put in. Aftershave.'

Anita opened the champagne; as Juliet would say, this conver-sation required alcohol.

'There's an alternating series of ten- and fifteen-minute breaks; each second break, chips are removed, twenty-five at the first break, a thousand at the last. With twenty-four levels: thirty minutes each. The tournament prize goes to whoever's left in at the end.'

Anita handed Carl clean underwear, trousers and a T-shirt. 'I think I'll give you a wide berth; sounds like big money and loads of concentration.'

*

Unlike their married friends Anita and Carl preferred their own routine. Carl would start at the craps tables, then take an anti-clockwise route to the sports book. Anita would head to the far end of the casino to play in the less busy area. Sometimes their paths wouldn't cross for days, which was why Carl suggested they meet at the Mexican restaurant at eight. Showered, shaved and changed, he headed to the casino. Forty minutes later, unpacked and freshened up, Anita headed for the lift.

The oversized casino daunted first-time visitors. In rodeo week the thousands of indistinguishable bull-riding enthusiasts wearing high-crowned, flat wide-brimmed cowboy hats who congregated around the gaming tables or bars overwhelmed even the most regular of visitors.

Anita manoeuvred through the smell of leather and headed in a random direction in the hope her preferred gaming area would be less crowded. When she emerged from a cluster of ranchers she spotted Carl in the sports book. This dedicated area provided a function equivalent to a betting shop in the UK, except this punter's paradise had luxury seats with a personal television monitor on each table and a provocatively dressed cocktail waitress available to bring you a free alcoholic or soft drink with the hope of a generous tip. One wall housed a number of small screens that showed live sports action including horse racing from a number of American tracks.

Carl watched football on a giant monitor that filled the wall. As soccer's popularity had increased in the USA, due in part to the Fox channel, which took the live feed from Sky Sports to beam premiership football games across the United States, the casino enticed punters with in-house bets for the televised games. Anita watched Carl count a number of bills to one of half a dozen tellers who lined the counter under the wall-sized odds board, ready to take any of the multitudes of bets advertised by the casino.

Anita tapped him on the shoulder. 'How's it going?'

As Carl's reply left no opening for further conversation she left him and headed in a different direction.

*

Anita ordered the Baja Miguel's signature margarita to wash down the tortilla chips she nibbled as she engrossed herself in the *What's On* magazine article about the life of a bull rider, then found herself gripped by the glossy exposé on the young women who trolled the circuit in the hope they'd snag a rich rancher or rodeo star. Her second margarita arrived at the same time as Carl, who kissed the top of her head and then gave her a summary of the craps game. He'd lost two hundred, so on his turn to shoot he broke another Benjamin. He'd rolled for an hour then crapped out. Anita enjoyed craps when she played with Carl at a quiet table, as this allowed her time to check her bets, although the stick man would remind her if a hard way went down or check if Anita wanted craps and eleven referred to as C and E for the come out roll and remember to switch her hard ways to off.

Anita continued to peruse the magazine as Carl's tale turned to woe when a few hands of Texas hold 'em had depleted his winnings. 'They're holding a country music awards on my birthday. Why aren't I going?'

Carl grabbed the magazine. 'I've planned something special so do as you're told. If you mither you'll spoil the surprise.'

As a child Anita had resisted the temptation to peek at the unwrapped Christmas presents on the top of her parents' wardrobe. No doubt due to a harrowing tale her mother had told to warn how the perils of peeking would result in Anita's nose growing six inches or some equally ridiculous affliction.

Once they'd finished their fajitas Carl, lured by the enthused sounds from a hot craps table, took a detour to join the game. Fatigued, Anita headed to the left where she bumped into Dylan Faulkner, who like the rest of the casino staff had donned cowboy attire to add to the rodeo atmosphere.

Dylan tipped his hat. 'I was on my way up to slip these under your door.'

He handed her a packet containing the country concert tickets Carl had ordered, plus two bonus seats to see Big and Rich. She explained to Dylan that Carl probably wouldn't go to the latter. Dylan convinced her Carl would love the concert as the band 'kicked ass' and attracted provocatively dressed women.

As Dylan shared Anita's love of country music she often joined him for a drink. She enjoyed flirting with Dylan. Despite his obvious good looks she didn't fancy him. She didn't need to; Dylan fancied himself enough for both of them. They made their way to the bar at the far end of the casino designated to the NFR for the duration of the rodeo, with a dedicated big-screen TV to show the full programme of events live from the Thomas Mac centre. Their chat covered an update on the headline concerts, new albums and Brooks and Dunn's announcement that they were going their separate ways. When the combination of Jim Beam and jet lag hit Anita she thanked Dylan, promised to catch up with him before the end of the week and returned to her suite.

It normally took Anita six days to acclimatise to the eight-hour time difference. Luck dictated her bedtime, though jet lag normally hit her by ten. Regardless of the hour she went to bed, she would wake at 2 am. To combat her mid-day fatigue she'd take a two-hour nap.

As the casino operated around the clock you could saunter into the casino at any time to find the tables open and the dealers ready for action. Alternatively you could play any of 2,563 ever-ready machines that flashed their neon enticements morning, noon and night. Carl often commented on the people he had seen playing a machine when he headed to bed and found sitting in the exact same spot when he returned hours later. If you tired of gambling or needed to break an unlucky streak then you'd find the all-day breakfast available at the twenty-four hour café.

As both of them regularly lost track of the time after days in the clockless, windowless casino Anita prepared an Excel spreadsheet to keep track of the events they'd booked. She ticked off the first day, then took the hire car agreement and rodeo tickets out of the safe and left those on the lounge table along with a note to remind Carl of their 4 pm meet-up time.

As the sun disappeared behind Red Rock Canyon the desert temperature dropped. Anita shivered under the industrial-sized heater used by all the hotels as Carl waited for the valet to sprint into the underground car park and retrieve the hire car. They left early to beat the 20,000 strong rush of cowboys to the Thomas and Mack Centre: home to the University of Las Vegas basketball team and host of the annual rodeo competitions collectively known as NFR. As Americans do they ignored grammar to call the event the National Finals Rodeo.

Anita linked arms with Carl as they moseyed past the NFR stands littered around the outside of the stadium, taking the opportunity to stop and warm the top half of their bodies beneath the umbrella of portable heaters spaced at regular intervals. Carl tucked into a second buffalo burger as he followed his wife into the beer tent packed with folks wearing cowboy boots and similar NFR branded attire. Carl ordered their obligatory drinks: a Jack and diet for her, and a large diet for him. Anita foot-stomped as the DJ played requests for Jason Aldean, Lady Antebellum, George Strait and every popular country artist in between. Carl's interest peaked when two scantily clad cowgirls electrified the atmosphere by hopping onto the bar to perform a hip-gyrating line dance. The cowboys swigged bottles of the sponsor's beer and showed their appreciation for the show as they tucked dollar bills into the top of the dancers' red snakeskin boots.

Forty minutes later the stadium opened its doors to a surge of rodeo-starved ticket holders. Carl pinched his nose when the pong of horse and cattle dung mixed together with straw greeted them as they neared their gold buckle seats. Anita thumbed through the programme to check the schedule. Each rodeo event consisted of a number of heats that culminated with the final on the Saturday. The person with the best aggregate score from the heats would be deemed the champion. The nightly winners received a small prize with the overall event winner presented with a larger cash prize; theoretically if you won the final of your event you could amass a sizeable amount, although compared to the money associated with other sports the value seemed meagre.

Bareback riding headed the event, followed by steer wrestling, team and tie-down roping, then the women's event, barrel racing, which involved riding a horse around four barrels without touching them; the fastest time won. When Anita asked Carl why women only participated in one event, he said if they got injured there'd be nobody to cook the beans for tea.

The organisers saved the main event for last. Bull riding involved a cowboy, kicked in the head more than once, staying on the back of a crazy wild-eyed bull for a grand total of eight seconds. Like most people Anita thought this would be an easy achievement for an experienced rider until she witnessed the first eleven getting thrown off in times that ranged from one to six and a half seconds. With everyone caught up in the buzz, anticipation for the last contestant to appear intensified when the commentator reminded the audience that if this bull rider beat the clock he'd scoop the cumulative prize money. The tension built as the noise of the crowd's whistles, whoops and hollering echoed around the stadium. Anita felt sure the rider could do without the extra pressure as he prepared to mount the back of the 'beast from hell'.

Anita's heart lodged in her throat as the camera zoomed in to project onto the big screen the bull rider's leather-gloved hand gripping the rope as the bull bucked, both impatient for the gate to open. The rider shot from the pen. Carl kept one eye on the clock that took an eternity to reach the five-second mark. Around the stadium pockets of the crowd screeched, 'He's gonna do it, y'all!'

With six point seven seconds on the clock most of the audience covered their eyes as the bull tossed his rider into the air. In slow motion the rider hit the floor. The outrider circled the bull. Rodeo clowns charged into the ring from various directions to distract the rampant bull from the immobilised body. Eventually an outrider hauled the broken-boned rodeo start onto his mount. They left the arena to sympathetic applause.

Back at the hotel, exhausted from the exuberance of the rodeo, Anita left Carl in the casino and headed to the suite. She ticked the second day off on her spreadsheet, then left the envelope with Carl's 'seat' for the poker tournament on the table with a good luck note.

Due to Carl's good run in the early rounds of the poker tournament combined with a profitable return from the tables, he avoided Anita more than usual. To pacify his wife Carl suggested dinner to catch up en route to the Wynn, winner of the most Forbes five-star awards in the world, where Anita had a front-row ticket to watch Garth Brooks perform at the Encore Theatre.

Carl tolerated Anita's love of country music to join her for the occasional concert, although the success of the Big and Rich experience threatened to change his perspective. Carl enjoyed the songs but showed an elevated appreciation for the efforts made by a high quantity of women in sexy outfits, some of which bordered on pornographic. Carl protested that the boob flashers who sent him into a muted cardiac arrest were a welcome visitor to a healthy man's life. The thrill extended throughout the night and resulted in their first sex session in months.

Carl preferred to take Anita to dinner at a cowboy bar; that way she could get her fix of country music and he could enjoy a succulent steak. As they'd eaten at Gilly's en route to watch Brooks and Dunn, Carl suggested Toby Keith's I Love This Bar and Grill. The perky tip-hungry waitress offered them a booth, then reeled off her well-rehearsed patter and the daily specials. With her fixed white smile she scribbled on a palm-held electronic device Anita's order of a Mason jar of whiskey girl with the fried catfish dinner and baked potato – butter, no sour cream – and Carl's order of a cowboy cut New York strip, medium rare with a diet Coke.

Carl's lacklustre demeanour told Anita the last round of the poker tournament hadn't gone as expected well before he explained how he had thought he was on for a big blind special but finished with a bee stinger. His alien terms of reference delivered the message that Carl's participation in the tournament had ended.

As they ate Carl updated his wife on the newly installed bank of 'progressive' slot machines he'd played. The object of the bonus game excited you with the prospect of getting three balls in one of three jackpot tubes. The prizes ranged from the Mini, which normally paid around $30, up to the Grand, which stood at over $3,000. Carl played for five minutes before the bonus game was initiated. Similar to a game a child might play on a handheld console, the screen transformed from the standard slot reels to an animated clown with a long tube that protruded from its mouth to scroll across the screen. As instructed Carl pressed the illuminated button. The clown spat a white ping-pong ball, which bounced between each of the jackpot receptacles, then landed in the Mini. Carl played Anita a video he'd taken with his mobile phone to record the fun of the bonus, which teased with two graphic white balls in the 'Grand' then two in each of the others, but then to Anita's amazement the unthinkable happened: the third ball dropped into the 'Grand' slot. The screen animated a firework display, then flashed congratulations to Carl on his $3,089.23 win.

With replenished funds Carl flitted to play a bank of machines in the Wynn casino as Anita revelled in Garth Brooks's down-home roots and charismatic informal performance. Rather than the traditional concert she'd expected to see, on a stool in the middle of the stage Garth performed his one-man show. He strummed his guitar to captivate his audience with songs that took them on the journey of his musical influences, entwined with personal stories. When Trisha Yearwood joined him on stage to duet for *In Another's Eyes* the intimacy of their performance could have melted the most hardened of hearts.

It was two days later when Anita next caught up with Carl; he woke her from an afternoon nap with the news that Dylan had left two complementary VIP tickets to see Phil Vassar that night at Green Valley Ranch.

Situated ten miles from the main strip area, the Station Casinos flagship hotel's moderately-sized entertainments room wasn't exactly the venue of superstars but their front-row seats ensured a position at the heart of the action, or so they thought. They shuffled towards the five-foot-high platform stage behind a line of middle-aged woman that Carl described as MILFs.

Carl laughed. 'Well, that's different; it's like sitting at the bottom of a cliff. If his guitarist takes a wrong step he'll end up in a MILF's lap. Though I expect he'll probably end up in her lap later anyway.'

By the rapturous applause from a four hundred strong crowd Anita assumed the front man had appeared. She watched the crown of his head as Phil sat at the grand piano positioned at the rear of the stage to perform the first number.

Carl's quips entertained her more than the concert. 'It's a good job you came to listen rather than watch him,' he shouted to be heard above Phil's piano solo. 'You know what this reminds me of?' Carl nodded to Phil, whose head bobbed up from behind the piano lid. '*Top of the Pops* from the 1970s when Gilbert O'Sullivan sang *Get Down*; but we want Phil to Get Up.'

'Maybe he heard you,' Anita shouted as Phil jumped on top of the piano.

Carl remarked, 'How funny would it be if the brakes failed and the piano skidded off the stage?'

They both yelled, '*The Music Box*!' They always named this Laurel and Hardy episode as their favourite, in particular the scene that involved the comic duo being tasked to deliver a piano to a house at the top of a hill. The slapstick geniuses leave the horse and cart at the bottom, then carry the piano up ten or twelve flights of stairs. During the sketch the piano ends up at the bottom of the steps at least five times due to various mishaps. When they finally get to the top of the stoop they meet the postman, who points to a road that runs up the hill around the back of the house. So they take the piano back down the steps, load it onto the horse and cart, then drive the piano directly to the front door.

Eventually Phil abandoned his piano and exuded a vast amount of energy as he bounded across the front of the stage, much to the delight of Anita and the MILFs.

At the end of the evening instead of stopping off at the craps table Carl followed Anita up to the suite to give his wife her birthday surprise. When she opened the envelope and checked the details she threw her arms around Carl's neck; her affectionate appreciation led to their second sex session in months.

Honolulu Baby

Cases packed, Anita logged on to the laptop to use the online check-in for their 11 pm flight. She e-mailed the girls that Carl's birthday surprise was a two-night break in Honolulu. Two new message alerts sounded. She read the general e-mail update from Donna and Juliet's one-line message, You'll never guess who's asked me out? Anita thought of eight men off the top of her head. As she opened up the hotel reservation for her stay at Chrystalmere a 'swish' sound alerted her to a new e-mail.

When Anita read the first line bile rose in her throat. Although Carl wasn't in the suite she lowered the lid of the laptop and looked around the bedroom when she realised Elliot had replied to her personal e-mail.

Anita
I'm sorry if you think that I've hurt you.
I value your input into my contracts and I hope to have your continued involvement to support Donna now and in the future.
You've made the situation clear: you're a married woman with no signs of leaving him.
Am I wrong?
Elliot

As she reread his empty words her heart deadened.

A limo driver greeted them off their six-hour Hawaiian Airlines flight. They exchanged pleasantries as their chauffeur opened the backseat cabinet to display the selection of complimentary refreshments available for the forty-five minute journey to the beachfront hotel.

On her birthday's eve, encircled by tiki torches they enjoyed a lavish meal of fresh fish served with local vegetables at the courtyard restaurant. Anita pulled a thin cardigan over her shoulders as they sat beneath the stars to sip Blue Hawaii cocktails, listening to a trio of Hawaiian musicians performing their ukulele rendition of Elvis songs. When they returned to their two-bedroom suite Anita realised she'd be sleeping alone when Carl asked which room she wanted.

She tugged hard at the white Egyptian cotton sheets to create a space large enough to slide under. Embraced by the oversized quilt that snuggled her like a lover's arms, Anita fell asleep until the date she'd dreaded since her father had died ten years earlier arrived with a continuous fanfare of text notifications, complete with kisses and smiley face symbols, to wish her happy birthday.

Carl put a cup of coffee on her bedside table. 'Come on, get up, I've booked a sunrise breakfast, open your cards on the beach.'

Anita walked into the bathroom to turn on the shower.

Carl banged on the door. 'Make it quick, wear something sexy and remember to shave.'

Carl squeezed Anita's hand as they waited at the waterfront podium for the maître d' to confirm their reservation. Reservation confirmed, they were introduced to the hostess who Carl greeted with a rehearsed, '*Aloha kakahiaka*.'

With a smile as bright as her red and white orchid print muumuu she responded with her own *aloha*. They followed her past the tiki torches that lit up the beach pathway to their private table cocooned within a fine cotton enclosure, where she introduced their waiter as Abdiel.

'*E komo mai. Noho ilalo*.'

Anita looked at an equally confused Carl.

Abdiel gave a deep, throaty laugh. 'I'm sorry; welcome, come in, please sit.' He pinned back the sides of the tent to unveil the sun, which shone a spotlight on the participants in the sunrise hula exercise class who moved in time to the beat of the pahu drum as the symphony of the surf sprayed against the shore.

The aroma from the floral bouquet of plumera blossoms, deep purple orchids and yellow hibiscus weaved through the bird of paradise centrepiece, mixing with fresh fruit platter and chilled juice cocktail, added to the ambiance. Anita nibbled papaya as she watched their waiter secure the trolley underneath two arched palm trees, then lift the large dome lids to reveal the assortment of hot food.

'*Hau'oli la hanau*. Happy birthday.' Abdiel placed a bottle of champagne in the cooler at the side of the table. 'Compliments of the hotel.'

Breakfast complete, Carl popped the cork. As she sipped chilled sweet bubbles Anita opened her birthday cards. She scanned the card from work to see if Elliot had written a message. He had. She wished he hadn't.

Anita gave Carl a peck on the cheek. 'I love the breakfast, the surroundings, everything.'

Carl looked at the sea. Aloud he shared his thoughts. 'What's going to happen with us? We can't go on like this.' His head rolled in sync with the surfers who negotiated the waves in preparation for their glide to the shore.

'I have been trying to talk to you for weeks.'

Carl continued to concentrate on the aqua ripples of the Pacific Ocean. 'I know. But we come on holiday and it's nice, like it used to be, then we go home where you're either wrapped up in work or fighting impending doom, and let's not forget your mood swings.'

'How could we forget? You remind me often enough.'

'Here we go.' Layers of fine sandy hair filtered through Carl's fingers as his hands gripped the side of his head.

'I get it, my temperament's difficult for you, but you're as bad stuck in front of the PC.'

He turned his head to deliver his sharp words: 'It's how I make my living. Remember?'

'Do we have to do this?'

'No, but January you'll be off down south. I'm sick of hearing how there's a lot riding on this contract. How's that going to affect us?

Anita banged the empty champagne glass on the table. 'I've asked you to come with me.'

Carl drained the champagne into her glass, then slammed the bottle neck-first into the cooler. 'I don't want to go with you. I want to stay in my own house. I'm happy with my life. You're the one who needs constant change.'

'Whatever. Why do you wait until my guard's down, then make an insensitive remark? Oh, what's the point? I'm sick of trying. Nice bloody birthday celebration this turned into.'

'A hundred sixty miles isn't the end of the earth. Let's see how it goes. Anyway, I don't want the house left empty.'

Carl left Abdiel a generous tip, then put his arm around Anita. 'Forget I said anything. Enjoy your day. I've planned a special treat for tonight; c'mon, give us a smile, you know you want to.'

Anita shrugged him off. As she stomped back to the hotel, she took a moment to scorn the couples that held hands to meander the golden sands of Waikiki beach.

For Anita's final birthday surprise an exotic lady greeted them aboard the sunset catamaran cruise with a Hawaiian lei and an ice cold mai tai. As they coasted from the Waikiki shoreline the sun slipped from the sky; a few nautical miles into the Pacific Ocean, strangers gathered to photograph the city, sphered in the orange hue. The waitress topped up the cocktail glasses as the waiters dished out teriyaki chicken skewers and BBQ ribs from foil trays in a makeshift galley; passengers stood in huddles around the deck with video cameras poised to capture the firework display. Carl cocooned his wife against the rail as they admired how the moon crowned the outline of Diamond Head to emboss it within the black sky.

The bell rang for the start of the firework display. Carl rested his chin on Anita's shoulder as they watched the adornment of sparkling colour illuminating the night sky to reflected shimmers of pink, gold and green on the ripples of calm Pacific waters.

The night ended on a nicer note when they agreed not to

discuss the future until after the holiday. As Anita retired to her own room she wondered how much more of her unorthodox behaviour Carl could endure as he waited for his wife to be cured of whatever ailed her and abandon her search for a life her husband couldn't provide, a life he believed didn't exist outside the walls of her imagination,

The next day, sat on the balcony they enjoyed their room service breakfast as they savoured the contrast of the Pacific Ocean against the beauty of the sedate island landscape, aware that later that day they flew home.

Whilst Anita headed for the spa's signature three-hour top-to-toe pamper treatment, pre-booked as part of her birthday surprise package, Carl, with his laptop balanced on his knee and a crushed ice fruit cocktail at arm's length, found solace amongst other Internet-hungry males, enticed to lounge in the luxurious hotel foyer by free Wi-Fi.

Anita inhaled until it hurt but failed to tighten the ten holiday pounds she'd gained which hung like a pouch over her bikini bottoms. With forty-five minutes until her treatment Anita checked her reflection in the full-length mirror behind the door.

She reflected on how with a tan the skin on her neck looked like an unfolded origami swan but her cellulite-dimpled thighs appeared less prominent. When she turned around she thought how Mark from work would say, 'Why worry about your arse? It's us men who have to look at it.'

Anita slipped off the oversized robe and slippers to dangle her feet in the Olympic-size pool before she lowered herself into the warm water; she couldn't swim, but liked to float on her back. As Anita strayed into the deep end panic prompted a frenzied splash to propel her far enough to find the bottom of the pool with her toes, much to the annoyance of the half-submerged woman who engaged in mundane conversation.

Bored of the inane chatter around the pool, Anita headed to the relaxation room, took a neck pillow from the warmer and reclined the chair to stretch her legs on the pouf as she waited for her appointment, designed to enhance her wellbeing.

The perky therapist introduced herself as Zoe. 'I see your husband booked this treatment; special occasion?'

Anita nestled on the heated treatment table. 'If you call another year older special; it's my fiftieth.'

Zoe used her fingertips to examine the texture of Anita's face. 'Your skin's in excellent condition; you don't have many lines.'

'Unfortunately looks are only part of the equation; I feel ninety-two today.'

The therapist presented a tray of products to show Anita the range of oils and an exotically-named mud she'd be using for the full-body treatment. 'What's wrong with fifty? It's the new forty, so they say.'

Anita felt like a Thanksgiving turkey when the therapist basted her salt-scrubbed body with moisture-rich algae mud, wrapped her in foil and cloaked her with a heated blanket. As Anita baked she flinched when Zoe smoothed repair cream into her hands and feet, then covered them with mitts and booties freshly warmed in the mini oven by the sink. Zoe dimmed the light, placed a warmed wheat bag over Anita's closed eyes, set the timer for thirty minutes, then left.

Unshackled, Anita reflected on how her life appeared to have evaporated. When she thought of her father's death she tried to recall the headline events of her last ten years. The search prompted the question: if she died at seventy-three what significant experiences could she expect over the next twenty-three years?

The solitude rekindled Anita's dark mood to make her recall the curtness of Elliot's e-mail. Despite her best efforts to push thoughts of him to the back of her mind, her consciousness wouldn't relent. Whichever part of her brain inflicted torture insisted on a vivid replay of how for the last four years she and Elliot had skirted the periphery of an affair and how the crescendo of their mutual desire had happened on the night Ryan had treated the team to a free night out to celebrate the success of their latest project.

As Anita couldn't trust her behaviour if she drank too much she drove that night. To make sure she stuck to her plan she offered to collect Pike, Henry and Joey on the way; they thankfully refused a lift home as they'd booked an overnight stay.

Anita's flesh-coloured gel bra gave oomph to the plunging neckline of her Lycra mix dress. As sexy trumped comfort, she wore the matching G-string she'd spend the night discreetly tugging from between her buttocks. With her hair curled she applied a generous spray of Gucci Guilty, a thick layer of mascara, thin charcoal pencil lines under her eyes and two coats of red lipstick a few shades lighter than her scarlet dress. Once she had checked the expensive silk tights, guaranteed to enhance her slender legs, for snags she slipped on her red high heels.

When they arrived at the venue the guys teased that Anita scrubbed up well for an old 'un. The night combined fun, good conversation, and free drinks. Five Diet Cokes later Anita needed the loo. As she approached the ladies', Elliot, who'd arrived late, came out of the gents'.

To be heard above the noise of drunken revellers in the crowded bar he stood close. 'You look gorgeous, titch; let me get you a drink?'

Elliot's intoxicating effect on her was greater than any alcohol. As he kissed her neck, breathless she declined. When Alan pulled Elliot's arm to drag him into the pool room he squeezed Anita's hand. Thirty minutes later, disappointed she was unable to find Elliot, she said her goodbyes and left.

The chill from the plummeted temperature caused her skin to goosebump; Anita rubbed her arms and wished she'd brought a coat. As she hurried to the far end of the dimly lit car park she recognised her name; she turned to see Elliot jog towards her.

'Hold up. Any chance of a lift home?'

Her keyless Toyota unlocked when she touched the handle of the passenger side door. 'It'll cost you.'

As she turned Elliot took half a step back, then pulled her body into his. His grip tightened as his mouth locked hers. The taste of his kiss lingered on her lips when he withdrew. Elliot relaxed his grip. Anita's bare flesh tingled from the rush of cold air. Elliot rubbed her arms with his large hands. Her head spun as her insides churned. She could hear her heartbeat vibrating through her eardrum as Elliot's hands cautiously roamed the outside of her dress. The passionate kiss that followed distracted her as his hands rolled over her breasts. He looked into her eyes as his hands slithered towards her hips. His fingers hooked the hem of her dress. She thawed at the touch of his warm calloused hands that roamed her thighs. Cognisant of their public location, Anita pulled back to check nobody had witnessed their display of passion in the cold mist of the unshielded car park.

As they drove onto the main road she searched for Elliot's hand.

Elliot broke the silence. 'I couldn't take my eyes off you tonight. You look hot, titch.'

'And here's me thinking you want me for my mind.'

'Trust me, titch, the way you look only an idiot would want your brain.'

Elliot suggested they pull into a secluded lay-by that truckers used to park overnight.

'Oh, titch, you've no idea how long I've wanted you.'

Cradling her cheek with his hand he stroked her face. His chapped lips replaced tender kisses with a renewed intensity. Her body jerked back as Elliot pulled at the bar under her seat. She wriggled to get comfortable as Elliot tugged the lever to recline her. His hands stroked the length of her arms until he found her wrists. He turned her palms towards his mouth, then kissed the full length of her arm. Anita squeezed her eyes shut, scared to look. His eagerness for the taste of her neck magnified her passion as she quivered at the touch of his long thick fingers that found their way over her neckline.

When the straps from her dress fell to her elbows, he released the clasp on her gel bra. Anita whispered 'no' but made no move to stop Elliot, who pulled the cups to expose her breasts. She quivered as his warm breath exhaled onto her bare flesh; his lips moved from her neck to taste the tip of her erect nipple. Anita winced as Elliot seized her nipple between his orthodontist-perfect teeth. An electric charge of excitement surged through her body when she wondered if his naked torso looked as good as she'd fantasised. She undid the buttons on the shirt fated to become her favourite, then like those of a sculptor whose hands embrace the texture of wet clay in preparation to mould a masterpiece her fingers ran over his chest. As Anita nuzzled into the curly soft chest hair that paved the route to his navel, to tempt her to move lower he clenched his stomach. Anita removed her tights and threw them onto the back seat. The crescendo of desire forced her legs wider apart. His hand moved inside her G-string; when he lifted her bottom she pulled her knees together. Elliot took a few second to register her changed reaction.

'Stop. If we do this we'll regret it. I don't want to be a ten-minute fumble. I can't, no matter how much I want you.'

Elliot stared at the steamed-up windscreen as he digested her words.

Embarrassed by her state of undress, she fastened her bra and retrieved her dress. As Elliot turned onto his side to fix his trousers she snuggled into his back and kissed the dark freckle on the nape of his neck.

'I couldn't face Carl. I'm sure you don't want to sit across from your wife at breakfast knowing you've cheated on her.'

Elliot held Anita in his arms. As he kissed her forehead the thud of his heart hammered against her chest. 'We OK, titch?'

'Yes. I'm sorry, you must think …'

Before she could finish Elliot put a finger on her lips. 'It's OK, you're right and you deserve better than a quickie in a lay-by, but if you want to change your mind …' He forced a laugh.

The mix of scents trapped within the car tempted her to rip off his clothes then straddle him to finally release the lust entrenched within her.

Instead Anita uttered the words, 'Sod off home and do it yourself.' She hung her head with a pang of regret.

'Looks like I'll have to.' Elliot got out of the car, then opened the driver's door. As his body eclipsed hers he whispered, 'I care too much to spoil what we have.'

Elliot kissed her, pulled up the collar of his Ashby waxed

jacket and headed home to his family. As Anita drove back to an empty house she skipped a number of tracks until the LEDs displayed her favourite song, *Relentless.*

Zoe lifted the wheat bag from Anita's eyes and raised the lights. A line of showerheads suspended from an arm sprinkled Anita clean with tepid water as Zoe scrubbed the desiccated algae residue from Anita's body. As Zoe completed the full-body treatment with an anti-aging facial and hot oil scalp massage, Anita thought how she may well look rejuvenated on the outside but her memory of Elliot left her feeling old and jaded on the inside.

Within twenty-four hours the location may have changed but their routine remained unchanged. To combat the jet lag Anita went to bed. Carl resumed his usual position for his fix to satisfy his gambling craving and to catch up with his cyber buddies on his betting provider's members' forum.

Mid Life Crisis

Fingers dipped into the second oversized box of chocolate-covered macadamia nuts as Anita multi-tasked to filter Ryan's priority e-mails, accept the recurring invitation to Ryan's 3.30 get-together, reject Mark's invitation to the Christmas party and share her holiday highlights with her work colleagues inquisitive about whether Waikiki beach resembled the opening scenes from Hawaii Five-O.

Anita arranged to call in to Juliet's on the way home, as Juliet insisted on seeing her friend's expression when she revealed the name of her mystery courter. They filled the time with a discussion about Carl's decision to stay in Liverpool and Elliot's e-mail reply until a dismayed Donna blustered into the office.

Donna made a motion as if pulling her hair. 'As you can see, Elliot's contract's still here. Kylie had a right argy-bargy with him. She refused to include the three documents he added without your agreement. He refused to sign it. Oh, and by the way he's off.'

'Don't tell me he's Christmas shopping with his hot new girl-friend or at breakfast with Kylie.'

Donna shrugged her shoulders. Anita did a quick check of the contract's contents, removed the additions Elliot had inserted, then phoned Kylie who reluctantly agreed to get the contract couriered to the client without Elliot's signature. Anita suggested Donna PDF the contract and e-mail it to the client.

Anita blocked nine till two from her calendar to peer review the perpetual scope documents with Donna. By three, up-to-date Anita handed her live files to Donna and turned her focus to Ryan's afternoon get-together.

Anita drained the dregs of the lukewarm coffee as Ryan passed her a list of the resources he intended to poach from the sidings.

'Have you given thought to the relocation package?'

Anita assured him relocation wouldn't be an issue as Carl could do his thing anywhere there was an Internet connection; all she needed to do now was convince Carl.

'I'd like to take Mark and Joey but they're picking up any slack when Elliot deputises for me. Where's Donna up to with the turbine hall contract?

'Gone today, but if Elliot's got enough on his plate, what if the client instructs us to accelerate the programme, seein' we've missed the January start date?'

Ryan checked his laptop. 'Didn't you know? Elliot's used the mild weather forecast to negotiate a flexible start date; he's got the contractor coming in Christmas Eve of all days for a meeting.'

Anita couldn't be sure how much Ryan knew of her turbulent relationship with Elliot. She guessed nothing, otherwise he'd have known Elliot didn't tell her diddly-squat these days. Anita scribbled a note on her pad to check the contents of the three sections she'd removed and prayed they had no relevance given this new information.

The aroma of garlic wafted from Juliet's small kitchen when she opened the front door to greet Anita with the question, 'So go on, chuck. Guess who's asked me to dinner?'

'It's been a shit day; can't you tell me without the guess-who game?'

As Juliet laid the kitchen table with two cups of coffee, a plate of toasted crusty bread and a pineapple upside-down cake she prompted Anita to offload.

'Usual crap with Elliot and I've told Ryan today I'll relocate to Chrystalmere.'

'Maybe you shouldn't go.'

'I'm going with or without Carl. Anyway, back to the quiz: who asked you out?'

The second slice of cheese bruschetta in Juliet's hand appeared destined back to the plate for a moment before she took a big bite. Her eyes closed as her crammed mouth hummed a sound of approval. She wiped the edge of her lips, then collected the crumbs lodged in her cleavage.

'OK, I'll play. I guess Nathan.'

'No. Guess again.' Juliet switched the convector heater to high. 'It's a bit nippy in here, feels like we might have a white Christmas after all.'

As the warmth circulated Anita reeled off the names of the men in head office, then every other male she could recall.

Juliet picked up her coffee. 'You're nowhere near close, chuck.'

Anita held the upside-down cake hostage. 'I give in. Tell me or this cake goes home with me.'

'Keep it quiet, it's a bit sensitive.' With her coffee cupped between her hands, she leaned forward to whisper her secret. 'It's Ryan, he phoned me last Saturday.'

Anita slid the cake towards Juliet. 'My Ryan! Good grief, could this be my cue to give you sensible advice for a change?'

Juliet stabbed her folk into two cubes of pineapple and popped them into her mouth as she answered. 'Actually, he phoned to ask if I'd oversee the change control element of the Big Contract, then he asked if I wanted to go for dinner and drinks with him before he moves to Chrystalmere.'

'You could give Kylie a lesson in sleeping your way to the top. What did you say?'

'Yes and yes.'

'Bloody hell, if you dare to give me your pearls of wisdom on how office romances end in disaster …'

'You know what the wise preach, chuck: do as I say, not as I do.'

'And Leo?'

Juliet had met Leo, the male participant in the affair she didn't mention in public, when she'd become a regular at the Palace bingo hall to get a few hours of respite from the nightly arguments with her now ex-husband. The night she stayed for the last-chance game, Leo joined Juliet's group of regulars for a quick drink in the pub. For the next three months Leo boosted Juliet's ego when he flirted and seduced her with outlandish compliments. He suggested they start a torrid affair. Juliet's unbearable home life encouraged her to go to bingo more often. When Leo offered Juliet the fun she desperately missed in her life she convinced herself that Leo's proposal made sense.

Juliet emerged from her divorce as a stronger liberated woman. She entertained Anita with her colourful cougar stories when she dated a string of younger men and tried a threesome on holiday for which both men took Viagra to satisfy her sexual appetite. She'd continued to date Leo on a friend-with-benefits basis.

'I've told Leo if I date a man with potential then he's history.'

Anita followed with two fresh cups of coffee as Juliet carried the remainder of the cake into the lounge. Unconvinced by Juliet's protests, Anita cajoled her for the details of her upcoming dinner date with Ryan.

Juliet played with her food. 'I must kinda fancy him; otherwise I wouldn't feel like a sixteen-year-old kid.' She hugged a cushion. As she beamed her face blushed. 'He's reserved a table Wednesday in the conservatory of that posh Moroccan restaurant in town.'

Juliet Googled the website. '"Enjoy our intimate retreat perfect for couples, with soft furnishings to ensure you"' – Juliet lowered the tone of her voice and added an unrecognisable accent – '"*experience the magnificence of a Moroccan palace.*"'

In the bedroom Juliet jangled three different styles of earrings by her lobes as Anita rummaged through the closet to select the appropriate attire.

''Ey, chuck, I could borrow your azure dress.'

'You can sod off; I'm saving that for my own special occasion.'

'Or you could borrow me one of your bingo dresses as Leo calls them. You know, eyes down, look in.'

They agreed trashy wouldn't be a good look for Juliet. Anita grabbed the perfect item, a turquoise and white silk dress.

Each of Anita's friends had stamped their mark in her heart but she connected with Juliet on a different level. Anita gave Juliet the appropriate responses to her proposals for how to handle the end-of-night kiss, and three ways to let Ryan down nicely if the date proved to be a mistake.

Wednesday afternoon Mark called Anita a miserable bitch, then sweet-talked her when he promised Elliot couldn't join them at the Christmas party. Five hours later Donna and Anita packed themselves into the reserved function room of their local pub. They joined the Yuletide merriment and mingled with the guys from the office, most of whom had brought their spouses or girlfriends. The younger crowd, who'd been in the pub since lunchtime, congregated under the speaker to sing the traditional Christmas pop songs the older members of the team had tired of hearing years ago. When Joey commented on Ryan's absence Anita amused herself with thoughts of how his date with Juliet might have turned out.

Anita's fun night came to an abrupt end when Mark called everyone to the window to admire Elliot's brand new Jaguar XK. Elliot guided his designated driver, his hot new girlfriend, to position the car within the white lines of the parking space. On the third attempt Elliot gave her the thumbs up. In a fleeting moment Elliot turned into a celebrity and the envy of every hot-blooded man in the pub. One of the engineers whistled as he bet the young woman, who clutched Elliot's arm like it was a bag that matched her shoes, couldn't be more than nineteen.

'Wow, what a body, classy, what I'd give—' Mark's wife hit him on the back of the head. 'I meant the car,' he protested as Paula dragged him from the window.

When Elliot introduced his hot girlfriend as Chantelle, although everyone present had heard her name already, she giggled her hello as she draped herself on Elliot's shoulder, then used her diamond-crusted nail to point to the silver name chain that glittered against the bronze shimmer lotion on her décolletage. Elliot thick rich chestnut-coloured hair, which matched his suede jacket, offered a sharp contrast to his arm candy who'd lacquered her long honey-blonde hair to such a stiffness her fringe stayed rigid when she pivoted her head like the star of a red-carpet event. Like most young girls she overused makeup to cover a blemished complexion. Donna called her a poor man's geisha. Nobody looked at her face; her black micro-dress drew their attention elsewhere.

Joey, one of the few single guys, put his head on Donna's shoulder to drool. 'Look at them legs; they'll be running through my dreams tonight.'

Donna laughed, dropped her shoulder and nudged him with her hip. The accompanied men waited until their girlfriends went to the toilets before they said hello to Elliot and introduced themselves to Chantelle. Donna checked to see if Anita wanted to leave; she declined and hoped Elliot would maintain a discreet distance. What an understatement that wish was; Elliot avoided her like a man who owed her money. Though Donna did comment on how amused she'd been when, like the picture in a black and white creepy movie, Elliot's head faced forward but his eyes moved to the side to look at Anita when he thought nobody could see him.

Mark dragged Paula from the group when she raised her voice to comment on the way Chantelle offered it up. 'She looks like a right sloobag.'

When Mark shushed Paula, she shot him a look that told him he'd be sleeping in the spare room if he tried to keep her quiet again.

Chantelle hung on Elliot's words as he bragged about the details of his new car to the guys. He used words like 'aerodynamic', 'sweeping' and 'light aluminium body' as the men nodded their approval at the automotive technology. Anita understood the phrase 'exhilarating to handle', though she couldn't be sure if Elliot meant the car or Chantelle.

Paula had more to say. 'Look at her; she's on him like a tramp on a kipper.'

Donna and Anita stood back and watched the disaster movie unfold.

Paula shouted to Donna to reiterate her point. 'He should know better at his age. What if his baby girl came home with a man old enough to be her father?'

Anita needed a drink. As the barman poured her order Elliot pushed in to stand next to her. He shouted above her head to check if Chantelle wanted dry or medium wine. Donna took a protective stance within earshot.

As Anita tried to hand a £10 note to the barman, Elliot

pushed her hand towards her purse and passed a twenty over the bar. 'These are on me.'

Anita sighed, bored with the drama, and stuffed her money back in her purse; she refused to stroke his ego further with a public display of her feelings.

An inebriated Elliot confirmed the gossip that Kylie had imparted to Donna a few days earlier when he announced he'd filed for divorce from his wife of thirteen years.

Chantelle hugged Elliot around the waist and snuggled her head into his chest.

'How old's Elliot's children?' Henry asked.

'Eight, eleven and fourteen.'

Elliot had complained for years of an unhappy marriage; the men in the office had thought he'd have a fling to get it out of his system. This assumption had influenced Anita's decision not to cross a line with Elliot they couldn't come back from; she had wanted Elliot to leave his family for the right reasons, so he'd never blame her.

An unyielding Paula continued. 'I don't care what he says. She jumped into bed with him before his poor wife had time to change the sheets.'

Chantelle appeared unperturbed by Paula's remark and stretched to nuzzle Elliot's neck. When Elliot suggested they leave Chantelle gave her audience a final show with a forced giggle as she searched Elliot's pockets for his car keys. When she found them she put her finger on her bottom lip and sucked the tip of her diamond-crusted nail.

Christmas Eve Anita woke in an irritable mood when less than four hours' sleep thwarted her intentions for a positive frame of mind. If Donna hadn't begged Anita to support her at the meeting Elliot had arranged with the contractor she'd have used the time in lieu hours she'd accrued over the last two months and left the Christmas party with the knowledge it would be six months before she had to set sight on Elliot again.

The menagerie of thoughts fogged her mind as she dragged

her dehydrated body into the bedroom and plonked her bare bum on the cold plastic dressing table chair. With a cat's lick and a promise she resigned herself to the fact no amount of makeup or skilled plastic surgeon could help her look twenty-anything.

As she shuffled the mail, Anita met her reflection in the hall mirror; she looked as if she should be out selling the *Big Issue* rather than delivering the multimillion-pound Big Contract.

With no reason to look as bad as she felt Anita stuffed a letter from the bank into her handbag, ran upstairs and lined up her anti-aging products. As the coolness of the cleanser soothed the coarseness of the exfoliator, she applied the pro-collagen serum to the dark circles around her eyes. The day cream with a hint of foundation combined with pink lippy, eyeliner and a quick brush over the eyebrows brightened her tired complexion.

The thought of food repulsed her, but heedful of her mother's words (*You go nowhere until you've eaten breakfast, young lady*) she buttered a slice of toast, ate the middle and tossed the crusts into the garden for the birds before heading to work.

In the car park she blinked a number of times when she couldn't recall the journey to work. Anita took the unopened letter marked 'confidential' from her handbag, ripped open the seal and read the computer-generated page. Unable to digest the relevance she stared at the competitive loan application figures.

Instead of being tucked up in bed Anita sat at her desk with two cups of strong black coffee and reviewed Donna's subcontracts as Shell Suit Cheryl the office cleaner, who'd called in to the pub for the last hour of the team's Christmas night out, joined in the post-party analysis of Elliot's behaviour.

Everyone expressed an opinion. The women empathised with Elliot's wife. Those with life experience rationalised Elliot's behaviour as a phase he needed to go through. The younger engineers expressed envy that Elliot 'banged' a girl half his age.

Anita listened to Mark, Alan and Joey as they detailed the infinite list of features for the Jaguar XK. They looked for the car's specification on the Internet and made noises of ecstasy when they imagined themselves driving the beast.

When Pike joined the conversation to speak of Elliot's girl-friend, they couldn't recall her name; they guessed at either Candy or Bambi, preferring to label her as Hottie.

Alan shared his summation of his conversation with Chantelle: 'I spoke to her for a few minutes; she's as dull as dishwater, though I'd still give her one.'

Pike added his uncharitable comment, 'If she's stupid enough to throw herself at Elliot she deserves to be used.'

Anita folded her arms. 'How can it be her fault she's immature and where a young woman likes to be, cast in the starring role of a man's melodramatic life? She's starstruck with his flash car and money, and flattered the way he shows her off. When she matures she'll cringe at the memory.'

The census of opinion in the office deemed that Hottie had one solitary function: to stroke Elliot's ego.

Shell Suit Cheryl, who over the years had turned out to be brighter than she looked, emptied the waste bins into an oversized clear plastic sack. 'I've read an article; Elliot's validating himself as attractive. Pulling a girl who wouldn't look twice at him in his twenties elevates his masculinity.' Cheryl plonked a sanitised plastic waste paper basket on the edge of each desk as she continued, 'It also proves, in his twisted mind, that it can't be his fault his marriage failed; nothing wrong with him if he can pull a young woman whilst his wife's home in tears praying for a chance to try again.' She took a fresh rag from her pinafore pocket and a spray cleaner that Anita, had she realised it existed, would have sniffed to dissolve her nose hair.

As Cheryl wiped the empty desk her statement drew the men's attention. 'A woman satisfies a man's emotional needs,' she said. 'Men can talk to their wives, probably an outcome from the way their mothers empathised with their boyhood troubles and wiped their tears. Their male friends talk of sport, work and women: an unlikely environment to share how alone and unloved you feel since your divorce.'

As Cheryl put her cleaning materials into her bucket, grabbed the rubbish bag and left, Henry pulled up a chair to confess his own divorce experience and the traits he shared with Elliot. He told Anita how he had taken three years to recognise the extent of his idiotic behaviour.

'Each change makes Elliot feel in control. The high's a drug. The experience will be temporary. Like any addict he'll want to maintain the euphoria. As a result he'll change every aspect of his life piece by piece.'

Anita understood why Henry gave advice on relationships regardless of whether he'd been asked for his opinion.

'He's oblivious to his actions; he'll realise the ridiculousness of this relationship one day.' Henry looked out of the window. 'I know I felt more ashamed of a fling with a woman five years older than our daughter than how I treated the wife. Though the Mrs did get revenge: she took me to the cleaners. She got the four-bed detached house; I ended up living in a caravan.'

Henry gave a nervous laugh that made Anita think he hadn't yet forgiven himself. 'Like me Elliot will need to fall flat on his face to accept his situation. Though when he does he's left with the cold hard truth that fifty is nearer than twenty, nor can he turn back time and get his self-respect back.'

'Will Elliot and I repair our friendship?'

'I doubt it; he reached out, you turned your back on him.'

At least Juliet's night showed promise when she messaged Anita to say:

Hi Nita

Hope you had a fun night. Did Elliot turn up?

I had the most wonderful time. Ryan looked dapper dressed up. I'm going out with him again. He's charming and interesting, we talked for hours.

Got to tell you this, talk about a back handed compliment. He said 'I don't know how much you paid for that outfit, but it was worth it.'

Will give you the details when I get back from Yorkshire after the holidays and yes before you ask he did wear a bottle and half of Brut. Ha ha.

Enjoy Christmas and Happy New Year

Ju. x

Juliet deserved a genuine relationship now she'd expelled her desire to be queen of the cougars. Anita hoped Ryan had genuine motives for his interest in Juliet both personally and with his surprise offer to include her in the Chrystalmere project.

Later that morning Anita switched to decaf as the caffeine rush aggravated the stress of accompanying Donna to Elliot's 11.30 contractors meeting. With no contentious issues on the agenda they agreed Donna should take the commercial lead.

Followed by a posse of contractors Elliot held the door open for Kylie; as she walked past he whispered a remark into her ear. Kylie paused to exaggerate her laugh. She looked at Anita, who'd positioned herself apart from the group, then sat opposite Elliot.

Elliot took the lead. Kylie took the minutes. Anita listened as Elliot reiterated his standards and expectations, with each statement preceded by 'I'. At the end of the meeting the contractors had no doubt of Elliot's self-proclaimed importance. Under 'any other business', Elliot instructed the contractor to disregard the contract documentation that had been couriered to them in haste, with a quick reference to Donna as the contract administrator.

Anita half-opened her mouth to interrupt.

Donna raised her hand. 'If I can stop you, I'm the contract manager. Note for the records, Kylie, I have Anita's full delegation. I must remind you all, contract issues come via me.' Donna pushed her glasses onto the bridge of her nose and scanned the unsmiling faces.

They waited for the room to empty then high-fived Donna's boldness.

Anita expected everyone to be at lunch, so when she spotted Elliot and Kylie at the foot of the stairs that ran outside her office she trundled. When she got within eight feet if she'd gone any slower she'd have been in reverse. Holding the handles of Kylie's handbag open, Elliot glanced in Anita's direction then turned away to continue his conversation. With five feet between them Anita caught the look of a smug child when Kylie glanced through her fringe as she rummaged through the contents of her designer tote bag. With each step closer Anita witnessed Kylie drawing her body further in to Elliot. Three feet away Kylie jangled her car keys in a manner similar to the way Anita had shaken Tara's lead for walkies. Heartsick Anita said a quiet 'thank you' as the odd couple walked towards the car park. Standing at the top of the stairs, she watched Elliot take another piece of her heart as he disappeared with Kylie.

At home, Anita dropped her bag on the hall chair and looked at her sorrowful reflection in the mirror. As she prepared for the Christmas break she hoped that too much damage hadn't transpired to sabotage all chance of a friendship with Elliot. She consoled herself with the hope that one day he might say sorry. If she'd known the revelation Carl had waiting for her she'd have taken back the wasted wish for Elliot's friendship.

When Anita woke in the middle of the night she prayed for a time machine to transport her back to the first day she'd met Elliot, or to any number of times where if she'd said yes she could be with him now. Then given her recent experiences she wondered if she should have her father's words, *be careful what you wish for*, etched onto a plaque so she could keep it in her handbag and hit herself with it whenever she acted like an idiot.

Christmas

Carl kissed his wife under the mistletoe, then handed her a gift bag. She undid the bow clasp as Carl marched from the kitchen to cover the festively decorated dining table with ceramic dishes overloaded with the breakfast delights he'd prepared.

As her mother had insisted that giving a wallet or purse without money inside would be unlucky, Anita looked inside the Gucci purse that matched the handbag Carl had bought her for her birthday.

Carl placed a ceramic dish in front of her with sausage and bacon still sizzling in the fat. 'I've put twenty quid in it. Your mother and her superstitions cost me a fortune.'

Anita presented Carl's gift, wrapped in jolly Santa paper. 'I know, but why tempt fate? We need all the luck we can get these days.'

'iPad; sweet.' Carl kissed his wife. 'Tuck in; I didn't get up at the crack of dawn to fix breakfast for you to let it go cold.'

Anita dipped a slice of sausage in the egg, rolled it in bean juice, then stabbed tomato, black pudding and a mushroom onto her fork. 'Since when's 7.30 been the crack of dawn?'

Anita half-listened to Carl, who'd squashed his breakfast mixture between two slices of toast and pulled the expression of a bored child. 'Christmas depresses me enough without the lack of a sport.'

Anita snagged the last piece of toast to mop up bits of black pudding smeared in yolk. 'What about the live NFL games on Sky Sports? Won't they pacify your gambling crave?'

Carl delivered his annual sermon. 'You get hardly any sport, then an overload on Boxing Day.' He reeled off his gambling strategy to split his funds to cover the football fixtures and a dozen or more horse race meetings. The success of Carl's plan hinged on the predicted overnight frost not affecting the ground conditions to a point where the stewards would call off a meeting or a referee would abandon a game.

Carl's twenty-eight-year metamorphosis from a Saturday-afternoon bookies' shop punter to the betting odds trader he'd become was attributed to three factors. The noticeable element came from advanced technology, which imprisoned Carl for endless hours at his home workstation, logged onto his online betting account, although he had moved at least once to get the Christmas tree from the loft.

The second had come when the deaths of Carl's parents, Anita's parents and a number of close friends had raised the issue of mortality and changed the couple's perspective towards money. They had abandoned their concern to save for their twilight years; instead they convinced each other to indulge their whims whilst still young enough to appreciate them.

The third element had come into play when Carl had turned fifty-one and duelled with his own mid-life crisis. Anita had expected he'd buy a motorbike or arrange a male bonding holiday to ogle half-naked babes an exotic beach. Instead Carl had announced that his life's ambition to become a professional gambler had gained momentum when his company offered selective voluntary severance. Due to Carl's thirty-four-year service his pay-off would be significant. To enable Carl to live his dream Anita had agreed that once they'd paid off the mortgage she'd authorise incremental portions of the balance to his betting fund. This also afforded Anita the opportunity to take a portion of cash for her own indulgences.

Thankful they'd made no plans other than the pre-booked Christmas dinner at a local restaurant from which she came home stuffed full of Christmas cheer, mulled wine and two brandy coffees, Anita sprawled on the couch. Unable and unwilling to move she retreated into a fantasy world to catch up with the television series she'd recorded. Anita ignored Carl when his huffs followed by a long sigh gained momentum with each rapid tap of the keyboard. He reminded her for a third time of the sizeable amount he required to lay the field in the King George at Kempton.

December 25th; the race commentator's words, 'And they're off!' boomed through the speakers. Anita studied Carl as his attention switched from left to right; his focus darted from the televised race to his computer, which monitored the fluctuating odds. At random intervals he incorporated a swift glance at the laptop which streamed a race courtesy of his betting provider.

Carl's preferred horse racing system relied on laying two or more runners at short odds. Throughout the race commentary fierce concentration reddened Carl's face. As the horses entered the final furlong, Carl perched on the edge of his seat to sit inches from the monitor, muttering words to encourage the odds to change from red to green; as this meant the bet had been laid, a close finish ensured a profitable result.

As Carl vented hostility at the television when the commentator recapitulated the action of the King George, Anita presented him with a cup of tea and a snack, aware from experience he'd starve to death rather than miss any betting action, then busied herself in the conservatory to dust, clean the windows and re-pot the outsized rubber plant they'd bought to fill the bare corner of the room. When Carl had called the full-sized plant the pod from *Invasion of the Body Snatchers* Anita had threatened to lock him in one night to see if it worked. She wondered if Carl had transformed the conservatory into a study in the hope his wife might emerge a cured pod woman.

By 8 pm, out of oomph, Anita poured a large measure from the bottle of bourbon Jon had given her into a glass of fizzless Diet Coke and sprawled on the couch. Downing her third drink she entered the merry zone with incessant chatter of Chrystalmere and the Big Contract. In response to Carl's sporadic updates for both the Washington Redskins and the New York Giants' American football games she made noises of interest; when Carl leapt from his chair to shout his encouragement to the quarterback who led the offence, raised his arms straight above his head to mimic a referee and then echoed the commentator's enthusiastic 'Touchdown!', Anita realised he'd wagered high. Carl tapped his keyboard to lay off a bet as the special team ran on to the pitch to take the field goal and then punt. In a close finish the Redskins beat the Jaguars twenty to seventeen to give Carl a reasonable profit. Carl's excitement expired with the news of the Giants' loss to the Packers seventeen to forty-five.

As Anita drifted into an alcohol-induced sleep Carl casually told her he needed money to subsidise his betting account for 'when his funds passed through cyberspace'. When she asked why, he got agitated and said he'd explained once. Anita couldn't remember and assumed she hadn't listened.

Four hours later Anita, disoriented, woke to an upright Carl snoring in his chair. She snuggled into the fleece throw he'd covered her with and dwelled on the prospect of six months without the man she'd shared her entire adult life with. Anita felt shame at how nonchalantly she'd accepted the decline of her marriage; her liberation had come at the expense of a man who'd done nothing but love her. As she returned to her slumber the Sky box whined to record another of her late-night programmes.

The second time Anita stirred, when she glanced at Carl's empty chair a sense of panic overwhelmed her. Fearful her brain might explode she used her hands as a vice to hold her head in place as snippets of her drunken rambling brought bile into her throat. She looked at the empty Jack Daniel's bottle and grabbed her notepad to scrawl an amendment to her new year's resolutions list to include a reduction in her habitual alcohol consumption. Despite her sense of unease she pushed the previous night's vague conversations from her mind, unaware of how her words would fester in Carl's memory.

New Year

Big Ben tolled for the twelfth time as Carl rang in the New Year. He stood in the hall and handed Anita a piece of coal and a £20 note. As fireworks lit the sky and the traditional chimes brought tears to her eyes Anita tossed the coal in the bucket and accepted the crisp new note from Carl.

Her mother had initiated the tradition to welcome in the New Year with the gift of money thirty years earlier when she'd opened the lounge window to hear the sounder from the BICC coincide with televised chimes of Big Ben, then handed each of the family a crisp green £1 note and a wish for prosperity in the year ahead; Father spent his on a gallon of petrol.

In the mid-eighties when the £1 coin replaced the pound note and inflation devalued its worth, Mother upped her New Year gift to a £5 note. This time, as a result of the 1980s oil glut, Father's fiver filled his car with a quarter tank of petrol.

Carl handed Anita a glass of champagne and sat on the arm of the chair. 'You know how you say New Year's a good opportunity to reflect on your past mistakes and set your short-term goals for the year ahead?'

Anita stayed at the window to watch a neighbour set off a firework display for the children allowed to stay awake past midnight, ignorant of how the rocket that exploded above the garden symbolised the detonation of her financial security.

Carl jumped when a rapid succession of bangers exploded outside the window. 'I don't know why they still sell them bloody things; they frighten the life out of pets. What's bangers got to do with New Year?' Carl paced in front of the fire. 'I've hit a serious losing streak. I tried to get out on Boxing Day. I abandoned my system and placed high-stake chasing bets. You know what it's like.'

A dejected Carl explained how, due to his low funds, he'd been tempted by a deposit match promotion and opened an index-linked betting account with a similar principle to the stock market. His downfall came when he targeted the full programme of premiership games. Enticed by the prospect of a big win, Carl had selected the multiple corners bet; in layman's terms, you multiplied the total number of corners from the first half by the total number in the second half. The unit index read thirty-eight to forty. This meant once each half's corners were calculated every unit above forty gave him a profit.

In the first match there'd been nine corners at half time; he needed five in the second half to win. Carl scowled; he still couldn't believe there'd been no further corners in the game. As Carl bet in high denominations and didn't lay off at the referee's whistle his losses stood at a grand after the match. With a further six low-corners matches his losses stood in excess of three grand.

Anita considered mentioning the letter from the bank but thought better of it. She took the laptop upstairs and manipulated the figures on her money manager spreadsheet. She calculated £8,000 could be released. Anita counted the slow stomp from Carl's feet as his slippers vibrated against each of the twelve stairs. He hovered outside her bedroom door until she shouted, 'I'll put four grand in tomorrow.'

When she heard Carl's bedroom door shut she submitted the electronic data that transferred the other four grand into the online bank account she'd opened in secret a week earlier.

As Carl prepared for the Sunday afternoon football Anita blockaded his workstation. 'We have to talk. I'm off tomorrow; I'll be worried if I leave you. Please come with me.'

He gripped Anita's delicate shoulders, heaved her out of his way and switched on the bank of plugs. 'I'm busy; do we have to do this now?' His PC flickered as it sprang into life.

'For crying out loud, this is our future.'

When Carl turned the red blotches on his neck deepened. The rapid tap of his foot on the floor shook his entire leg. 'I thought we'd settled this; I want to stop here.'

'I don't understand why.' Anita nodded towards the PC. 'Maybe the change would give you a fresh perspective.'

'I think you should go alone.'

'What, so you want a separation?'

Carl pointed the remote control at the Sky box and tapped the numbers four, one, five into the handset. 'No, I'm wondering how moody you'll get when you're bombing up and down the motorway, I'm trying to be thoughtful. Forget I spoke.'

'Suit yourself. I'll make a drink.'

Carl followed her into the kitchen. 'I've got an idea. Vanessa invited me to the Gold Cup Trials at the end of Jan; it's a couple's invitation. Given Cheltenham's a few miles from Chrystalmere, we can make a weekend of it.'

Carl did this every time they had a serious row; he'd say something mean, regret his angry words, then speak to her as if nothing had happened or he'd reminisce about the good times. She'd convinced herself their marriage was over, yet he'd asked her to spend the weekend with him. Confused, Anita wondered if Carl's request could be a feeble attempt to reconcile or maybe he needed sex.

'Come on, it'll be fun. Do you remember the first time we went?' Carl tickled under her chin.

As Anita hit the button on the coffee percolator, she played Carl's sports trivia game. 'December, 1989; Desert Orchard won if I have my dates right.'

Carl asked her if she could still recite the Dickinson five from the 1983 Cheltenham Gold Cup. Anita closed her eyes to picture them as they came up the hill for one of the most memorable races she could recall. Her robotic tone recited the names: 'Bregawn, Wayward Lad. No, that's not right, Captain John second, then Wayward Lad, Silver Buck and Ashley House.'

Aware resistance was futile Anita agreed to accompany him. As she waited for the slow drips of caffeine to dispense she opened her calendar. 'Tell me the dates.' She watched the red blotches disappear from Carl's neck.

Chrystalmere

Anita slung her suitcases into the boot, and programmed the sat-nav for Chrystalmere. To keep her company on the long journey she loaded six CDs into the player and clicked the random play button. As she headed onto the M62, she performed her duet with Reba McEntire to Strange and Consider Me Gone. At the M6 interchange she hit the repeat button when Sara Evans's A Little Bit Stronger ended. This dealt with her feelings for Elliot. Anita couldn't find a song to discharge her feelings for Carl. As she counted down the motorway junctions Anita continued to sing with the songs that lifted her spirits and skipped the ones that made her sad. Three and a half hours later, she followed a one-way gravelled road carved through the thirty acres of private land and headed for the trademark spires of the Victorian Cotswold hotel. In awe Anita slowed the car when the structure emerged in its entirety, unveiling its stunning elegance against the waves of snow-filled sky that clouded a backdrop of rolling hills.

The fragrance from a large bouquet of lilies behind the desk filled the air as an Eastern European lady with exquisite manners confirmed the reservation. She used a pink highlighter pen to mark a map of the hotel with the route to Anita's bedroom and handed the map to Anita, along with a pass key to the top floor meeting room Ryan had reserved.

Standing under one of three crystal chandeliers that illuminated the foyer, Anita waited for the porter to fetch her bags. She watched two ladies, who wore similar military tweed suits with walking boots, pause as they descended the grand wooden staircase to read aloud the brief history etched onto a plaque below the large wooden-framed portraits.

Anita followed the porter to her room, which reproduced the

website description of a connoisseur room 'incorporating period features and exposed beams for that authentic taste'. Although the room had been freshened a musty smell hung in the air. She pushed open the original stone window frames to expose acres of exquisite frost-crisp landscape. Anita exhaled and studied the cloud of her frosty breath as it swirled in the atmosphere like cigarette smoke.

Despite the chill that rushed into the room, Anita imagined summertime with ladies shielded by a parasol as they sat around a white carved wrought-iron table, where they'd sip Lady Grey tea and eat jam and cream scones as they watched the gentlemen play croquet or crown green bowls.

Anita took the lift to the tenth-floor meeting room where Ryan was engaged in a telephone call with Gerry. Anita couldn't glean much from the one-sided exchange of words, although the familiarity of Ryan's tone suggested an alliance.

As Ryan concluded his guarded conversation with Gerry she stood by the large glass window and looked into the distance at the boom and jib arms of the cranes at Chrystalmere dockyard.

Ryan's familiar twitch prompted Anita to listen carefully.

'Mr M's told me to handle the Gerry situation.' Ryan emphasised the word 'handle' as he placed the four files from his briefcase on the glass-top table. 'We have our work cut out. This Big Contract will be harder than I first thought.' Ryan updated her on the few days he'd spent in Chrystalmere. 'Jake Burrows, project manager: I can't tell if he's the reason this contract's failed or the one who's kept the project afloat. Every time I ask him a question I follow a maze that leads back to Gerry; when I speak to him, the trail leads to Jake. Oh, and Beryl, contract manager: she's hard work. You'll have fun with her.'

The hostility with Elliot seemed mild in comparison to Ryan's tales; she wondered if she might live to regret her decision to move to Chrystalmere.

Ryan passed Anita three of the four files. As they discussed the contents he raised the subject of Juliet's eventual arrival to support Seven Point and the potential Marsh Moore project.

Ryan seemed unusually prescriptive with regard to what information Anita could discuss with her friend and work colleague.

'I can tell there's something else; I guess by the way you're acting it's sensitive. Does it concern Juliet?'

Ryan's mouth twitched again. He shook his head no.

Ryan rested his hand on the fourth folder. 'I took this from Gerry's cabinet.' He kept his hand on the black file. 'You know I trust you implicitly. I wouldn't ask if I had an alternative.' He slid the file towards her, then paused as Anita stared at it. 'Raymond suspended our involvement in the Marsh Moore framework agreement.'

Anita asked Ryan how serious the damage could be.

Ryan stroked his chin. 'Gerry may have offered bribes to influence his advantage to win the work. If they can prove cohesion Raymond will want Mr M's blood.'

Anita paid attention as Ryan continued, '"Inseparable friends" our lecturers called Mr M, Raymond and me. When we graduated from Liverpool University Mr M's dad, Mason Senior, offered us a position in his company. We jumped at the chance to work together until we realised the old man's connection to a band of unsavoury characters.'

Ryan continued the story of how Mason Senior transgressed from normal practice to win work at a time when bribery and intimidation ran rife within the construction industry.

'The old man's unscrupulous dealings with some serious players from the City and the money he owed a guy who ran an illegal loan business from a rundown garage on the old dock road came to a confrontation when the old man refused to pay the extortionate interest rates.'

Ryan summarised how they'd resolved the stalemate when Mr M had paid off a large part of his father's debt with mutually beneficial favours. When Mason Senior had a stroke the loan sharks sent their leg breakers to take over the business and frighten the boys into joining them.

'Young and scared, I took a job with BP and headed to the other side of the world. Raymond's old man, with friends of his own, got him a job in London. Like me Raymond went his own way and, well, you know the rest. Mr M took over from his dad. He survived the investigations of the early nineties into the dubious contracts he won. His business flourished when he married Gerry's mum and merged her engineering company with his own business interests. This contract's our first contact with Raymond for years.'

Anita jumped from her chair. 'Shit, Ryan, it's difficult to plead ignorance when we've already briefed the staff on the updated bribery policy. Gerry could be jailed for up to ten years or at best an unlimited fine; doesn't he realise the laws have changed since the old days? Today they punish those who offer backhanders to win work.'

Ryan took back the black file. 'Nathan's looking into things for Mr M but I need you to check for any irregularities.' He passed her the relevant papers from Gerry's private files and a copy of the documents Juliet had filed as the company's business manager.

When Anita thumbed through them, Ryan's request to censor what she discussed with Juliet made sense; at least Juliet could claim deniability.

Anita stood and looked at her reflection. The large glass window superimposed her within the barren winter landscape. 'Will this be investigated by the police?'

Ryan opened his briefcase. 'Unofficially, Mr M's had the heads-up from a friend who works with the serious fraud squad. Gerry insists he's clean. Mr M has his doubts. Raymond won't take a chance; I've countersigned for funds. I want to know where we stand.'

'In the witness box, that's where you'll stand. With me behind bars 'cause I've perjured myself.'

Anita snatched the black file off the desk. 'I didn't say I wouldn't help.'

Hunky

The orchestra of sounds that echoed from the adjacent room to announce the occupants' imminent departure to Bristol airport woke her an hour before the alarm, so she pulled an overstuffed armchair closer to the window, sipped coffee and watched the moon disappear behind the dawn's grey cloud. The light that flickered behind a distant row of pylons the solitary indication that civilisation existed beyond the horizon.

She sipped her second cup of instant coffee as she watched the sun drizzle the sky with caramel swirls to awaken the day. The mist rolled across the landscape to create a mirage of a frozen lake, then entwined with the trunks of the sparse brown stick-figure trees. Anita imagined a painter obscured by the frost, sat at his easel to capture the serenity of the daybreak. She'd be encapsulated as the lone female figure that waited at the window.

An up-tempo country song burst from her mobile alarm loud enough to wake the entire floor. Anita swiped the screen and reduced the ringer volume, then hit the snooze button.

Anita's mother regularly told people, 'Our little girl's not what you'd call a morning person.' Since Anita's first day at infant school at the end of each night she'd prepared her clothes for the next day with clean underwear dangling off the neck of the clothes hanger and her polished shoes sat below. As a teenager she'd wake after a heavy night on the town to find her best dress skew-whiff on a hanger.

For today she'd selected an elegant block colour dress with a tag that boasted the inclusion of stretch fabric and guaranteed the garment as an instant figure shaper. She heated the straighteners to flatten her bed head. Since she'd paid £130 for a pot of pro-collagen marine cream she avoided face makeup; to give her face colour she chose a mauve lipstick. On the second snooze reminder Anita applied the slightest spray of Gucci Envy, slipped into her beige stilettos and made her way to the hotel annex for breakfast.

The high carved ceiling gave the breakfast room an air of grandeur; the long wall of velvet-draped windows gave the illusion of space. Anita picked a newspaper from a small table in front of the wall-to-wall bookcase. The headline talked of a crackdown and threatened to force companies to turn over their client lists, to name and shame tax avoidance scheme partici-pants. Anita turned to page four to check that Mr M's name didn't appear. The announcement seemed ironic given how the government had created the double taxation treaty with the Isle of Man fifty years ago, no doubt to facilitate their own tax affairs more efficiently.

The article failed to highlight this as a shameful example of British justice or focus on the underhand way the government had orchestrated the closure of the loophole. Dissatisfied when the 2008 budgets had changed the law, the Chancellor had proposed to apply the law retroactively from 2006. This would be akin to increasing the price of a speeding ticket today from £60 to £100 and saying in addition that everyone who's been fined in the last two years has to pay the £40 difference too.

The aroma of fresh ground coffee and sausages that sizzled on the hot plate made Anita hungry, although her mouth salivated most when she watched a woman plunge toast soldiers into a runny egg, especially when the yellow centre oozed over the side of the eggcup. Anita asked for a full English, extra toast, black coffee, and make it snappy. She said the last statement in her head and hoped her telepathic message would motivate her server to hurry.

With a full tummy and ready for the day ahead she programmed her sat-nav for the Zeus Business Park. During the thirty-minute journey she noticed the lack of obstacles she'd routinely encountered in her urbanised life. The contrast with home was stark; there her two-mile journey to the local super-store consisted of four sets of traffic lights, three pedestrian crossings, at which all children felt a mandatory compulsion to press the button, one major roundabout and congested roads from backed-up traffic when two or more buses arrived at once to pick up commuters packed into bus stops. Her one criticism of country drivers came when a tractor pulled into rush hour traffic. The vapour trail from the tractor, which smelt like the old glue factory back home, travelled considerably faster that the hay hauler which trundled along the 'A' road. It irritated Anita further when the four cars ahead reduced their speed rather than overtaking.

Anita parked in the car park at the far end of the Zeus Business Park, then sat for a moment to marvel at the endless miles of greenery weaved amongst a backdrop of rolling hills: a stark contrast to the unimaginative design of the office structure. The complex appeared to have been constructed with the building block birthday gift her brother had received when he was called 'Mummy's precious little boy'. The three shades of brown bricks had sat in a trailer shaped like a train, which he dragged over the thick Axminster carpet as he made choo-choo noises.

Anita used her wing mirror to check her lippy and fluff her fringe, then followed the 'Visitors' sign. The steady pace of her short strides broke the silence as her heels echoed off the pavement until Anita heard a creature scuttling in the hedge. She quickened her step, abandoned the path and continued her journey across the car park. Anita wondered if the glass room submerged within the decorative roofline could be the war room reputed to be where Gerry conducted his private business meetings. She'd heard Mr M tell Gerry to give Ryan the key and Ryan to scrutinise the files; this was no doubt where the black file came from.

Distracted by a rainbow reflected in the large glass window, Anita failed to notice the cracked concrete until she stumbled from her shoe wedged into the ground. Anita cursed as her toes scraped against the leather. Her oversized handbag took on a mind of its own and sabotaged her efforts to balance like a tightrope walker. Her freshly painted toenails plunged beneath a large puddle. Submerged in freezing dirty water she used the ball of her foot to stabilise herself as she contorted her body to pull the shoe from its vice without leaving the heel behind; one final yank salvaged her scraped heel. As Anita scoured her surroundings to check nobody had witnessed her performance the shadow of a man at the second-floor window moved from view.

Anita pushed open the heavy glass door as a tall slim-built woman rushed towards her. The air of sophistication implied by her chocolate brown pinstriped suit and polished court shoes contradicted her overuse of Charlie Red perfume and straight home-dyed blonde hair with pale pink streaks. Anita's first impression was overshadowed when the woman, who Anita placed between mid-forties and early sixties, asked in her farmer's twang if Anita had had any problem on her journey from a place she pronounced as Glar-sterr.

Anita watched her reflection disappear as the imitation 1960s pink wingtip glasses, decorated with black and rhinestones in the corners, slipped off her greeter's nose.

'You 'right, me babba? I've been waiting for you to arrive.'

Anita studied the woman, who tucked a hardback historical romance novel under her arm and balanced a small plastic lunch box on top of her oversized rose-coloured Cabas Square neoprene shopper's bag. The bag banged against Anita's arm as the woman vigorously shook hands with her.

'Abigail Clarke, facilities manager, I've been asked to help you get settled.'

If she witnessed Anita's car park performance she didn't comment.

As they made their way to her office Abigail stopped anyone deemed worthy for an introduction.

'This one's your office. I'm at that desk outside your door, holler if you want me.'

She returned moments later with a large mug of black coffee. Anita tossed Abigail her car keys when she offered to have one of her staff fetch her files from the car.

Anita stood at her desk and questioned why she'd thought her secondment was a good idea. A few seconds of fear consumed her as she contemplated the daunting tasks ahead when Abigail shouted a ten-minute reminder for the start of Ryan's weekly progress review.

It's natural for a woman to check the talent when she enters a room. Macho men think they hold the exclusive right to eye up the opposite sex. A woman remains discreet when she scans the range of males, as if shopping for a new handbag or seeking out a specific product brand at the supermarket. One glance will confirm if anyone's worthy of a closer inspection.

As Anita made her way to the coffee machine, she glanced at the worried faces seated around the table. She selected rich roast from the dispenser. When she waved to Alan and Pike from the sidings, the chatter became background noise, as her eyes drew to a bulky figure seated among them. She wondered who this eye candy could be. She would think of him as Hunky.

With both elbows on the table Hunky used his large hands to cradle his chin as he tilted his head to look at her. Anita was awestruck by this handsome mystery man; his rugged face intrigued her. As Hunky tilted to balance on the back legs of his chair he absorbed the complete length of her body. As the sunlight broke through the cloud to shine on Hunky's face, for a brief moment Anita saw her late father's eyes. She saddened at the thought of his cloudy blue eyes, filled with kindness, his face alight with pride when, as a child, she'd run to him arms outstretched; the beam of his smile would confirm the depth of love for his daughter. The moment faded when someone closed the blinds.

Anita poured a second cup of coffee and took a seat next to Alan, who conversed with an older woman with dyed chestnut-coloured hair backcombed and fluffed up. Next to her sat Hunky. More obviously than she intended, Anita looked past Alan to take a closer look.

'I take it you're thirsty?' He nodded towards Anita's hands as she placed both cups of coffee on the table.

'To keep awake; Ryan gets tetchy when I snore at his meetings,' Anita gave a nervous laugh. 'I'm Anita Richardson.'

Before Hunky could reply Pike interrupted. 'I see you've joined the circus folk.'

Anita gave him her best gormless look.

'Your car park wobbles.' Pike held his arms outstretched to mimic her balancing act. 'You had an audience at the window. Alan bet a pound you'd leave the heel behind.'

Alan shrugged his shoulders and nodded towards Hunky. 'Soft lad here wanted to rescue you with a hacksaw.'

Anita rolled her eyes to disguise her embarrassment. 'So long as I kept you two amused.'

Hunky shouted, 'If you need me to check your heel I have a hammer on the desk.'

Ryan stood to open the meeting. He wished his new team a happy new year, gave a brief summary of the agenda and ran through the usual fire alarm procedures, then summarised his previous day's discussion with the client. Anita surveyed the eyes of each person seated at the table, aware that behind each false smile lurked suspicion, resentment and anger.

'We'll start with introductions.' Ryan gave a summary of his career history, set his standards and expectations from the team then leaned against the window ledge.

Anita recognised this move; Ryan wanted to observe how his new team reacted without the pressure of the spotlight. Seated, Ryan would be the focal point and the dialogue would be directed towards him.

Ryan introduced Tammy Stone. Anita put her age at nineteen or twenty. She had a small round face, big brown eyes and a mop of blonde corkscrew hair. She gave a wave of acknowledgement as Ryan explained her role would be to record actions and any salient points of the meeting. Anita could see two engineers mimic Ryan's twitch. She glared at them. They'd soon learn the extent of Ryan's intelligence.

'We'll go around the table; introduce yourself, your responsibilities, and summarise the status of your current work.'

Ryan pointed. Anita stood.

'I'm Anita Richardson, senior contract manager.' She gave a sideways glance to check she had Hunky's attention. 'I'm responsible for the contracts associated with this project. I'm the NEC champion. I've been with the company more years than I care to recall.' Anita returned Pike's smile. 'I've spent the last four years working for Ryan at the sidings, where we've delivered a number of successful high-value projects.'

Anita looked to Ryan. His nod confirmed she'd stated enough. Ryan took a step forward; everyone focused on him. He strode to the other end of the room, then nodded to Alan.

'Alan Turpin. Also from the sidings, I'm here to finalise the indicative plan. Then I'll be here on and off until we have a schedule the client likes.'

Next to Alan sat the older woman with the bouffant hairstyle. She wore a plain brown pantsuit colour-coordinated with her costume broach; the large blood-red stone matched the oversized diamante buckle on her wide bronze belt and the clasp on the gold handbag she'd hung on the back of her chair. The bag no doubt carried a ton of cosmetics, judging by the makeup she'd plastered on with a trowel. She remained seated. By the monotone of her voice Anita guessed she felt insulted that Ryan had failed to recognise her importance.

'Beryl Dobbs, contract manager for more than twenty-five years.' As she spoke it drew attention to the red lipstick smudged on her teeth. 'Not as *au fait* with NEC as Ms Richardson but I know how to deliver contracts. I'm currently preparing a document to negotiate damages for the design element of this monster.'

Ryan waited a moment to check she'd finished, then nodded to the next person.

Hunky, who'd resumed his original position to use his hands as a chin rest, looked up to run his hands through his short fair hair. 'I'm Jake Burrows. Project manager for this works.'

This Adonis couldn't be the pain-in-the-arse mastermind behind their problems. Jake hadn't introduced himself that way, although a frustrated Ryan had referred to him that way during a recent rant. Anita estimated Jake's height at six-eight, maybe six-nine, by the way his shoulders enveloped his chair when he sat upright to deliver the rest of his monologue. As the ceiling light shined off the top of his head, she thought he had a monk's patch, which turned out to be a tuft bleached blonder that the rest of his hair. Signs of a bald spot would have been a definite turn-off.

'I work with an excellent team who've done a superb job. Beryl's been a diamond, bless; the client's repeatedly changed his mind.' Jake smiled at Beryl, who tilted her chin with a regal manner.

Anita pinched her eyebrow as Jake's sanctimonious attitude pissed her off.

'Good grief, why now?' Anita muttered under her breath.

The furnace that was stoked in her body forced the burning sensation to rise from her feet to engulf her entire body, erupting at her hairline. Anita snatched a handful of tissues from a box Alan slid toward her and absorbed the beads of sweat that trickled down the back of her neck. She closed her eyes and fanned herself with a jotter from the table.

When Anita opened her eyes Pike smiled from across the table. Anita took the tissue from her bra strap to dab her top lip. The action caused Jake to pause mid-sentence.

'You OK, Ms Richardson? Can I get you a glass of water?'

'She's fine. Hot flush,' Alan and Pike said in unison.

Jake looked perplexed as he concluded, 'It's great you're here, Ryan, but if you want a scapegoat look at the sales people.'

Jake's team nodded their agreement. One of the engineers jumped on the bandwagon. 'Jake's right, sales people promise this and that, take their commission and leave us to deliver the impossible.'

Beryl fidgeted as she contributed her support for her team with 'yes'es in the appropriate places.

Despite Anita feeling irritated and patronised her flush subsided. Still pinching her eyebrow, Anita raised her index finger.

'Did you want to say something?'

Anita directed her reply at Jake. 'What a load of crap.'

Everyone's eyes focused on her; the smile dropped from Jake's face.

'The sales people get us the work and do a damned good job. They earn their commission. As the project team we're paid the big money to deliver, we're supposed to be the "experts".' Although she hated it when anyone else did it, Anita used air quotes to emphasise her last word.

Tammy's eyes widened as she scribbled. Jake and Beryl both tried to interrupt. Anita drowned their words with her raised voice.

'If the contract hadn't gone badly we wouldn't be here. Nobody wants a scapegoat; we're trying to resurrect this deplorable project, make a healthy profit for the company and satisfy the client. Government-funded work attracts fierce competition. Delivering a good project this time will play a big part in securing a healthy order book for the next five years; no offence, Jake, but get off your high horse.'

Beryl sucked in her cheeks to give her a look of disgust, then looked at Jake as she retorted, 'Well, if you don't mind me saying, I suggest you hold fire on expressing your opinions until you've been here longer than a day. I have to say I'm perturbed by your tone of voice and strenuously object to your implications.'

'Beryl, I speak as I find. I can assure you I've been involved with this contract for two months. I sat alongside Ryan at the client's meeting. You mightn't like my attitude and I'd sooner work with you, but make no mistake: I won't pussyfoot around.'

Anita could tell by the way Alan used his hand to shield his eyes that her Scouse twang made her sound more aggressive than she meant to.

Ryan positioned himself opposite them. 'Enough.'

Anita continued to fan herself to ease the blush from being scolded. One day she'd learn to keep her big gob shut.

Ryan moved to the head of the table. 'This project's haemorrhaged money. We're months behind schedule. We have a limited opportunity to recover overspend through acceleration.

Raymond Philpott has given us one chance to turn this project around. I need a team that can work together; if anyone has a problem or feels pushed out, get over it. Put your differences aside and act professional.'

Beryl opened and closed her mouth like a goldfish.

'Won't this be fun?' Pike commented to Alan as they left the meeting room.

Anita headed back to her office. When she arrived, Abigail placed a mug of fresh coffee between two piles of multi-coloured files.

'How'd the meeting go, babba?

Anita inflated her cheeks, curled her lip then exhaled. When she couldn't muster the words to answer, Abigail smiled.

'First day's the hardest.'

Anita removed the project files from the desk to stack them against the wall. Although he hadn't asked, Ryan would expect a report. Anita logged on to the network and followed the prompt to change her password. With the mammoth task ahead her mind became preoccupied with her newly acquired pain in the arse Jake and the queen bitch Beryl.

Anita pinned up her Vegas calendar, then, like an incarcerated prisoner with an early release date, she crossed off the first day.

Getting to Know You

When Jake left the office at eleven for the third time that week, Anita, on the pretence she needed technical information, asked Abigail to find out when he would be back. Abigail twisted her monitor to show the large blocks of time Jake's calendar allocated to a series of private appointments. Irritated by Jake's complacency when he showed up mid-afternoon, Anita held back two subcontracts until Jake grabbed his car keys. She asked Abigail to give Jake the contracts and record the time and date of issue.

Eight thirty the next day Anita found the subcontracts reviewed with substantiations noted on her desk. Impressed by the quality of Jake's response and embarrassed by her unkind assumption, she made a point to thank Jake. Later that week Ryan passed her a folder and added how Jake had produced the most articulate reports submitted by a project manager. Anita suspected they'd both modified their initial opinion of Jake.

Alas, as Anita spent time concerned with Jake, she'd taken her eye off Bitchy Beryl who evened the score on Jake's behalf when she complained to Ryan twice in the same day that she found Anita's brashness offensive. Ryan told Anita to manage her. Although Beryl's negligible contribution created more of a headache, Anita scheduled a 10 am review in the hope for a more productive discussion with Beryl without an audience for her to perform for.

At Ryan's Friday action review meeting Anita was dismayed when she failed to recall the names of three people she'd met earlier in the week, then found herself distracted as she adopted Libby's trick of reciting the alphabet in the hope a letter would pluck their name from her subconscious. As Anita's menopause veiled the efficiency of her younger years, when she'd impressed her peers with the ability to recall the finer details of a contract or recite the elements others overlooked, Anita worried that her work colleagues would mistake her failing memory for ignorance.

Ryan tasked Jake to confirm each element of the job had been surveyed, photographed, planned and catalogued on the shared drive. Ryan escalated Anita's involvement with Jake when he directed her to attend the team brief to close issues and actions, which Tammy shortened to 'the CIA review' as a result of the acronym-obsessed culture.

At Jake's second CIA review Anita entered the room to face Tammy and Bitchy Beryl, who sat either side of Jake like a panel for the Chrystalmere's Got Talent competition. Anita suspected Beryl stopped mid-sentence to add to her discomfort and doubted Beryl would have offered her a warm welcome even if she'd entered the room on a unicycle, juggling oranges. As Jake reviewed the action list he asked Anita for an update on the documents overdue for review; Anita looked at an equally vacant Tammy who searched the register. Unable to confirm when they'd been issued, Beryl made a song and dance about having to print them off again, but aware of Jake's timescales she'd add the task to her list of priorities. If anyone else noticed the coincidence that the only documents missing were the ones Beryl needed to submit to Anita, they didn't comment.

Anita followed Bitchy Beryl back to her desk. As the light reflected off Beryl's brass pyramid earring to blind Anita she whispered into Beryl's ear. 'I'm on to your little game.'

Beryl grabbed the sleeve of Anita's jacket to retort. 'Or maybe you're just not as efficient as you think you are.'

At the end of what felt like an extra-long day Anita's posture slumped as the tension eased from her shoulders. She put a cross through day twelve on the calendar, then stood to stretch. She glanced at the clock as she spoke to herself. 'Seven fifteen on a Friday night and here you are up to the eyes in paperwork.'

She peered into the well-lit car park to see who else from her office block didn't have a life. She counted five cars; amongst them were her own and Jake's four by four.

Extending her stretch to sneak a peek into the open plan office, Anita took the stance of a visitor to the Museum of Modern Art and marvelled at the three-dimensional sculpture of Jake's torso. She focused on his neck bent forward to study a document. Anita fantasised about rushing to kiss the full length of his tanned neckline, elongated from beneath the collar of the sports branded T-shirt that hung loosely on his back. She exhaled when Jake muttered and ran his long thick outstretched fingers across the top of his eyes. Jake swivelled his chair and stared at Anita, who froze like an animal caught in the head-lights. Flustered, Anita waved, then took a sideways stride to stand at the printer to collect her fictitious papers.

Jake shouted, 'Hey, do you have a minute to review a specification?'

Her heart beat like a Cozy Powell drum solo. As her throat tightened she grabbed a random file from the cabinet beneath the printer. 'Yes, sure.'

Anita held her stomach muscles tight and clenched her buttocks, then prayed she stayed upright on her heels as she made her way to Jake's desk.

She perched on the edge of his desk. 'You're a right Billy no mates. Can't you find an engineer to do a review?' She skimmed the flimsy file that contained the specification.

'I take it that's a Scouse expression; where in the Pool you from?' Jake leaned back and clasped his hands behind his head.

'Actually I'm a woollyback.'

At Jake's request Anita explained the term. 'It's for people who live on the outskirts of Liverpool. Before the 1974 re-zoning I'd have been called a Lancashire lass.'

Anita acted like an excitable schoolgirl. As Jake asked another question, she focused on his misaligned teeth, masked by his plump kissable lips, and found herself magnetised to Jake who looked even hunkier up close.

'What's the spec for?' she asked.

As he answered Anita wondered what worries caused the puffy bags of flesh that hung under each eye. 'Seven Point want to replace all the fire doors in the engineering areas, then make good current office fire barriers with intumescent sealant, fire batt, fire sleeves and fire collars: usual stuff. I'm hoping you can turn the engineers' open-ended statements into a contract.' Jake's gaze made her heart beat faster. 'I see you have a fixture list pinned on the wall; who do you support?'

Anita could sense her body temperature rise, which no doubt illuminated her cheeks. 'The Toffees; I used to have a season ticket until I worked the bar at Goodison on match days.'

He winced. 'I felt sure you'd be impressed when I told you I'm a red.' He screwed his nose up, and then froze his expression. 'You can't be a blue nose? I'd just started to like you.'

Anita blushed again.

'I had the best time a few months ago when I took my son BJ to a Europa League game at Anfield.'

Disappointed at the thought Jake might be a happily married man with children, she searched his hand with her eyes. No ring. Anita made a note to ask Donna if men wore wedding rings any more. Carl didn't.

Anita chuckled at the funny comments Jake added to his animated tale, and the way he mimicked heading the football into the net as his arms widened and retracted to enhance his football story.

Anita felt swept away until Jake tapped her knee with his pen and repeated his question. 'Review next Wednesday; does that give you enough time?'

Anita accepted his invitation and slid off the edge of his desk.

'Before you go, look, did you get time to review the documents Beryl left on your desk?'

Anita recognised this as another of Bitchy Beryl's plans to set her up. 'Oh, sorry, I haven't; I'm afraid I've got a little behind.'

Jake's white teeth radiated his smile. 'I wouldn't say your bum was that little.'

Anita clenched the cheeks of her bottom and toddled back to her office. She hated how a minor comment from a man made her feel self-conscious. Unsure of the intent behind Jake's remark she checked her distorted reflection in the office window.

Abigail

The second week ended on a better note; she had been befriended by Abigail, who insisted Anita join her Sunday afternoon to watch the skittles final at the village pub which Burt, Abigail's husband, captained. Anita ignored her initial instinct to decline the invitation as the alternative meant another night alone in her hotel room and arranged to meet Abigail at the Duck and Goose at four. Pike and Alan, who lodged at the pub midweek, warned Anita the bar would be full of yokels and the car park would look like a John Deere convention.

Abigail greeted her new friend at the door of the Duck and Goose, then took her coat from across the seats she'd reserved at the table allocated to family and friends of the Duck Eggs skittle team. The visitors from the Brown Barn occupied a large table beside the twenty-four foot, hard, shiny-surfaced lipped skittle alley that ran alongside the wall of the bar.

Burt's yokel accent impeded Anita's attempt to interpret the rules of the game. 'You knock them there over with a ball.' He pointed to the nine wooden barrel-shaped pins, ten inches high, at the far end.

As if Anita came from Mars rather than Liverpool Burt held the wooden ball in his hand like the world cup trophy, then swung his arm back; he imitated rolling the ball, then ended with a noise Anita presumed replicated the sound of the ball as it hit the pins.

Anita sat in awe of the Duck Eggs who stole the show to win the close-fought battle for the tournament trophy, after which Abigail accepted the challenge for her and Anita to play a group of younger yokels. Two of the boys nudged each other out of the way to help Abigail and Anita with their swing as a group of three hovered at the far end of the alley to admire their opponents' cleavage when Anita or Abigail bent to roll.

When Burt left to celebrate with the team the bar emptied out. Ronnie the landlord's bored expression changed when Abigail flirted him into parting with two packets of crisps and a bowl of nuts from the stash reserved for the function room. Anita guessed Ronnie, a one-time leading seaman from the Royal Navy with a drinker's nose and a lived-in face, was quite a lad in his day by the way he flustered Abigail when he flirted back.

Abigail drank a quick succession of screwdrivers, then stimulated Anita's interest when she confessed that since her teenage children had excluded their mother from their lives and her husband preferred a pint and skittles at the Duck and Goose, she had embarked on an affair.

You didn't need to know Abigail long to realise the art of discretion had been extracted from her DNA. Anita made a rule that if a story revealed uncensored personal details with the possibility of being overheard they'd give the topic of their conversation a nickname.

'I'll call him Dickey or Woody; no, definitely Dickey.' Abigail followed her announcement with a husky laugh. 'He's the night shift security supervisor at one of the properties on the park I'm facilities manager for.'

'I can't place him, what does he look like?'

'Short. Tubby with a bald patch he likes me to kiss as he nuzzles my breasts.' Abigail pushed up her boobs and gave a series of throaty laughs.

Anita encouraged Abigail to continue, then shushed her when she slurred the next detail: 'He's flexible for an old man, babba.' Her voice tailed off into a whisper for the last part: 'He can get me into a few good positions in a small space.'

'I shudder to imagine.'

Abigail explained how Dickey liked roleplay. 'Sometimes I'm the corporate spy sent to steal confidential info. Dickey strip-searches me to check for hidden devices, though last time I wore his security uniform; he wore nothing but a cleaner's apron.'

Abigail continued to tell how she'd taken a tape measure to record Dickey's vital statistics, then held her hands apart to indicate the size of his impressive erection.

'Please spare me the details; it's enough to put you off men for life.'

'So, babba, do you want to hear how I took revenge on that pig of an ex-boss of mine?'

Abigail explained how each Friday her pig of an ex-boss had summoned her to his office, given her a fiver and sent her to the mobile cafe for a breakfast bap. Without a 'thank you' her pig of an ex-boss would take the bap from the wrapper, butterfly the bun on his desk, smother the contents with brown sauce then devour the entire thing between grunting noises. This Friday Abigail had amused herself with the thought of him butterflying his breakfast bap, with the knowledge her bare buns had been spread on his desk the previous night.

Anita looked at Abigail. 'Sodding hell. As Mark from the sidings would say, the rate you have sex you'll end up with a fanny like a hippo's yawn.'

Abigail slapped Anita's hand, then continued to tell how, under the ruse of a facilities inspection, she'd arrive in work at 6.30 to coincide with the end of Dickey's shift.

'Good grief, in work?' Anita exclaimed. 'I'll warn you now if you have sex on my desk, I'll kick your bare buns out of the door.'

Abigail raised her right hand and promised never.

Ronnie used his belt to pull up his trousers, then leaned over Abigail to get a bird's-eye view of her cleavage as he cleared their empty glasses. Abigail flashed a smile, then pouted at Ronnie to fetch another round of drinks over to the table as her feet hurt. She slipped her foot out of her court shoe and extended her foot to wiggle her toes. Anita looked at the landlord, who took out a large handkerchief and wiped his brow and neck.

'If he keels over you can give him mouth to mouth.'

Abigail threw her head back. Her throaty laugh echoed in the empty bar. Anita mused on how Abigail could be a worthy contender for Juliet's title as most sexually liberated woman in her circle of friends.

Anita's mind boggled when Abigail lifted her trouser leg to reveal the cuts, scrapes and bruises from her daybreak quickie. Abigail gave a blow-by-blow account of how she'd attempted to balance her foot on an overturned mop bucket as she gripped a brush handle secured to the wall by two black clip straps. As Dickey got her into position the straps snapped open.

Abigail tittered. 'All I'll say, babba, is if we hadn't landed on the toilet rolls the accident book would have made an interesting read.' Abigail's blasé attitude disappeared. 'It's more than sex, babba. It's real.'

Anita gave a sigh of support. Many of her middle-aged friends shared feelings of invisibility; although each one chose a different course of action, the common denominator was the attention only a man could bequeath. Like Anita her friends gave their hearts to men who remained oblivious to what a precious gift a woman bestowed.

By the end of the night Anita had managed to desensitise herself to Abigail's coarse sense of humour, although she liked how Abigail clinched her punch lines with a husky laugh.

Back at the hotel she discarded memories of the sidings to a distant corner of her brain and went to bed thankful she'd made inroads with Jake, increased her work camp friend count to one and mastered the art of skittles.

Bitchy Beryl

Like the hostess of a party, over the previous two weeks Anita had introduced herself to the revolving mass of people she met at the perpetual round of meetings.

During the initial days of Anita's career her father had reminded her that success wasn't merely a measure of her hard work; it assimilated the effort of others. He'd quoted the well versed, 'Be careful who you stomp on to climb up the career ladder, as you're sure to meet them on the way down.' As a result of his advice she'd learnt the value of a helpful hand.

As her career had progressed Anita had found people at the lower end of the career chain could be a reliable and untapped resource when you had a deadline to meet; the truth of her belief was evident as Abigail helped monitor Beryl's expanded list of deliverables whilst Tammy printed the surmountable number of actions Anita had accumulated on colour-coded post-it notes so she could track progress. Tammy exceeded Anita's expectations when she produced a printed seating plan for each regular meeting with a memory jogger to help Anita recall the names of the key attendees.

Anita tucked her fingers in the waistband of her bottle-green pencil skirt when Bitchy Beryl sauntered into the Wednesday contract review for a second time without the updated issues summary for the design contract. With less than two weeks until Jake and Anita were to present she reminded Beryl for a third time of its high priority.

Beryl avoided eye contact when she answered. 'I'm sorry but I've worries on my mind; it's difficult to concentrate, I know it's presumptuous of me but would you mind preparing it?'

Beryl picked up Anita's grimace when she told her she'd be happy to help, but wouldn't do Beryl's job for her.

'Do you have any idea how hard it is to ask you for help?' Beryl played with the imitation vintage flower necklace around her neck. 'You have no idea what it's like to compete with a youngster who thinks they know it all.'

'Actually, Beryl, I've a very good idea, and for the millionth time I'm trying to work with you, not against you. I'll prepare the matrix but I want you to put the report together.'

'Yes, well, I want to go home; will that be a problem for you, Ms Richardson?'

Anita knew with Beryl away from the office she'd get more done, but chose to keep that comment to herself. 'Do you understand the consequences if we don't have your data?'

Beryl returned a blank look. Anita couldn't be sure if Beryl was a mean vindictive old bag or plain stupid. Anita told her to go. When Beryl smirked Anita wanted to punch her lights out.

Sat at Beryl's desk, Anita sifted through the perfectly indexed files only to find the information she needed wasn't there.

She found herself mesmerised by Jake. She liked how he switched his phone to voicemail and turned his chair to face Tammy when he reviewed a file or document she'd prepared for him. When Pike asked him to peer review his project execution plan Jake offered Pike a cold drink and moved to the coffee table.

Tammy, who picked up the slack in Beryl's absence, walked into Anita's office with a matrix printed on plotter paper. Anita ticked off the completed items on her to-do pad and turned the page. Tammy had marked the first item with a red felt pen 'Beryl's Report – Status URGENT'.

As Abigail handed Anita two copies of the folder she'd put together for the fire door upgrade review, Anita was sure Jake, walking towards them, gave her the once over. 'Ready. I've booked room three.'

Room three, otherwise known as 'the broom cupboard', could fit three people at best if they squashed up around the antiquated steel table with the rubber end cap missing from one of the legs, or sat in each other's lap. Self-conscious as her relaxed knee rested against Jake's firm thigh, Anita tugged the hem of the knee-length pencil skirt she had thought looked perfect last night.

Jake opened the discussion. 'These specs for the ten-floor area they call the cauldron block. Do you know why one side of the fire doors must be painted green?'

Anita shook her head no.

'Seven Point Power Station paint all fire exit doors green, so if you find yourself trapped in a fire on site head for the green door; it could save your life.'

Jake tapped his pen against the relevant sections. Anita watched the light reflect in his tired blue eyes as he widened them to refocus on the small print specification. With her intense concentration Anita came to recognise the pertinent details by the pitch of Jake's deep voice, and how his tone heightened towards the end of a statement. The motion of Jake's rapid tap with his foot against the table leg prompted the uneven desk to wobble. When the vibration caused Jake's spare pen to roll off the edge, destined for the floor, Jake snatched the ballpoint from mid-air then looked at Anita as if he expected rapturous applause.

Anita considered herself intuitive but Jake sent mixed signals. She couldn't weigh up this man of contradiction. As Jake drummed the desk with his left hand Anita tried to picture him naked. Aroused, Anita licked her lips. Jake stuttered then coughed, unable to avert his eyes from her mouth. When Anita blushed, she practised a tip she'd read for dealing with embarrassment, which suggested you should concentrate on something else to distract your thoughts. Anita wafted her notebook to use as the distraction. When she felt her cheek with the back of her hand she questioned the effectiveness of the advice.

The review concluded when Anita offered to have a draft contract on his desk by the end of the week. She made her way back to her office unaware of how their work affiliation would blossom.

*

When Anita face-timed with Donna she updated her friend on how Bitchy Beryl had set her up and summed up every conversation she'd had with Jake.

'Sounds to me like you have a crush on Jake.'

'Don't be sodding stupid; given my temper tantrum at our first encounter he probably thinks I'm a basket case and he takes Bitchy Beryl's side every time.'

'You mention him every time we speak, and you're the one who calls him Hunky.'

Anita put her tongue out at Donna, who laughed from the frame of her laptop screen.

Donna asked Anita how she felt about Carl's expected arrival Friday afternoon. Anita shrugged. As she sipped her second whiskey from the hotel room minibar Donna rushed through the news from the sidings and an update on the contracts she now called 'her' contracts, not 'your' or 'our'.

'Nothing's changed with Elliot; actually people seem surprised he's still hot and heavy with Chantelle. Oooh, I forgot to tell you about Kylie.'

Donna spilt the gossip: how the animosity towards Kylie had reached its peak when the new office manager had called Kylie into his office to give her a poor performance notice. Kylie had dropped a less than subtle hint of her influential boyfriend's importance. The new office manager had taken Kylie's implication as a threat and reported the incident to human resources.

HR had interviewed the procurement team. Each person had given a similar account and expressed concerns for Kylie's immaturity and lack of experience for the role.

'Although HR kept their report confidential, rumour mill suggests that Kylie got her promotion because she'd slept with the head of training and development.'

'I thought you suspected the head of procurement had been the recipient of her "leg over" for a "leg up" the corporate ladder.'

Anita couldn't place Kylie's benefactor. Donna described him. 'Forty-nine and a BOBFOC.'

Anita stared at Donna's smirk framed in the middle of the screen.

'You need to get with the lingo, girl. Guess.'

Donna ridiculed Anita's suggestion that it sounded like some kind of Freemason-esque secret society, then explained the acronym: 'Body off *Baywatch*, face off *Crimewatch*. BOBFOC.'

'That hardly narrows the list.'

Donna continued to tell Anita how as the rumours spread Donna had warned Kylie how her questionable relationship could backfire.

'What a madam, she chewed the end of her pen and pouted. I couldn't hide my irritation when she pushed back her fringe; you know, like she does, to reveal that look of defiance or victory, I'm never sure which.'

Donna fumed as she recited the rest of her conversation with Kylie. 'I asked her, did she know how many women had affairs with their boss, and what did she think happened when the bubble burst?'

Kylie had retorted, *If this is a lecture, save your breath; I'm not interested. You're all jealous.*

Anita shook her head. 'She probably learnt the "not interested" phrase from Elliot; he says that to me.'

'I know it's cruel but I wanted to smack that smarmy-faced cow.'

Apparently Kylie showed substantially less emotion when she endured the walk of shame from the procurement office with a cardboard box of personal items and no self-respect.

'I feel a bit sorry for Kylie,' Anita said. 'With age comes wisdom. She'll learn the hard way.'

'I've got to see your expression for this snippet of news.' Donna pulled her glasses from her head and pushed them onto her nose. 'According to the gossip mill, Elliot and Mark went to a friend of a friend's party over Christmas. Kylie allegedly made a play for Elliot. Rumour mill says he had a threesome with her and her mum. Mark says he can neither confirm nor deny the allegations against his friend.'

'I know Elliot acts like an overgrown schoolboy, but he's a good guy on the inside; I don't think he'd do that.' In truth Anita had no idea to what depths Elliot might sink, and with her own worries she couldn't care less.

'Also …' Donna bent her head to peer over the rim of her glasses. 'HR moved her to Elliot's team. Kylie told me she's set her sights on him now you're out the way. Do you still feel sorry for her?'

Donna's words played on Anita's mind as she drifted to sleep. Anita couldn't recall any man from her past who could ignite this level of jealousy. The thought of Elliot with another young woman massed as a tight ball in her chest. Given her experience with Elliot she thought about Jake and questioned whether she needed another flirty friendship, doomed for failure.

Cheltenham

A motorway-fatigued Carl arrived Friday afternoon to collect his wife from work and drive her to Cheltenham. In the hotel lobby Vanessa greeted them with their hospitality package.

In the room Anita sat on the bed and waited for the kettle to boil. For half of a couple who'd been together for over thirty years Carl showed the nervousness of a man on a first date.

Carl's hand shook as he passed her a cup of coffee. 'Takes you back a bit; I can't remember the last time you came to a race meeting. I bet it's four years since we last flew to Paris for the Arc.'

The famous horserace, the Prix de l'Arc de Triomphe, took place the first Sunday of October. Anita had fond memories of the times they had travelled to Newmarket for the Cambridgeshire then caught a late flight to Paris for the Longchamp meeting on the Sunday.

Carl continued his trip through memory lane to recall Dancing Brave, the American-bred British-trained racehorse. Although Carl hadn't backed the horse they'd screamed him home at the 1986 Arc; the time Carl did speculate a sizeable wager, they watched the colt fail to win the Derby.

'I know you've heard it before but I do love you. Remember how all our friends called us Salt and Pepper?' Carl kissed her.

Like an old married couple, they headed to the bar to meet Vanessa and her other high-end clients. Anita engaged in polite conversation with two of the wives on their first visit to a race event. Carl relaxed in his comfort zone, surrounded by enthusiastic conversation of racehorses past and present. When the topic changed to dog racing and the group shared their horror stories of the unscrupulous world of greyhound fixing the younger men listened as if the older gentlemen recited a chapter from a Dickens novel.

The ladies appeared as interested as the men when Carl showed them his original bookmaker's ticket from 1983, which he kept in his wallet for luck. Inscribed across the middle: 'Carl Richardson, Turf Accountant', with the large print ticket number at each end.

Anita wondered how an ornate object could provoke your mind to dig up a long-buried memory. The ticket took her back to the time when Carl received his bookmaker licence to start his professional gambling journey on a rented bookie's stand at a rundown dog track. The track sat at the top of a hill in the middle of a one-horse town, famous for two things: dog racing and Neville Southall, who played for Winsford United before experiencing the greater glory of Everton Football Club.

Carl quipped that he'd raced greyhounds, then added he hadn't beaten one because he couldn't get out of the traps quick enough. He went on to recall the race history of Black Bob, the greyhound he part owned with his brother. He relived a couple of close finishes and the excitement of the wager. He went on to discuss the perils of greyhound racing and how his naivety had plunged him close to bankruptcy.

When Vanessa asked if Anita had been Carl's bagman, this encouraged Carl to amuse his audience with the embellished tale of how Anita had tic-tacked for him one fateful Tuesday night when they had arrived at Winsford dog track to the message that Carl's regular tic-tac boy had rang in sick.

Anita's mind played a different movie to the one Carl recalled from that awful night twenty-seven years earlier. Until that night Anita had performed no function at the races other than to float Carl's bag from a local cash machine when his bank depleted. As Anita could recite enough betting terms to hold a conversation Carl offered to give her a crash course on the finer points so that Anita could tic-tac for him. Her mission required her to stand on an overturned milk crate and mouth the odds with the applicable action to Carl, who stood on a wooden crate alongside the other uniformly positioned bookmakers, and his bagman, who stood at Carl's side to record the bets in a ledger. Carl would then chalk up a price depending on how much his bagman said they were 'in for' competitive with the odds his tic-tac had relayed.

Carl had become enthusiastic as he'd explained tic-tac slang to her and demonstrated how they identified the odds by what part of the body you pointed to.

'Wrist is five to four, half arm's six to four, full arm seven to four, eyes five to two, top of the head two to one and chest three to one; you make a sweeping "L" shape with your hand if it's four to one.'

Anita had mimicked the gestures three times before both Carl and his bagman had agreed they could translate.

'Each dog's got a slang name. Trap one's "the top". Trap two's "owt"; that's two spelt backwards.'

'You don't say. Tic-tacking's a bit more complicated than I thought. Are you sure I'll be OK?'

Carl's bagman's words of reassurance consisted of 'The box men here aren't the brightest bulbs in the box. If they can tic-tac I'm sure you can.'

'Your confidence inspires me.'

Carl interrupted. 'Listen. Trap three's "the middle" in five-dog races; trap four's called "ruof".'

'Let me guess: four spelt backwards. The ingenuity of the slang underwhelms me.'

'Trap five's called "the deck".' Carl held his hand palm down to demonstrate the gesture.

Carl's bagman took over the crash course. 'If Carl wants to know the price for trap one he'll shout, "What price the top?" as he pats the top of his head. If the price on the next board shows five to two, yell "eyes" and use the first two fingers from each hands to point to your eyes.'

Again a demonstration of the appropriate arm gestures deemed her suitably qualified.

In response to Carl's famous last words, 'You'll be fine. What could go wrong?' Anita accepted the challenge.

Punters' eyes fixed on the floodlit track as the whining noise of the mechanical hare gained speed. A wire released the lids. The greyhounds catapulted from the traps. The first few races passed without incident. By race four, a sizeable crowd had formed as a few bookies had priced up. Anita resumed her position.

'What price the top?'

'Eyes.' Anita put two fingers to her cheekbone.

Carl chalked the price up and took one bet for £20. Horrified by the realisation she should have shouted 'evens', Anita waved her arms ferociously at Carl, too late for him to guard against a stampede of greedy punters with fists full of cash who knocked Carl off balance. His odds board and cash bag wobbled with him. His bagman scrubbed the price. The rush of people retreated.

Despite being called a stupid bitch. Anita held her post until Carl scrubbed the race odds off the board, then she burst into tears. Carl terminated her services as his tic-tac but Anita could still act as the person who replenished his cash bag when he had a bad run of luck.

When their weekend companions headed to the bar for a nightcap Carl and Anita went back to the room for him to log onto his account and check the early trade prices. As Carl blu-tacked pages from the *Racing Post* to the wall, he read the form and asked her opinion on his choices. Then he muttered his regular complaint of the inconvenience imposed by the laptop ban at racecourses and how he wouldn't be able to lay off his online bets in running to make a good book.

Anita pondered on how much their relationship had changed since their courting years. As a twenty-something woman, eager to be a part of Carl's world, she'd grab the newspaper from the letterbox and read the back page as she ate her breakfast. On a Saturday afternoon between three and five her father would sit at the kitchen table and listen to the football on his transistor radio. He'd shout the updates to the Everton and Liverpool scores to Anita, who sat on the couch with her mother to watch the afternoon matinee on TV. When the final whistle sounded Anita would watch her father sit at the kitchen table with a copy of his football coupon and mark off the score draws. Once he'd confirmed they hadn't scooped the jackpot she would leave to meet Carl and stop off on the way to buy him the *Football Echo*.

They arrived at the racecourse and made their way to the car park bay inscribed on the pre-paid voucher Vanessa offered them. The steward directed them to the far corner of a large field and manoeuvred them into a space wide enough to open the car door.

Vanessa greeted them on the other side of the turnstiles and led them to the hospitality room. 'Open bar, as usual. Lunch will be served before the first race; if you'd like to follow me.' Carl followed Vanessa through the open glass partition that lead to the top tier of the stand and into their private balcony a yard past the finishing post.

Carl scoured the time form card as he drank his tea. Anita drank the large whisky that the waitress had discreetly added to a coffee as she exchanged texts with Juliet and Donna. Anita told them how Carl's pleasant behaviour the previous night had made her question if she'd been too harsh, with a comment that maybe, if she made more effort, they could salvage their marriage. Wisely they told her to wait until the end of the last race before she made a decision.

At the end of the third race an agitated Carl emerged. Anita gave him her debit card. By the time Carl appeared at the end of the fifth race she'd lost count of the number of Glenlivets she'd downed.

Carl told her to 'sup up and get her coat', then moaned for the entire thirty minutes' walk back to the car and for the five minutes it took for the engine to warm.

Anita couldn't be bothered. As they joined the queue of other drivers who'd run out of funds before the last race she drifted into a world of her own. 'I feel sick; put the AC on, will yer?'

'It's minus eight outside.'

'I'm 'ot.'

The sickness subsided as the cool air flowed through the vent towards her face.

Impatient drivers honked their horns as three men battled

the weather to push a broken-down transit van across the car park's grass verge. As they waited in the stationary traffic, a car edged into the space ahead of them.

'Can't you go another way? It's taking forever.'

When cars joined the line from various directions Anita broke into a rant on discourteous drivers and the lack of stewards or traffic police to keep order. Carl turned up the radio to listen to the result of the last race. They surged forward then stopped two cars short of three stewards, who each wore an official bright orange tabard. The trio ignored a couple of drunks who blocked the exit. One of the drunks swayed as the other leaned on a car bonnet to taunt the young woman driver with two elderly passengers in the back.

'Yer can't run us over.' Car horns sounded from the long line. 'Ah, shurrup. What's your rush?'

Anita flung open the car door. Carl shielded his eyes.

'Oi, you lot.' Anita marched towards the stewards. 'We want to exit the car park. Can't you move them two idiots?' The stewards looked bemused and turned to ignore her.

One of the drunks took a couple of steps towards Anita; the other followed. 'Now, me darlin', you need a drink.'

Anita tapped on the window of the Vauxhall Nova and told the young girl, 'Drive. If they don't move, run over 'em.'

The stewards scuttled off to watch from a safe distance.

One drunk staggered back towards the car. 'She won't run us over, will you gorgeous?'

Anita gestured to the driver of the Nova to move. 'No, but I effin' well will. So move your fuckin' arse. Now!'

Carl opened the car window as he pulled up beside Anita and yelled at her to get in the car.

The drunks waited until she'd put on her seat belt before slurring, 'No need for foul language; Scouse bitch.'

Before Anita could retaliate Carl put his foot on the accelerator. The two drunks shouted obscenities as they jumped out the way; Anita looked behind as they shook their fists and staggered to block another set of drivers.

*

The short walk from the car park felt like an eternity as Carl grumbled how his banker bet had fallen at the last, and how a succession of failures by horses to clear a fence or hurdle had contributed to the afternoon's results. Though he caveated his sermon with the statement that he'd 'sooner lose money than see a horse injured'.

As they approached the hotel Carl stormed off ahead to arrive at the revolving door at exactly the same time as a stout man with a trilby. Neither one showed the other courtesy and they proceeded to enter the same cylindrical enclosure.

The large man tipped his hat. 'Excuse me, sir, but you appear to be stuck in my compartment.'

Carl stayed put to shuffle like a participant in a three-legged race. The large man spilled into the foyer as Carl came full circle.

Without an interruption to the motion Carl snarled, 'If you dare laugh …'

Anita entered the next empty compartment and stayed a few paces behind a red-faced Carl who walked past the lift and up the stairs.

When Carl dropped her off the next day he apologised for his grumpy mood and promised to make it up to her when Anita came home Valentine's weekend.

Old People and Computers Don't Mix

Abigail collected the Monday tea club money, then handed Anita a coffee and a comment that took her by surprise: 'Do you know when you enter the open plan office you look for Jake?'

'Tell me, Miss Marple, how did you deduce I look for Jake? I could be looking for Tammy, or you as you're never at your desk.'

'Now, babba, you know I'm in the kitchen making you coffee. I know you look for Jake 'cause when you find him you smile.'

'Rubbish.'

'Look at you.'

Anita proved Abigail right when she stopped mid-conversation to look at Jake as he rose from his chair. Anita felt her cheeks blush as he strode towards her office.

'Go away.'

'Jake can't hear you.'

'I mean you. Go away.'

'Though maybe he can with those antennas on the side of his head.'

She had a point; Jake looked cute but had ears like FA Cup handles.

'That's mean. Go away.'

'Message received and understood, boss.'

With a nod Jake passed her door. He raised his voice to tell Abigail he had no idea when he'd be back. Anita watched. As the heavy burden of his workload rested on his shoulders, he no longer walked with grace; instead he slumped and plodded clumsily. Unaware he'd become her prey, or a victim of her lust as her friends would tease, he disappeared into the distance.

'Told you.'

Anita pushed the door shut and went to the window. She watched Jake cross the car park. Maybe Donna and Abigail had a point, although Anita wouldn't admit she liked Jake, since the fool she'd made of herself with Elliot.

For the next couple of days Abigail investigated her friend's newfound object of fantasy to update Anita with the latest instalment of what she'd learnt. Today at lunch she informed Anita that Jake had turned forty-five last October, which made him a Libra. On acquiring this information Abigail insisted on reading out his horoscope.

'I'm pretty sure he's single, although his dating status remains unknown. Rumour mill says Beryl fancies her chances.'

'That'd be my luck: cast aside by Elliot for a string of young girls, then eclipsed by an age-withered Liz Taylor. Anyway, why are we having this conversation? Leave me alone.'

'You know, he could be "the one". I have a gut feeling, women's intuition. This could be the love you've longed for.' Abigail read aloud excerpts from her recent romance novel and childishly changed the characters' names to Jake and Anita's.

Anita hid her amusement from Abigail. 'Give it a rest, just because you're on the pull.'

As Abigail reached the end of the page she slammed her book face down on the desk to exclaim, 'That explains it to me, babba!'

The way Abigail's mind worked remained a mystery to Anita. 'Explains what exactly?'

'The connection, the way he looks at you. You're like this woman from my book: a femme fatale Jake will be powerless to resist.'

'I bet you don't have a clue what that means.'

'Yes, but look at the way you blush, babba, when he's around. It's soooo cute.'

'I can distinguish between love and lust. This thing with Jake's better known as infatuation.'

'So you admit it's a thing?'

'Remind me again what they pay you for? I'm sure it's not relationship advice.'

'Oh yeah, I forgot to tell you, Jake's mum's ill; that's why he's got time blocked in his calendar.'

As Abigail scoured Wikipedia for the definition of her 'femme fatale' comment Anita made a mental note to control the desire to observe Jake to times when she'd confirmed her colleagues couldn't see her; especially Abigail.

With nine days until Jake and Anita presented their recovery strategy, Ryan worked late nights, Abigail duplicated the files at the close of the day so Anita could work on them at the hotel, Tammy finalised the issues matrix and Beryl phoned Ryan to say she'd be back at work the next day. Ryan told Anita he wanted Beryl's report on his desk by noon. Anita went to her action list and put a big red box around the action and exaggerated two exclamation marks.

At 9 am the next day Anita called Beryl into her office and demanded the report.

'Sorry, but I appear to have misplaced or accidentally deleted my report file. Rob from IT will have a look this afternoon.'

Her matter-of-fact attitude wound Anita up. 'Ryan wants the report by noon today.'

'Well, what do you suggest I do? Rob said IT's backlogged.' Beryl turned to leave.

'What do you plan to submit if Rob can't recover the file?'

Beryl opened the office door; as she turned her skirt twirled from the waist. When she stopped each pleat rested in place.

Beryl spoke loud enough for the occupants of the open plan office to hear. 'If the computer man can't find the folder, dearie, then it's lost.'

Anita resisted the urge to pinch her eyebrow or punch Beryl's lights out.

With as much calm as she could muster, Anita stepped in front of Beryl and closed the door. 'You know this report's vital to our presentation. You do have a paper copy or handwritten notes. Don't you?'

'I'll have records within various files, I suppose.' Beryl stuttered her reply. 'I'll look once I'm sure it's lost.'

Anita could see Beryl look to see if Anita would pinch her eyebrow. She did.

Beryl's voice became calmer but her face flushed. 'No need to panic, sweetie, you've a few days yet.'

Anita stood with her back to the door. 'Ryan wants his section by noon. I want the full report by eleven, not one or three. I suggest you get your arse in gear, as they say back home.'

Beryl moved towards the window. Anita wondered if her nemesis might jump.

'No wonder this bloody contract went badly with that attitude.'

As Anita continued Beryl pulled a lace handkerchief from her sleeve. Beryl's shoulders wobbled as she released tiny cries and dabbed her nose. Anita gritted her teeth in anticipation of offering an insincere apology for her abruptness. Beryl told Anita she felt unduly stressed and would have to go home.

Anita watched Beryl and half the staff jump when she slammed the office door.

At lunch Abigail joked how Anita had gained a reputation as a ruthless manager when they'd seen Beryl leave the office in tears for a second time and assumed she'd been sacked.

For a second time Anita sat at Beryl's desk and searched every file and failed to find what she needed. Rob from IT phoned Anita at eleven to say he couldn't retrieve Beryl's files and added his unhelpful comment that old people and technology weren't a good mix.

Although Anita spent the next two days with her trusty companions Abigail and Tammy for a joint attempt to retrieve the information Jake needed to complete the presentation, she couldn't wait for the support she'd get from Monday when Juliet officially started at Chrystalmere.

A thick black line marked her fifth week off the calendar. She looked at the red heart Abigail had drawn around the fourteenth. Anita dreaded what would be waiting when she went home for the weekend. She was pretty sure it wouldn't be a romantic surprise.

In need of moral support Anita phoned Juliet and suggested they meet up in Bristol on Saturday afternoon for a girly lunch and a little retail therapy.

On Saturday Anita sat in a city coffee shop and replied 'OK' to Juliet, whose text said Ryan would drop her off outside the Brazilian restaurant at two. In preparation for her official start and to pass the time until she met Anita for lunch at the waterfront in Bristol, Juliet had offered to call in to the office to help Ryan put a business report together.

With time to spare Anita ambled along the high street until she found herself musing on how the russet brown suit which looked fabulous on the shop window mannequin would be perfect for the client's presentation with Jake. The sales girl rubber-stamped the idea when she coaxed her to try a size twelve. Impressed by how the cut hugged her curvy figure Anita studied her reflection in the cubicle mirror. She admired how the cut of the jacket exposed a discreet amount of décolletage and how she could wear the once-worn two-tone burnt umber suede platform stilettoes she had back at the hotel. Anita struck a number of poses to determine her best feature. As men complimented her double Ds more than her eyes, this answered the question. She ignored the price tag and charged the suit and the sales girl's recommendation of a chic vanilla silk blouse to her credit card.

Outside the restaurant Juliet hugged Anita as if they hadn't seen each other for years rather than weeks. They gabbled as Anita showed Juliet her new suit. Then Juliet updated Anita on the news of Mr M's tax avoidance scandal, which she believed had initiated the tax audit that had postponed her move to Chrystalmere.

At the restaurant Juliet fiddled with her napkin, then rearranged the condiments, water glasses and her knife and fork four times as they waited for their food. 'Ryan's asked me to move in with him.'

Anita choked on her latte. 'Living over t'brush; how common.'

'I know it's a bit quick, chuck, but I've fallen for him. He's been asked to stay here to oversee this work and the Marsh Moore job if it moves into full-blown implementation.'

'It must be the high mineral count in the water. They should sell it as a love potion.'

Juliet picked up her wine glass then put it down. 'We both have failed marriages. We want to take a chance. At our age time's a depleted luxury.'

Anita sensed her friend's search for approval. 'Ryan's a good man. You deserve to be happy. What did you tell him?'

Juliet smiled; her tone picked up speed as she excitedly explained, 'I'll use my relocation allowance to rent a place, Ryan can move in with me; that way, chuck, if the relationship sours he can sling his bloody hook.'

As they ate their lunch Anita listened to Juliet's concerns about the business report she'd put together and how Mr M and Ryan had checked up on her returns. She asked if Anita could shed any light on their behaviour. Anita said no; she hated the dishonesty and how Ryan's trust forced her to split her loyalty. Anita reminded herself how, if Juliet realised the full extent of the situation, it could compromise her ethically; she might not report her findings.

''Ey, chuck, I almost forgot: two guesses who showed up at the office. I double-checked with Ryan to be sure.' Juliet gave Anita no time to answer. 'Jake.'

Juliet had Anita's full attention.

'And guess who came to see him.'

Anita snatched up the wine bottle as a hostage until Juliet told her the story without the guess who game.

'Bitchy Beryl.'

Anita filled Juliet's empty wine glass.

Juliet imitated Beryl's false polished accent. 'She came to put together a business report for Jake. The one you've been working on. Apparently she couldn't let Jake down, aware he presented to the client next week.'

'That bitch-faced cow.'

'You should have seen her fuss Jake.' Juliet looked at her sour-faced friend. 'Oh, chuck, don't tell me you're jealous.'

*

The euphoria of the afternoon brightened Anita's disposition until back at the hotel she took the papers Ryan had given her from the safe. With the information Juliet had imparted Anita scrutinised the documents. She delved deeper to unfold Gerry's discrepancies and hints at Ryan's involvement. Anita studied her logic as random words from Ryan's guarded conversation with Gerry clarified a number of anomalies. Anita went to bed with one question unanswered: would the lawyers call Ryan a victim or a collaborator?

Anita and Jake
Present

Armed with a briefing pack and travel arrangements, Tammy hugged the pile of papers as Anita approached her desk. 'Raymond phoned; he's rescheduled. He's brought the presentation forward to on site Wednesday at nine. Here's the hire car agreement. I've put you and Jake on the drivers list. Sign here.'

Anita scrawled her name on the dotted line as indicated by Tammy's glittery fingernail.

'You're booked into the Grange, two miles from site. Ryan told me to book a room for Tuesday and Wednesday in case you have to go back Thursday. I've also booked a conference room for tomorrow afternoon.'

Anita nodded her approval as she'd stayed at the Grange in November.

Tammy's concentration wrinkled her forehead. 'A single en-suite for you, single for Jake; countersign please as Ryan told me to cost this to your budget.'

Pen ready, Anita checked the budget code then initialled each page as Tammy continued.

'There's the report, agenda, list of project objectives. Ryan said to double-check they're included in your presentation.'

Tammy left; Abigail appeared with a large black coffee in exchange for the weekly tea club money.

'I should ask maintenance to install a revolving door.'

Abigail ignored the sarcasm. 'You know Tammy tries to impress you; she hopes to be as successful as you when she gets old.'

'Cheeky bitch, I'm like a vintage car. More valuable and sought after the older I get.'

Abigail nodded towards an A3 flip chart on a stand in the corner of the office. 'I thought with the number of items on your to-do list this might be more effective; you can blu-tack the sheets to the wall.'

Abigail may have procured the flip chart as a joke but Anita liked the idea.

Anita made her way to Ryan's Monday progress review where she maintained a stony face as they offered thanks to Beryl, who'd used her super powers to defeat the evil contract manager and pull out the stops to finish the report vital to Jake's presentation and in her spare time save the world.

Anita groaned to Juliet how Beryl had as much use as an ashtray on a motorbike and ignored Beryl for the rest of the day.

During the afternoon Anita locked herself in the office to draw up an exhaustive list on flip chart paper and stuck each sheet on the wall. Meticulously Anita struck through each item as Abigail supplied countless cups of coffee.

By 4 pm Abigail had procured Anita a coffee maker, with enough supplies to last a year. Abigail tapped the side of her nose when Anita asked where it had come from.

'Need-to-know basis, babba, and you don't need to know.'

When Anita phoned Carl to tell him she'd be home Thursday night, not Friday, his stern 'we need to talk' thwarted any hopes of a romantic weekend.

As Jake had won the toss to drive the hire car Anita stood outside her hotel with one small holdall that contained her new suit and a sparse range of clean clothes; she'd stuffed her suitcases of dirty clothes into the boot of her car. Jake pulled up five minutes early.

As they headed to the Tudor-style Grange Hotel she'd stayed at in November, they combated the tedious journey with a friendly debate about the weekend football results. Jake bragged of the Reds' one-goal win over Chelsea; Anita retorted with the biased details of Everton's fine form where thanks to Saha, who'd scored four, the Toffees had beaten Blackpool five goals to three.

As they pulled into the hotel car park a country song sparked life into her mobile. 'Can I call you later?' she asked. It took four seconds for Juliet to guess Jake as the reason Anita couldn't talk.

Jake asked the name of the song.

'Keith Urban, *Who Wouldn't Wanna Be Me.*'

'Who'd you call him?'

As they waited in line at the hotel's reception desk Anita described herself as a country music fan and explained how Keith Urban ranked first of the country artists she'd seen play live. Jake looked unimpressed until she enlightened him with the news that the country singer had married Nicole Kidman; in Jake's eyes, that somehow gave Keith Urban a credibility that being a hugely successful country star lacked. Jake offered a backhanded compliment when he said Anita looked too young for country and western, then insulted her when he added how his dad listened to Johnny Cash.

Her stout reply hinted at annoyance. 'Johnny Cash, that's a bit before my time. I like new country. It's still steel guitars that twang songs of broken hearts, but with the influx of younger talent it's more of a pop country. Why, what type of music do you listen to?'

Jake winked. 'Anything except country.'

An hour later they met in the conference room Tammy had booked. Jake connected the laptop to the overhead projector and wrote the agenda on a flip chart. Anita double-checked their information, then together they checked the timelines and technical data aligned with Jake's PowerPoint presentation, which had been colour-coordinated by Tammy with Arial black font words projected in bold colours for a dramatic effect. By 7.30, exhausted, they tidied up the room and called it a night.

Anita sensed Jake's presence as she waited for the lift. Too nervous to look, Anita tapped her toes and willed the doors to open. As she stepped into the lift, Jake jammed the door with his foot.

'Do you fancy a walk to the Indian on the corner? I don't know about you but I could do with a change of scenery.'

Anita suggested they meet at the bar at 8.30 to give her time to freshen up.

'Sounds good to me, though can we avoid talk of contracts? I've had as much as I can take today.'

Anita nodded her agreement as the lift door closed.

From the pile of discarded clothes strewn across the bed Anita chose the plain, knee-length, lust-red dress, shaped to gather under the bust then flow to conceal her middle-age spread.

She stood in the foyer and watched Jake chat to the barman who mundanely wiped drip trays. As Anita entered the lounge her heels echoed off the stone floor to alert Jake to her presence; when he turned she hoped the bulge in the front of his faded jeans, stretched to capacity by his firm thighs, was the outline of his room key.

His tousled hair looked damp or gelled. The way he wore a navy V-neck jumper over a cream shirt, combined with his stubble-free strong jaw, reminded her of a six-year-old wearing a school uniform. Jake left half a pint on the bar. As he placed his arm on her back to guide her through reception, the scent of Yves Saint Laurent Eternal prickled her senses.

As they entered the restaurant the aroma of spices wafted by when a customer with an armful of takeaway bags pushed past them in the doorway.

The enthusiastic waiter welcomed his first eat-in customers of the night into his restaurant and ushered them to a table by the window, no doubt to impede any attempt to leave.

As they sized one another up as if they were on a blind date the waiter handed her a Jack and diet and put a cold glass of beer on the table in front of Jake.

'I've a joke for you: what do you get if you play a country song backwards? You get your truck back, your dog back, your girl back and life is good.'

'The old ones are the best.' Anita pretended to yawn.

Jake used his finger to tap the centre of the two complimentary poppadums, then dipped a large piece into the condiments. 'Did I hear right: you go to Vegas on your own to watch concerts?

Anita answered Jake like a contestant in the quick-fire round of a competition to win a major prize. She rattled off the twenty-two country artists she'd seen in concert, fifteen of whom she'd seen play live as a result of her eleven solo visits to Vegas.

'Yes, but on your own? My ex wouldn't go the shops by herself, let alone Vegas. Most women would go with a friend at least. Though I bet you're not on your own for long.

Anita's Scouse accent emerged. 'Why do men assume if you're alone you're on the pull? You know, I don't need to go five thousand miles to cop off.'

Jake struggled for the right words. 'No, I wasn't implying – I – erm, I meant you're an attractive woman, look. Can I start again? Me and my big mouth.'

Anita paused to allow the courteous waiter who'd anticipated a break in the conversation to dart over to take their order. The waiter repeated their request for chicken pasanda, lamb balti, egg rice and a well-done naan bread, smiled and gave a small bow.

The conversation drifted slightly, but before long Jake apparently felt brave enough to risk the topic of Vegas again. 'Anyway, Vegas: tell me more. I fancy going one day, although the long flight puts me off.'

'It's only ten and a half hours if you fly direct. With the eight-hour time difference you arrive late afternoon. I went in December. The pilot's approach took us above the Colorado plateau. I could see the north rim of the canyon, Hoover Dam; the views were stunning.'

The waiter interrupted with their food and another round of drinks.

'What dictates the pilot's approach? Isn't the flight path static?'

Due to Carl's interest in aviation Anita understood enough to answer the question. 'The flight path's determined by prevailing winds. The landing's a bit weird as Vegas sits in a basin so summer months the warm air rises more rapidly; the blistering temperature increases the winds.'

Jake stabbed his fork into a piece of chicken and swabbed it in Anita's pasanda sauce. 'I do understand the principle of convection currents.'

Anita picked up the naan bread and ripped off a burnt section. 'You can wind me up like a two-bob watch, consider yourself warned.'

Jake raised his eyebrows.

'Is this all stuff you already know, then?'

Jake shook his head.

Unsure of Jake's interest Anita studied his reaction as she continued. 'When warm air meets the winds that come over the mountains it can lead to severe crosswinds.'

When Anita paused Jake zipped his mouth with his fingers, locked it and tossed the imaginary key over his shoulder.

Her words picked up speed. 'This can cause the aircraft to pitch and roll without warning. The approach unnerves you a little as the pilot comes in to land on an angle, and then straightens at the last minute.'

Jake focused on her mouth as he spoke. 'I read Vegas has some of the world's biggest hotels but it's actually a small desert town.'

Anita sounded like a tour guide as she rattled off her repartee of how if you landed in daylight you'd think you could walk to the strip. How the gigantic hotels created an illusion they were closer than they actually were, then how at night you would land to an oasis of neon.

Before Jake finished his question of which hotel had a big light Anita answered, 'The Luxor; did you know the beam is supposed to be clearly visible from outer space and has been listed as the world's strongest beam of light? Oh, and it's over 40 billion candlepower.'

'That's impressive; you're like a Vegas encyclopaedia.' Jake put his glass on the table and cradled his chin with his hands. 'Tell me more fascinating facts, Mrs Wicker.'

Embarrassed, Anita exaggerated a pout. Jake hesitated. Anita wondered if her dinner companion had been on an active listening course. He appeared to have mastered the art of asking one question, then waiting for an answer regardless of how long she took to answer. Anita described how the billboards advertised headliner shows and the Jumbotrons on the strip used creative video or animation to promote upcoming events.

Jake looked at Anita with a serious expression. 'Are you married, kids, or is that too personal a question?'

Anita agreed to answer on the condition that once she'd finished he had to tell her a fact that would impress her. She sighed. 'It's weird at the moment. Carl stayed in Liverpool. If I'm honest I couldn't tell you the current state of my marriage. I don't have children; I suppose that's why my job's important to me.'

'I couldn't help noticing you don't wear a wedding ring.'

Anita played with the third finger on her left hand. 'No, I stopped wearing that a couple of years ago. I wanted to regain my lost identity. It's a mid-life woman thing. I wanted to liberate my independence rather than be branded. Carl took it well. He's secure.' Anita ran her fingers across her lips and tossed her own imaginary key over her shoulder. 'Your turn.'

Jake gave a big grin. 'Did you know Cary Grant was born in Bristol, down the road from me?'

'I'm underwhelmed. Tell me something I might find interesting.' Anita looked at Jake, suspicious that he'd said little about himself. She took the bold approach. 'Tell me your life story, then I can finish my drink.'

'Honest, I'm boring. I'm a divorced footy fan with a six-year-old, BJ, who I see two nights a week and alternate weekends, look. You mightn't believe it but I'm a bit shy, though I feel comfortable with you.'

Anita took it as a compliment.

She'd avoided personal questions in case Jake gave an answer that ruined the fantasy. Anita took a deep breath. 'You said your ex before; is that BJ's mum or are you married?'

'Divorced two years now, look. Usual story: shotgun wedding, a few years on we realised we wanted a different life. We tried to make the marriage work but agreed it wasn't fair to us or BJ.' Jake swapped his empty beer glass for the fresh one the waiter handed him. 'We both spent time on our own, my ex met someone else but I've been too busy with work to commit to a relationship. Most weekends I do a bit of DIY at the parents' house, look. Mum's in hospital to recover from her second stroke, I spend most nights with Dad. My sister can't help; she's got three kids under six and lives in Eastbourne, look.'

'Is that a Bristol trait, to add the word "look" when you speak?'

'Yes, look.'

Jake's thoughtfulness captivated her as he explained the details of the home improvements he'd undertaken to make life easier for his dad and to prepare for his mum's return from the hospital. Jake asked if Anita's parents still lived in Liverpool, which Anita supposed seemed a reasonable question from a person whose parents were still alive.

The smile dissolved from her face. 'Father died ten years ago and Mother's been gone four years last September.'

'I'm sorry, I shouldn't have assumed; me and my big mouth again.'

Jake ordered coffees and broke the solemnness. 'I've heard Abigail say you're off to Vegas in August with your mates; any room in your suitcase for a small one?'

'Six foot six isn't small. But you're more than welcome.'

As the night concluded they walked back to the hotel where Jake gave her a peck on the cheek. When Anita bade him goodnight she felt like she'd known him forever. Exhausted, breathless, swept up by his enthusiasm and display of endless energy, Anita took a hot bath to help her relax.

Slightly subdued from her late night, Anita held a napkin under the cup to protect her expensive russet brown suit from drips of coffee as she watched the women congregated in the foyer. Almost as one they turned to watch Jake, who appeared from the lift dressed in a taupe two-button vested suit.

'You only need sunglasses and that lot'll think you're a celebrity.'

Oblivious to the attention an equally subdued Jake reviewed the format for the client's presentation. Confident they had their bases covered, they left for Seven Point Power Station.

Trish Ireland greeted them at the security gate with their visitors' pass, then escorted them to the boardroom where Raymond Philpott concluded his team brief. Anita took it as a good sign when Raymond greeted them with a smile.

'Mr Philpott, it's nice to meet you again.'

'Please, Mrs Richardson, call me Raymond.'

'Then you must call me Anita.'

Jake mimicked her when Raymond walked out of earshot.

Raymond's project team appeared more receptive to their presence. Anita got the impression they appreciated the advanced copy of their presentation and Jake's brainchild the red tape challenge report, which highlighted onerous processes with alternative solutions to bypass the bureaucracy associated with government-funded work.

By coffee break the pace of the symposium relaxed. The previous five weeks' effort to prepare felt out of proportion when Jake concluded their formal presentation with a summation in under seven hours. When Raymond realised they were booked into the hotel for a second night he insisted they attend his Thursday project appraisal.

As they strolled back to the car Jake nudged into her. 'We make a good team. I underestimated you, look.'

'We could be the Nick and Nora Charles of Elite Engineering.'

Anita felt old when she had to explain the *Thin Man* detective film characters. She protested against Jake's ignorance when he teased he hadn't heard of them as he'd have been a nipper at the time. Anita emphasised that she'd been a young girl herself when she'd watched re-runs of the films with her mother.

A nervous smile accompanied Jake's tentative suggestion. 'We deserve a treat; how do you fancy a celebratory dinner at that Chinese in that village we passed on the way from the hotel?'

In her best nonchalant tone Anita replied, 'Meet you in the bar at 7.30.'

The bar mirrored the Tudor style of the hotel with vertical black panels on a white background, wooden beams, narrow doorways and small rectangular windows. It felt crowded, although Anita counted no more than six businessmen, no doubt with an expense account. She ordered a Diet Coke when Jake, who'd ordered a pint, pulled up a barstool.

'You smell nice. What perfume's that?'

'Gucci, I have the whole kit 'n' caboodle. It's my favourite.'

Anita leaned forward to offer Jake her neck and was left disappointed that he didn't nibble her lobe. He obviously hadn't watched *Dr Love* on TV.

When they had finished their drinks, as Anita slid off the stool Jake took her arm.

'I mightn't have said it but I appreciate your help.' Jake tilted his head to the side as he smiled. 'Today went well, look, and it should keep Ryan off my back.'

'I enjoy working with you. You're easy to be around; I find most project managers a bit too self-serving for my taste.'

'So you think I've got off my high horse, then.'

She'd hoped Jake had forgotten her outburst at their first encounter. 'It's early days yet. I'll think about it and let you know.'

Jake grabbed his coat. 'You're a hard woman to impress.'

'I know, but keep trying.'

They laughed as they left the bar to stroll into the village. Anita quivered as the dusk wind prickled her wine-coloured woven dress. Jake placed his leather jacket over her shoulders and shoved his hands up the sleeves of his pullover.

As they waited for a table in the jam-packed Ping Pang Pong restaurant Jake, excited by the all-you-can-eat offer, scanned the menu.

Anita looked at the armload of dishes the waitress carried to see if one of them took her fancy. 'I must confess I rarely eat Chinese. I hate chilli but I like chicken.'

'Lucky for you I'm an expert.' Jake listed three starters she apparently had to try.

The waitress cleared glasses and a cutlery box from a table beside the kitchen door. A naturally pretty Chinese girl used her hand to flatten the plastic tablecloth as another set two places. She nodded to the waiter, who guided Jake and Anita to their seats.

Jake munched prawn crackers as he started the conversation. 'Your turn to tell me your life story tonight, so what was life like in Liverpool?'

The conversation evolved as Anita divulged how naively oblivious she had been to the despondency that lay ahead of her school years and how on her last day of term she had sat in the assembly hall to listen to the headmaster. Instead of a speech to inspire, he had apologised and explained how the economic climate meant fewer job opportunities for school leavers. The precision of the headmaster's words left no room for misinterpretation.

'Each of you joins thousands of young adults in the North West who leave school this year with hard-earned qualifications and no jobs to go to.'

The waiter delivered four dishes, one of which Anita recognised. She pulled the plate with the spring rolls towards her and cut them open to cool.

'I left school in the early eighties,' Jake said. 'Graduated from Oxford with a Civil Engineering degree. We celebrated our future. Bit different from you, look.'

Jake devoured the ribs covered in a thick sauce as Anita rambled on how she got a job the same month she left school and whenever she complained to her father how hard she worked, he reminded her of the thousands who'd happily swap their place in the dole queue.

The conversation deepened. Jake told Anita how his dad had worked at Seven Point, which proved recession-proof as 'you can't stop generating electricity with the push of a button'. This led to Anita's recollection of the scheduled blackouts they had endured.

'When the 'lecky shut off Mother would stick thick slices of bread on the end of the poker and toast them in the flames of the coal fire, then put a sock on her hand and used the fire's light to do a shadow puppet of a crocodile and a bunny on the wall.' Anita mimicked the action with her hand.

The waiter brought duck and pancakes, which Anita recognised as an intermediate, but the plate of shredded lamb and a lettuce head bemused her until Jake ripped off a leaf, dropped a scoop of lamb into the centre, then rolled it like a cigar.

'Another disappointing era of Northern life' was how Anita described the three-day week and the later horror when victims of the miners' strike replaced optimism with anger as the aftermath tore communities apart.

Jake tucked into two main dishes of duck and pork with Shanghai noodles. Anita picked at the chicken and pineapple.

Jake, who'd been raised in the country, could only empathise with her sadness at how the economic decline had impacted her industrialised hometown, reducing a hive of vibrant factories like the BICC and the Huntley and Palmers biscuit factory to a distorted landscape of derelict buildings covered in graffiti.

The waiter pointed out a shortcut to the hotel through the car park. As they walked past rows of practically new cars with their wing mirrors tucked away, parked with precision within the white lines of the parking bays, she commented that she'd not seen any indication of public transport on the approach road to Seven Point.

Jake couldn't recall his father not owning a car, as he calculated the walking distance from the nearest village, Anita thought back forty years to when the BICC factory's whistle signalled 'knocking off time' and thousands of industrial estate workers fled through the gates to jam on to a stream of Crossville busses parked up to drive them home.

She recognised their paradoxical memories of the same era as the North-South divide she'd heard about as a youngster. For the first time Anita appreciated how the rewards for her hard work meant these days she did a job that thousands of other people couldn't do.

Robert Bull, or Bobby Bullshit as Anita nicknamed him after listening to three hours of the usual drivel you'd expect from a habitually arse-covering middle-aged senior project manager, stank of denture cleaner when he stood too close, ended his monologue with a reminder of the site's safety and compliance priorities; he waffled on with company speak, then introduced the industrial safety representative who read the two recent safety events. Raymond closed the management brief with the statement that in the spirit of collaborative partnership he mandated Jake and Anita's attendance at his on-site weekly project appraisal. The three men left the office.

Elise Potts, the contract manager who'd taken over from Donald Turner, shouted at Anita, 'We wait for the bosses to leave, then we start the real assessment.'

Frank Fisher, the lead engineer, reached into his bag and put a large tin of chocolate biscuits on the table. Unlike Ryan's formal progress review Frank's informal forum encouraged the team to debate and challenge, which gave Jake and Anita an insight into the constraints and important issues. Frank tabled a number of concerns to which Jake's red tape challenge report offered proposals without the need to upset fragile egos.

Anita followed Elise, who shared her caffeine addiction, to the coffee machine. As they became better acquainted Elise asked her counterpart for help, explaining that this project was her first NEC contract. As the boys engrossed themselves in layout drawings, wiring diagrams and AutoCAD reprints of building structures as if admiring a special playboy edition of Pamela Anderson photographs, Anita tutored Elise on the conditions of contracts and the responsibilities and obligations of both parties.

At the end of the project appraisal Anita's happy bubble burst when she overheard Frank discussing a performance specification for the proposed refurbishment of the turbine hall. He asked Jake to work up an indicative cost and programme for discussion at next Thursday's project appraisal.

As they made their way to the car Jake explained his lack of turbine hall experience and asked if she'd had any previous involvement with similar work.

Although the thought filled her with unease Anita suggested the obvious route for expertise. 'Elliot from the sidings is your man. His forte's turbine hall refurbs; I've helped him with a number of projects. I know Ryan will tell us to contact him.'

'I'll take help from anywhere; I can give him a call, or would you sooner speak to him?'

Anita struggled to smile 'No. Be my guest.' She jotted Elliot's number on the back of the specification. 'I'll e-mail Elliot with an overview to prep for your call. I'll ask Donna to send us his last project execution plan.'

Jake dropped Anita at the Victorian Cotswold hotel to collect her car. As he headed to the hospital to visit his mother Anita headed towards the M6. She switched on her earpiece and phoned Donna to ask her to e-mail Elliot on Jake's behalf and forward any useful documentation.

They spent the next hour contemplating what bad news Carl might have in store for her. Anita told Donna if she hadn't seen the letter from the bank she'd be ignorant of Carl's tentative enquiry for loan rates, and hoped he hadn't done something daft.

Donna assured her friend no company would process a loan application, especially one secured on the house, without both of their signatures.

Valentine's Weekend

Carl tossed the chocolate heart and card, hidden beneath a deep red envelope, on the hall table. He waited until Anita took off her coat before he announced, 'I'm skint.'

'Happy Valentine's to you too. I'm great, thanks; yes, I'd love a cup of coffee; the journey, work, well, now that you ask …'

At the sight of Carl's forlorn expression Anita wondered why she bothered to use sarcasm as an ice breaker.

In Carl's words, his luck had 'taken a nosedive to submerge his gambling funds so deep into the abyss it would take a deep-sea detective team to salvage them'; he then listed a number of reasons that forced him to 'dip into' his emergency funds to float his gambling business.

When Carl had entered into what he now referred to as his 'gambling business' they had agreed he'd have a portion of their nest egg transferred into his betting account with an incremental amount deposited each month to cover incidentals or indulgent purchases. Anita controlled the remainder of their funds from a high-interest account to protect against, well, this.

'A grand should be enough to tide me over, or make it two, give me a bit of a cushion.'

Anita rushed upstairs to run a bath.

Carl shouted, 'I need funds now.'

Married to Carl for thirty-two years, she should have known better than to enable his gambling when his luck was depleted; instead she rushed down the stairs.

Carl pressed a few buttons and her bank log-on page filled the screen. 'Can you do this first? I want a bet on the Europa League match.'

Anita tapped in her passcode as she listened for the sound of the bath filling up. 'How will our marriage survive this?'

Carl glared at the card reader as he waited for the authorisation code. 'Our marriage is the least of my worries.' His leg wobbled against the chair as he waited for the transaction to complete. 'Oh, by the way, your gift's on the chair.'

Anita picked up the padded envelope; too thick for divorce papers.

The tension released from Carl's face. 'It's gone through?'

Carl's mood became amiable with his replenished funds; any further remark would be pointless. She knew her husband would beat himself up in his own private hell. Anita put her bankcard back in her purse. With the start of the football, fatigue from the journey and exhaustion from the drama in her life. Anita took her envelope into the bathroom; she poured in a generous amount of muscle-relaxing bath oil, fluffed up the bubbles, rested her head on the waterproof neck pillow, submerged herself in the hot water and opened her present. The note from Carl said no more than, *I saw this and thought of you.*

Advancement in technology allowed Anita to preserve precious moments on her iPhone, her palm-size HD digital video camera or Carl's iPad. Memories from her childhood she stored in her mind. The lack of snapshots from her younger years made Carl's gift precious.

Anita flicked through the black and white photos of the old promenade in New Brighton that had been dismantled when she'd been nine. Anita could hardly recall the tower or the ballroom that at its heyday showcased local bands that included the Beatles.

As her vivid memories unfolded they roused the smell of sand. Anita looked over the black and white pages that depicted a typical summer's day from her childhood. School holidays, her father worked overtime to cover shifts for his work colleagues who could afford family holidays, whilst her mother took Anita and 'Mummy's precious little boy' on day trips to New Brighton.

Anita stroked the photograph of the Royal Iris, and visualised herself dressed in a pink and white pinafore dress with a large daisy on the front, white plastic sunglasses and a floppy hat. Anita would grip the handle of the silver cross pram that

Mummy's precious little boy had been bundled into. Early morning the three of them would board the workers' bus to the pier head and embark on the ferry to New Brighton. Anita's mother, done up to the nines, would sit on the deck with the baby on her knee and shout her usual warning for Anita to stand back from the edge or she'd slip through the rail and fall into the Mersey. Anita remembered how she took two steps backwards when she watched her mother empty the contents of the baby's nappy into the river.

To a young child, New Brighton had held the magic Disneyland did today. She'd squeal like the seagulls as they neared the ferry pier, then feel dizzy as she looked between the old wooden boardwalk slats at the ebbing dirty salt water. When Anita mithered at her mother to win her a fluffy toy or shoot a duck or buy candyfloss as they passed the fairground stalls, Mother'd threaten to leave her at home next time.

On the promenade Anita would skip faster as the throb of loud music, combined with screams of excited dodgem riders, lured her to the indoor funfair. In the arcade her mother would hand her a bag of pennies for the one-armed bandit; Anita would jump up and down when she saw a cherry in any position to pay two large brass pennies that would clank in the metal tray. Her mother drummed into her young daughter that if Anita got lost she should make her way to the movie star game. The plastic Perspex arch with large glossy face shots of Marilyn Monroe, Betty Grable, Jane Russell and her favourite, Jayne Mansfield, could be seen from anywhere in the arcade. To play the game you dropped a penny in the slot to select a Hollywood starlet. When the time period ended, if the light stopped on the face you'd selected you won. If you lost, the display flashed a reminder to 'Bet Now' for a chance to win.

As an eleven-year-old Anita watched the local news report the sad dismantlement of New Brighton's landing stage and pier. She'd been seventeen when the pier's promenade had suffered the same fate. Later in life Anita reversed roles when she took her mother to New Brighton. They'd sit on the promenade with a bag of bread to feed the birds. She'd buy her mother a chippy tea and listen as her mother reminded her for the umpteenth time how once, as she'd settled the baby, Anita had tried to help but hadn't realised the chip shop sold tea and the white stuff on the counter was sugar until she'd sprinkled it on the open bag of chips.

Anita studied the more recent images of this bygone era, which captured her courting years with Carl. Back then the name Las Vegas belonged to a seafront arcade. Carl and Anita, ignorant of the part gambling would play in destroying their relationship, would spend an hour or two in the arcade, then visit the ten-pin bowling alley. They'd end their night with a stroll along the pedestrianised seafront, then stop at the café for a fish supper.

New Brighton could no longer be deemed a seaside resort. The history of her childhood memories had been knocked down or boarded up, with the exception of the indoor funfair and the lighthouse. Anita looked again at the newest addition to her memory box.

Nine thirty on Saturday night found them standing outside a fancy restaurant in Liverpool. Carl handed his wife a cellophane-covered rose from the fresh-cut selection, if you believed the handwritten sign on a piece of cardboard shaped like a heart and stuck to a bucket.

Carl's interest in the teatime football match from which he'd made a tidy profit aided cordial dinner conversation. As he updated his wife on the day's football injustices, they debated inconsistent referee decisions, goal line technology, footballers who earned a fortune and 'couldn't hit a barn door with a banjo' to inadequate players who 'went down in the box' looking for a penalty.

As they indulged in five courses of fine dining the ambiance encouraged frivolity, and Carl and Anita took turns to recall moments from their past as two irresponsible lovers united to experience life's unbounded possibilities. Memories of their naivety, justified as the folly of youth, subdued the atmosphere. Both of them ended the night lost in their own thoughts.

At home a pang of guilt encouraged Anita to challenge Carl. 'Answer me honestly. What do you expected from me, from us?'

Anita expected Carl to retort with the chauvinistic remarks he often used to deflect his true feelings.

Carl fidgeted. 'I want a companion, friend, partner to share my life. Someone I can trust.'

His sincerity unnerved her. The moment overwhelmed her, forced her to open her heart and plead her case to start afresh. 'Come to Chrystalmere with me. Let's get our marriage back on track. We can't go on like this. And if you're left to your own devices what state will our finances be in?'

Carl's demeanour remained unmoved. 'I'm not a child.'

'Then stop acting like one.'

Carl's face tightened. 'Just shut up; don't make me say something I'll regret.' He bolted into the kitchen.

Anita screeched after him, 'Let's resolve this once and for all. I can't live like this!'

Carl stormed back into the lounge with two empty cups. His reply came from left field. 'Is your beloved Elliot going down south?'

Anita's heart thudded. 'No, and why bring him into the conversation?'

Carl waved a dismissive arm, then stomped into the kitchen. Anita heard the cups slam on the worktop. Carl stormed back into the lounge. 'It's always you, isn't it?'

Anita gulped, unsure what she'd said to anger him. She felt her face flush.

'Well, I can't put up with your crap any more either. If Elliot did go, I doubt you'd want me imposing. Well, would you?'

Anita tried to protest but Carl spat his venomous words. 'Little tip for you: next time you've drunk half a bottle of JD think twice before you confess your feelings for another man.'

Her mind raced through the exhaustive list of nights she'd drunk too much.

The lids of Carl's brown eyes reddened. Anita thought he might cry. 'If you had, we might have a future. I give you everything but it's not enough. I know you'd be with him if he'd have you. But he likes them younger than you. Doesn't he?'

Anita absorbed his anger. 'That's cruel, nothing happened with Elliot.'

The calmness in her voice defused his hostility, but Carl's emotionless words still stung. 'Yes, well, who wants a wife who longs for someone else and a life you can't give her?'

Anita felt like a human punch bag. Out of fight, she conceded. 'You win, Carl, I'm done. I'm off to bed.'

Anita gripped her head, which throbbed, as she stood by the bedroom window and wondered if her parents looked on from beyond the array of stars that glistened against the twilight sky. Anita said her prayers; she thanked God for the good in her life, her health and her friends. Then she asked her father for a sign that would tell her what she should do.

As the church bells rang to alert the local villagers to Sunday worship, Anita's clarity of mind answered her prayers when Carl apologised for his churlish behaviour then reiterated that his mindset remained the same; he wouldn't join her in Chrystalmere, nor would he stop gambling. He suggested a break, then insisted it wasn't a separation; he called it a cooling-off period. Anita told Carl she would rent a property in Chrystalmere; if he changed his mind he knew where to find her.

Aware she no longer had a home in Liverpool, Anita felt a degree of fear creep in as she buried sections of her marriage piece by piece in the boxes she packed with her personal items. As she stacked the last container in the spare room she picked up the tiny wooden coffin that contained Tara's ashes and put it in her bag.

The Chapel

On Monday the expression 'misery loves company' ran through Anita's head twice, the first time when the ringtone of Jason Aldean's Relentless roused her mobile. A picture of Elliot illuminated the screen. Anita shut her office door.

With the phone on speaker Elliot's words echoed in the office. 'Turbine hall, Ryan said the work's escalated to a project and you'd send me the details.'

'I'm fine, Elliot, and you?' Like everyone else he ignored Anita's sarcasm. 'I'll send them now. Is that all?'

'Yep. That's all.' Elliot hung up.

The second time occurred when Bitchy Beryl stood by the open window. Anita engaged her usual fantasy, to shove Beryl hard then feign surprise when questioned by the homicide police. Anita's irritation dissolved when Beryl dabbed her nose with the fresh lace handkerchief she'd taken from the large silver bag that accessorised her belt.

'I need to speak to you in confidence,' Beryl said. 'If I don't tell someone I'll go mad. I know my work's suffered. I live alone. I can't afford to lose this job.'

'Oh, Beryl, I'm not trying to get you sacked.'

She interrupted with a wail. 'Please listen.'

Beryl unburdened her pain with a story of Millie, the cousin she hadn't spoken to in forty years. The unkind thought of how Anita wished she could be as lucky as Millie flashed across her mind.

'I'm an only child. I'm ashamed to admit that I don't value loyalty or friendship.'

Beryl's tale sounded like a chapter from Abigail's book. She continued to tell how forty-two years earlier she'd turned into a green-eyed monster when Millie had announced her engagement to a fine local boy, Harold Walter Barrow. Beryl had made it her mission to lure Harold from the cousin she detested. Her plan had materialised when Harold had succumbed to the intimate favours Beryl offered.

'Pregnant. I shamed my parents. They planned to send me to live with a relative in Scotland; 'twas different them days.' Beryl gave a long sigh. 'I lost the baby at four months.'

Anita could see Beryl's torment unravel in front of her eyes as she explained how Millie, traumatised by the betrayal, remained a spinster.

Dry of tears, Beryl looked at Anita through red puffy eyes. 'The outcome split the family.'

Like a priest in the confessional box Anita waited for Beryl's sacrament of penance. No amount of words could give absolution to Beryl as she concluded this heart-rending tale.

'Two months back Millie sent me an invite to a family reunion. I refused to go.'

A few weeks later a relative had made an unexpected visit to beg Beryl to reconsider. She'd refused. Two weeks ago a cousin had phoned Beryl to say Millie's cancer had spread, and that Millie had something important to tell. Beryl had relented and visited Millie, who had revealed the second element of this traumatic story. As Millie had organised her personal papers to prepare for her death she had found a letter written by her mother. The letter explained how she'd engaged in an affair with her sister's husband and that Beryl was Millie's half-sister.

'One stupid selfish mistake and I lost the chance for a sister. I'm beside myself with guilt. What do I do?'

Anita guessed nobody had cared for Beryl in a long time. She held Beryl the way her friends held her and offered an opinion that Millie still had a few months to live. She suggested Beryl reduce her hours and spend time with her sister. Anita offered to speak to Ryan, without a breach of Beryl's confidence.

When Beryl had left, Abigail barged into the office with a document that required Anita's signature. 'The staff feel sorry for Beryl, the amount of times she leaves your office in tears.'

'So they should,' Anita joked.

Abigail countered with a cheeky grin, 'No wonder they think you're a tyrant.'

When Anita thought how Beryl's plight put her melodramatic worries into perspective she shed a tear for Beryl.

Anita gave Tammy a list of requirements and asked her to contact a local property rental agency to see what they had on their books. An hour later Anita scrutinised the printed details for each of the three vacant properties the real-estate company had sent Tammy. She discarded the first two and arranged to meet Susan Stubbs from the letting agency Stubbs, Stubbs and Potter on her way home from work to view an unoccupied three-bedroom detached property ten miles from work and within her budget.

Anita stood in the driveway of the eighteenth-century converted chapel, fanning away flies and the stench of manure as four cows flopped their heads to nibble the grass that sprouted from the base of the wall. Anita looked beneath the strategically placed foliage that secluded the headstones for the dead people laid to rest in the front garden. Once Susan confirmed the landlord's responsibility for the upkeep of the cemetery Anita resumed her interest and followed the letting agent inside for the hard sell.

Susan gushed about how olde-worlde the décor of the bought-to-rent property looked; Anita thought of it as dark wood ceiling beams and charity shop furnishings. Throughout the house the oatmeal matte-finished walls, Aertex ceiling and deep patterned threadbare carpets improved the welcome. When Anita opened the toilet door she expected a decomposed animal sitting on the loo.

Susan shut the door quickly. 'That'll be the chemicals for the septic tank.'

Anita huffed as she struggled to find polite words to reject the property. A commission-hungry Susan took advantage of the lull and ushered Anita upstairs the way a collie herds sheep. Other than a mass of dead flies on the window ledges, which

Susan passed off as a consequence of a living near grazing fields, the spacious rooms looked clean. Anita imagined the smallest of the three bedrooms as her dressing room. The middle room would be the main bedroom and overnight visitors could use the room by the bathroom.

Susan encouraged her indecisive viewer to study the view from the bedroom window.

A zip-a-dee-doo-dah moment pounded in her chest. A painter could not have portrayed a more perfect scene. The edges of the drifting grey clouds flared, irradiated by the sun's glow as the flaming orange ball settled on the horizon. Anita watched a Land Rover from one of the two private houses at the end of the narrow country road drive up the brew en route to civilisation. A lone noise came from the tractor, which purred as it travelled between the farmhouse and the cow field that surrounded this property. Given her current state of mind Anita welcomed the isolation, and given her depleted financial status she paid Susan the upfront deposit, signed a six-month lease and agreed to move in the next weekend.

The Memory Box

On moving in day Anita sat in the lounge of her new home with Juliet's housewarming gift on her lap. She opened the card stuck to the front of the neatly wrapped package. Curious at Juliet's words, 'I thought it might feel like home if you had your family with you, chuck', Anita peeled back the wrapper; her eyes clouded at the two pictures Juliet had framed. One of Tara with her head on Anita's leg when they both fell asleep on the couch, the other a twenty-five-year-old photograph she'd taken of her father and brother sitting either side of her mother who cuddled Sheba, the German shepherd pup Anita had given the family for Christmas.

The father-and-son delivery duo pulled up at eight to unload the contents of the removal truck in exchange for a cuppa tea and bacon butty. To a chorus of 'Where d'you want dis puttin', love?' Anita directed her able-bodied assistants to place her prize possession, a forty-two inch flat-screen TV, in the corner and the two-seat cream leather sofa flat against the opposite wall. She ran her hand over the cracked leather seat. The cool soft comfortable couch had a few years left in it yet.

When she topped up two mugs of tea and left them on the hall window ledge beside an open packet of chocolate biscuits the men sat on the stairs for elevenses. Anita fished through an assortment of household items from the boxes in the kitchen. She opened the sturdy box marked 'FRAGILE' and picked at the sellotaped bubble wrap to find her four authentic hand-painted colour-rich pots, in which the crafter had depicted his Indian landscape with a mixture of blue, red, pink and lilac colours melted onto strokes of black. She placed her favourite piece on the coffee table, then absorbed the beauty of the large pot with its deep red neck that faded to pale pink above a scene recognisable from any Wild West film. The black imprint of an Indian warrior, his fist raised to the gods of the sky as his horse bows to drink from the blue river, evoked strength. During their many trips to Vegas, to give respite from the intensity of the city, Carl and Anita would take a two-night break in Zion. They'd stay a mile or two from the entrance to the National Park at an adult-only hotel with no mobile reception and a strict noise curfew. Each visit Anita roamed the stores for pots to add to her collection. The white pottery with the black stick figures still took pride of place in her glass display cabinet at home.

When the clang and bang of the bed as it hit every wall and wooden structure en route to the bedroom stopped, Anita went upstairs. She loved her bed, the refuge to heal from illness and upset or to contemplate life. As her mother would say, 'everything looks better after a good night's sleep.'

Anita searched through an oversized storage bag crammed with sheets and pillowcases for a set that matched the quilt that spilt onto the bed from the split bin bag. As she tossed a selection of bedding similar in colour onto the bed, the removal men brought up the dozen or more boxes that stored the guts of her life and the wooden rocking chair her late father bought her for her thirtieth birthday.

For the removal duo's journey home Anita filled up their Thermos with tea, gave them the half-finished packet of biscuits and a £20 tip, then waved them off.

Upstairs Anita dragged the worn leather-seated antique rocker in between the bed and the radiator, sat down and pulled the edge of the powder blue fleece she used when she slept on the couch under her chin. Anita tucked the edge of the fleece into the neck of her sweater to snuggle. Her eyes flickered like a light bulb ready to blow as the chair rocked like a metronome. As she sat at the upstairs window below the spired roof of the chapel and swayed, Anita was amused by the thought that to the farm hand in the tractor she'd resemble Norman Bates's mother.

Due to the lack of light pollution Anita woke to the bleakness of a black night sky. The dark room felt like a coffin. Anita listened to the house's structure creak as the infrastructure settled for the night; a murmur whispered through the window seal from the wind or a dead spirit at rest in her garden. The radiator under the window rattled as its innards cooled; the house gave a long groan, then silence.

Anita fumbled for the bedside lamp. Her attention was drawn to a box taped up and marked 'memory box'. As a result of an inane conversation with Carl in which they had discussed what items from the accumulation of junk, trinkets, holiday souvenirs and unwanted gifts they'd save if the house caught fire, at the same time they had shopped for a millennium capsule, Anita had bought a grey padded box as a hive for her treasured memories.

Anita peeked inside to find her New Brighton book on top of the '*Fifty and Fabulous*' sash wrapped around her birthday cards. She placed them on the bed, along with the sealed dusty pink envelope that contained memories of Elliot. Then like catching up with an old friend Anita delved into the contents, which transported her to the times she liked to remember.

When the chill of the outside temperature emitted from the bare stone wall Anita took her treasure chest downstairs, made a hot drink and pulled the armchair close to the electric fire set to high. She opened the leather-bound album and flicked through endless photos. Anita looked at the picture taken in the late forties of her mother in the dance hall at the top of Blackpool Tower, then recalled the discontentment she'd witnessed on her mother's face when she'd found the old photo in a drawer. She'd told Anita the tales of her youth, then saddened as she wished to be young again.

When Anita had looked at her mother, she couldn't imagine a young vibrant woman. Until recently Anita hadn't truly understood why her mother had spent a lifetime wishing she could be anywhere but where she was. Anita compared the black and white picture to one Carl had taken in the hospice when they'd all faked a smile as Anita held the frail hand of her mother's listless cancer-ridden body.

Anita recalled her whispered words. *I thought I had more time; don't let your dreams slip away.*

Mournful Anita turned to the back of the photo album to remember the deceased family pets: five dogs, one cat and the two budgies Father bought Mother as a present for their fortieth wedding anniversary. Anita had a thick bundle of Tara pictures from the day Carl brought the ten-week-old abandoned puppy home to the day the vet was to euthanise her.

'1971' labelled a pack of Polaroids she'd taken with the instant camera her parents bought her for Christmas. She flicked through the stack of her mother, who posed like a 1950s movie star. The catalogue of her childhood seemed like somebody else's memories. Anita cringed at the sight of an awkward eleven-year-old whose dad challenged her to outsmart him, if she wanted to take his photo. A plastic cover preserved the four pictures she'd taken of her camera-shy father. The one photo her father had posed for showed him dressed in his Sunday best, standing at the side of the silver artificial Christmas tree Mum had bought from Woolworths. Her failed attempts to photograph him included the one she'd taken when she had waited behind the door for him to come from the kitchen with a cup of tea. Anita had succeeded in taking a snapshot of her father with a tea towel hung over his head. Her second attempt had captured him hiding his face behind his hands when he couldn't get the cat off his knee to dart from the room. The last snap Anita had taken from the bedroom window when she had spied him on a pair of stilts he'd made her from cuts of wood he'd found in the shed. As she looked at the photo she recalled how her father strode up the path to check he'd secured the footholds before he'd let his precious princess have a go.

Anita's trip through memory lane continued when she picked up a metallic Walkman, home to the BASF audiotape that contained the old 78s and 45s Anita had taped for her parents the year they'd bought her a cassette recorder. She'd spent Christmas day with the microphone up against the speaker of the blue and cream Dansette record player. Father would play the poor-quality ninety-minute tape when he decorated. Anita plugged in the earphones to listen to the tape she'd played for him in hospital, in the hope the songs from his past would spark happy memories into his paralysed mind and give her father comfort for the final weeks of his life. As she sang along to Guy Mitchell's *Look at That Girl*, and a combination of Dean Martin and Johnnie Ray hits, the songs sparked the memory of her father standing on the stepladder with a paintbrush and a tin of white emulsion. He'd sing out of tune to irritate her mother, who'd then chastise him for spoiling the songs when he sang the wrong words. Anita turned the cassette over and enjoyed Val Doonican's version of *Elusive Butterfly*, Ken Dodd's *Tears for Souvenirs* and Des O'Connor's *I Believe*. Anita didn't need photographs to remember her father; his presence lived in her heart and her memories.

Anita recalled a quote by Tennessee Williams, *Time is the longest distance between two places.* Like many others Anita admired the works of the man considered one of the greatest playwrights in American history. She looked on the Internet to find the quote she couldn't recall further than the first line. Anita read it aloud: '*Life is all memory except for the one present moment that goes by you so quickly you hardly catch it going.*'

Relentless

Late again, Anita rushed down the stairs. She'd worked so many weekends she'd lost track of the days. Pretty sure it was Monday, she tipped change from the slummy pot by the phone to hunt for a pound coin for Abigail's tea club and noticed the green light flicker on the answerphone. She hit the play button.

''Ey, chuck, wanted to catch you before you left; call me back.'

Anita hit redial; she heard the engaged tone. She checked her watch and put two slices of bread in the toaster. With the toast trapped in her mouth Anita searched her bag for her keys and purse, which she found in her pocket. Snuggled into her weatherproof coat to shield from the cold rain that made her face smart, she dashed to the car. As she waited for the car to warm up she dialled Juliet's number. No reply. Anita sent a text.

Stuck behind a line of cautious drivers, Anita slowed as the car ahead drove through roadside puddles to engulf her car with a spray that mixed with the horizontal rain, looking like steam as it lashed past her windscreen to impede visibility further. Anita fished a country music CD from the glove box to relieve the tediousness of her prolonged journey. In the car park the introduction to her favourite song Relentless sparked thoughts of Elliot. Already late, Anita stayed in the warmth of her parked car, closed her eyes and hit the rewind button. She played the song twice, then pulled up the hood of her coat.

The parallel rain lashed in her direction as she dodged parked cars to fight her way across the car park. A gust blew the hood from her head. Her freshly washed and curled hair stuck to her drenched face. Anita turned to use the force of the wind to propel her tangled mane back to its original position. The howling winds caused the branches of the old oak tree to wave a ferocious warning to the cleaning lad, whose repetitive attempts to erect a plastic yellow sign in front of the entrance to warn of a slip hazard failed. He stood with his hands on his hips, dismayed, as each time the yellow noticeboard appeared secure a gust collapsed the legs and forced him to chase the plastic frame as it skidded across the car park.

A few steps from the entrance Abigail opened the glass foyer door a fraction. 'In like a lion, out like a lamb, they say.'

Distracted, Anita plunged her foot into a puddle of water to send splashes of dirt up her nude-coloured tights.

'You're late; Ryan wants to see you as soon as.'

Anita slipped off her ankle boot and used the doormat to blot her wet foot. 'Did he say why? Surely he can wait until the progress review.'

Abigail had no time to reply as Ryan's secretary popped her head over the handrail.

'Nita, Ryan's office, *now*.'

Anita handed her dripping wet coat to Abigail. As she approached Ryan's office she ran her fingers through her knotted hair.

'Sorry I'm late. Mind if I grab a coffee?' Anita poured tepid black liquid from the percolator into a large mug. Ryan nodded yes to a refill. 'What's happened since Friday? Don't say Gerry's been arrested.'

A knock on the door sent a sense of unease to tense her shoulders. The door opened. Ryan paused.

'Excuse me. Elliot Parker's here. Mr Parker, this way.'

Dumbstruck, Anita waited for a voice to confirm her worst fear. Dare she believe?

The strong presence of Ryan's aftershave couldn't overpower the scent of white jasmine and mint body wash. As Anita ventured to turn she locked on to the sparkle from Elliot's hazel eyes. Like a lighthouse that guides a ship to safety his smile lit up the room and her heart. Anita flushed with the familiarity of her pounding heart. Mentally she thanked God for sending the storm from hell for her first encounter with Elliot in months. Anita poured a coffee and checked her appearance in the plastic coffee dispenser. She pulled the tissue from her bra strap to wipe under her eyes to check for mascara residue. Although Anita maintained a calm demeanour, inside her stomach held a party to celebrate the jubilation at her old friend's presence.

When Ryan took an important call from Raymond, Anita studied how the roadmap of hurt on Elliot's face had replaced his youthful good looks. His slightly grey temples aged him. As she passed Elliot to stand by the window she squeezed his shoulder, then let her hand stroke across his back. He contorted his head to keep her in his line of sight. The end of Ryan's phone call suspended eye contact.

'Raymond's concerned the turbine hall job's escalated. I want a stand-alone project.'

Elliot's attention didn't waver from Ryan and Anita's didn't waver from Elliot as she scoured his face in search of the man who visited her dreams. The last time he had appeared the experience had felt so real Anita had roused groggy and disoriented to find her arms outstretched, the vision so vivid she'd tried to touch him.

Anita looked at Ryan when she heard her name mentioned.

'I want you both to do your thing on this contract. It's high priority.' Ryan looked at her. 'Abigail's sorted a desk; get him up to speed in time for the Friday progress review. Oh, and introduce him to Jake when he gets in this afternoon.'

As they left the office Elliot bent towards her. 'You look good, titch.'

'Yes, sure; the bedraggled look's on the cover of *Vogue* this season.'

As they entered the open plan office Juliet unfolded her arms, walking from Abigail's desk. Anita introduced Elliot to Abigail, who with no time for pleasantries gave Elliot the orientation talk and led him to his workstation. Anita went to the ladies' to comb her hair, touch up her makeup and send Donna a text to tell her of her surprise encounter.

Abigail stood in the doorway of Anita's office with a hand on her hip, having left Elliot to cart his own belongings from his car rather than getting one of her staff to help. 'Are you OK with him here? Does Jake know?'

'Yes, I'm OK, and my friendship with Elliot's none of Jake's business.'

'Oh, babba. Don't sacrifice a potential relationship with Jake by being stupid.'

In her time here Anita had gathered genuine friends, Abigail firmly entrenched in the group.

Out of words, Anita remained silent. She'd kept the full extent of her friendship with Elliot from Jake; maybe with hindsight she should have told him.

Juliet appeared next. 'Oh, chuck, tell me you aren't going gooey-eyed over him again.'

Anita listed to the lecture that Juliet delivered from the heart.

'You know, chuck, I'd hate to see you hurt like that again.' Juliet closed the office door as she left.

Unable to repress thoughts of Elliot's unexpected presence in her life, her subconscious took a pickaxe and tunnelled its escape through the migraine that formed in her temple.

That night when Elliot penetrated her subconscious with a visit to her dreams he said sorry as they sailed off into the sunset, lovers destined to be together forever, until Jake appeared and challenged him to a duel. Elliot chose his weapon, a foot-long spanner. Jake had a sword; Anita found Jake the swashbuckler rather sexy.

Anita watched her old friend emerge when Elliot used the rest of the week to assess the state of the project and put together a plan. Whenever Anita looked into the office she'd see Tammy, who'd promoted herself to Elliot's unofficial personal assistant, at the printer or the photocopier to organise Elliot's paperwork or at his desk to manage his calendar, like today when Tammy scheduled a series of meetings and reminded Anita that Elliot had insisted she attend. Despite the previous months of hurt Anita felt like a teenager with a crush when Elliot came into her office and shut the door. Like Tammy she thrived on the attention he showed her.

A gaggle of noise preceded the line of invitees who marched into the conference room single file. Juliet and Anita suspended their chatter to listen to Alan and Elliot banter with their Southern counterparts on the finer points of rugby league verses rugby union. A couple of local guys suggested the Northern scumbags should reserve their judgement and join them for the next Gloucestershire rugby union game. Alan and Elliot, who had often arranged a boys-only get-together to watch St Helens rugby team play at Langtree Park, accepted the invitation.

Pike laughed. 'Would you guess it's only Elliot's second week? They never ask me to go out.'

As Anita fixated on Elliot, Juliet kicked her hard under the desk. 'I still think he's a moron. Tell the truth, chuck: if you met him today would you fancy him?'

'He's my unrequited love. I still wonder if he's my destiny.'

'And tonight's Oscar goes to ...' She made a faint drum roll sound on the desk. 'Anita Richardson!'

'You're nowhere near as funny as you think. Hopefully Ryan knows what he's let himself in for.'

They both watched Elliot make his way towards them.

Juliet whispered, 'That suit makes him look like a dummy in a charity shop window. Jake's a lot nicer.'

Juliet's face remained expressionless. Elliot left a gap and took the seat directly opposite Anita as she returned his smile.

Ryan congratulated the team on their significant progress. 'Remember the dangers of complacency. Raymond Philpott's been extremely complimentary of your efforts. Let's stay focused.'

Abigail looked in Anita's direction and curled up the side of her lip as she whispered to Ryan, then stepped back as he read the note she passed him. Tammy hit the keyboard. The Primavera plan flashed up. Alan stood to talk through the programme. Tammy tapped a key. The project activity schedule filled the screen. When everyone turned to watch Ryan step into the side office Alan raised his voice to hold their focus. Anita watched Ryan stutter into his mobile. The more frustrated he became the harder he jammed his finger onto the glass. Ryan slammed shut his mobile. As he barged from the annex Alan lost his concentration; Tammy tapped her magic keyboard and the previous slide appeared.

Ryan held a hand up to Alan, who halted his presentation. 'Raymond's got an issue with the turbine hall. Elliot, what do you know?'

Elliot's puzzled look caused loose skin to wrinkle under his jowls. Anita couldn't dislodge the thought of the old Minced Morsels advert with Clement Freud and how Elliot wore the same hangdog expression as Henry the bloodhound.

When Elliot and Ryan looked at Anita, she shrugged her shoulders. Ryan looked at his mobile as he took his seat. Alan recapped, then huffed when Jake burst into the room.

'Sorry, Alan. Ryan, can I speak to Nita? I can't wait.' Jake placed his arm around her waist to guide her into the stairwell at the end of the hall. Anita caught the scent of Gucci for Homme. 'I've screwed up.'

Jake explained how he'd authorised the replacement of the monitoring equipment in the turbine hall. He jolted his arms to animate the installation. 'When the contractor removed the cable the VIR crumbled like a biodegraded carrier bag; the work's on stop.' Jake wiggled his fingers to demonstrate the cable crumble.

Jake's civil engineering background lacked Elliot's adeptness with power stations. This, combined with the lack of historical documentation, meant that Jake had failed to take into account that the legacy cable might be VIR: vulcanised Indian rubber. Jake's costly error would delay the project due to the metres of essential cable that now needed to be replaced prior to the installation of the new equipment.

Anita nodded. 'I think that's why Ryan's had a thrombo. Raymond's been on the phone. You have to tell Ryan what you've done. Elliot's the best person to assess the risk to the project.'

'Raymond's here to see Ryan this afternoon; I think this might be top of the agenda. Can you find me a get out of jail free card?'

Anita hadn't seen Jake fraught. He looked cute. She offered to ferret through the contract paperwork as they hurried back to the conference room.

As Jake spoke to a solemn-faced Ryan, Anita took her seat next to Juliet. Ryan took Jake and Elliot into the side room. At that moment, as she became aware of Jake's similarity to Elliot, she realised maybe she did have a type.

Juliet thought the same. 'They could be brothers. The Marx brothers; Jake can be Zeppo and Elliot's a combination of the other three clowns.'

As they left the conference room, halfway down the hall Anita heard Elliot shout, 'Nita, can you spare a mo?'

As they stood in her office Anita avoided his eyes. She was perturbed when he took a step closer. 'I'm busy at the moment; what can I help you with?'

'What's this Jake character like? If he's screwed up my project he can carry the can to the dole office.'

'You're horrible sometimes; you don't even know him. He's worked his bits off to fix this contract.'

'I thought Ryan blamed him in the first place.'

'No, he wasn't to blame, so whaddya want?'

'A copy of the turbine hall contract would be useful.'

Anita hated to split her loyalty. 'I'll send Tammy over with a copy.'

Jake waited for Elliot to leave, then came in. Aware the blame lay with himself, he asked Anita if she'd found a clause in the contract that could help take the sting out of the problem.

She offered a long shot. 'They've said we must inspect cables prior to installation but it's noted their schematics aren't up to date or available, therefore we could argue we couldn't have reasonably foreseen this. However Raymond will argue as competent contractors we should.'

Raymond arrived with Bobby Bullshit at 2 pm. At 2.05 Ryan called Jake and Anita into the war room. As they entered Raymond threw the installation paperwork for the monitoring equipment across the desk. The flimsy file slid to a halt in front of Jake. When Bobby leaned back and folded his arms Anita looked at the colourful glossy poster above his head, one of a series dotted around the building. This particular poster demonstrated the second of five teamwork tools. The first insisted on a safety-first attitude. The second promoted a no-blame culture with a quote: *Learn from your mistakes.*

Anita opened a copy of the contract and concentrated on the precision of Raymond's carefully chosen words.

'This equipment can't be down for longer than forty-eight hours. What's your corrective action plan?

Jake looked at her. They both looked at the door when the cavalry arrived in the form of Elliot, whose silver tongue stole the show. Bobby Bullshit stammered his objection to leave a spray of spit over the desk, then jolted his head back when the ingenuity of Elliot's suggestion penetrated his brain. Jake and Anita were bystanders. Within an hour Elliot had Raymond eating from his hand and offered to follow Raymond to Seven Point.

Elliot escorted Raymond to the car park. Bobby followed a few steps behind. Ryan told Anita to leave. She waited outside.

When Jake exited the office he looked at Anita and shook his fingers across his neck to mimic the 'cut' action from the movies. 'It's a good job we work in a no-blame culture, eh, mate?'

They marched side by side. Rebels against the tension, they playfully nudged one another each time they came to a door.

In the office Anita texted the girls to ask if Jake's 'mate' comment meant he viewed her as a friend.

Aren't They a Lovely Couple?

The gloomy Thursday couldn't dampen Anita's spirits as she waited for Jake to finish his phone call. When he held up his hand to indicate another five minutes she passed the time standing at the window to marvel at the tightly woven birds' nests scattered in the trees high above the ground. She favoured the black and white house martins. Back home she'd only seen sparrows; at the Zeus business park staff often hung bags of sunflower seeds off the large ash trees in the picnic area and attracted a spectrum of birds.

Anita watched Elliot strut around the office as Tammy scurried to prepare his paperwork for the weekly project appraisal at Seven Point. Elliot's voice boomed across the office as if the engineers who hung off his every word belonged to the hard of hearing institute. Anita suspected that, as Elliot lodged in the Duck and Goose with Pike and Alan, the younger engineers joined them most nights for an after-work drink. Elliot no doubt impressed the lads with his tales of conquest over a twenty-two-year-old hottie and Kylie on the side line waiting to jump into his bed, if she hadn't already. Anita scolded herself for the mean thought. As a project manager with a magnitude of shrewdness there wasn't much that fazed Elliot. Abigail described Elliot as 'large and loud'. Elliot called Abigail 'rough as a bear's arse.'

Elliot's confab with his team presented the perfect opportunity for Jake and Anita to leave without him, as neither of them wanted a chaperone to impose on their weekly date.

'Oi, you ready? I'll bring the car to the entrance; no point both of us getting wet, look.'

Since Abigail had watched Anita like a hawk when Jake had first suggested they stop for lunch on their way to the Thursday project appraisal at Seven Point, Anita had nonchalantly agreed, then spent an inordinate amount of time Wednesday night selecting the perfect clothes to wear.

Over the weeks that followed their contribution at the Thursday project approval get-together embedded them into the client's project team. Even Trish, a renowned stickler for the rules, issued Jake with a pass for the staff car park. Their work affiliation flourished as Jake and Anita perfected their good cop, bad cop routine. To the amusement of the commercial administrator Elise, Anita played the bad guy and used playful sarcasm to fetch conditions of contract into play in order to formalise good guy Jake's amicable solutions for Frank's complex issues.

Over the same period their lunchtime pub meal encouraged unscripted conversation that revealed past traits as if they were characters on a weekly soap opera. Whereas Anita's uninhibited nature talked freely she learnt Jake's life story from the bare facts he revealed, like when a waitress served mixed fruit sponge. Jake said the congealed odd-coloured custard that plopped off his spoon reminded him of school dinners; Anita recalled an article that said during the 1970s prisoners had been served a better quality of food than school children; this led Jake to relive the traumatic tale of a battleaxe dinner lady force-feeding him sprouts, which they both agreed probably never happened in prison.

Their personal relationship blossomed further when Jake suggested they forgo their meal deal lunch and stop at his local, the Quarry Lodge, on the way home from Seven Point. The locals called this traditional public house Casey's as for the last forty years it had been owned by Billy Case and his wife of longer years Ester, who the regulars called Tess.

The pub attracted an older clientele, who played dominoes in the corner as they grumbled of life today versus the good old days. Anita and Jake sat at one of the tables near the log fire, reserved for couples who wanted an intimate place to talk.

The first time they called into the pub, which smelt of best bitter, Jake pulled his chair closer to Anita's. Tess shouted over the bar, 'Aah, Billy. Aren't they a lovely couple?' A red-faced Jake pushed his chair back.

Billy shouted, 'Leave 'em alone, Tess, you're embarrassing Jake,' and sent over a drink. 'On the house.'

Jake returned Billy's toast as he complained to Anita he felt like a teenager in his grandparents' parlour.

The following week Jake exchanged pleasantries with Tess and Billy as he ordered the house special, homemade steak and kidney pie with chips and peas, then joined Anita at the table tucked in the corner where he passed her a bundle of photographs.

'I take it this cutie is BJ; you sure he's yours?'

Jake nudged Anita with his shoulder, then grabbed her arm when she almost fell off the stool. 'With them good looks he couldn't be anyone else's.'

Jake summed up a story to go with each snap of BJ. Anita studied how the young boy had Jake's blue eyes and fair hair but not his stature. Jake's face lit up with pride as he told her of BJ's school 'recycle or reuse' campaign and how his little tyke complained if people dropped litter on the floor.

'He talks like an old man. He has a Think Green poster on his bedroom wall. At his age I had a poster of Susan Day.'

Anita studied the photo of a proud young man who cradled a tiny baby in his arms. 'Bloody hell, who's this? He's a right tatty head.'

'That's me when I had long hair, before this look.' Jake bowed his head to show off his crew cut.

Anita ran her hand over his scalp. 'It feels like puppy fur.'

He didn't recoil. Anita tried to reassure herself with that knowledge when Jake changed the subject. She fretted she'd been too familiar.

'Oh, I know what I wanted to say. Abigail said to ask what film you appeared in. I'm intrigued.'

'Abigail has a big mouth.'

Anita explained how when she had been to Vegas to see Keith Urban she'd seen an advertisement for movie extras. 'I appeared in *Rocky VI*.'

'If I get the DVD will I spot you?'

'Doubt it, I had bleached blonde hair. I know where I stood but I haven't watched the film.'

The advertisement had been for extras to sit in the audience at Mandalay Bay when they taped the fight scene. She related the experience of watching the actors do tireless retakes to get the scene right.

'Then Rocky makes his way from the boxing ring, the winner of the match declared. I stood right at the front.' Anita searched her mobile for the picture she'd taken of Sly when he posed for pictures. 'He stopped right by me; I couldn't help but shout, "Hey, Rocky, take your best shot."'

'Wow, you make the simplest event sound fun.'

'Stallone's expression amused me no end. He looked as if he wanted to call security.'

'I get the impression you did something you aren't sharing.'

Anita guessed Abigail had told him she'd taken pole-dancing lessons. She decided to keep that tale in the memory banks for a more appropriate time. 'I'm telling you nowt else. You know the rules; you have to tell me something.'

Jake told her of the time he'd been arrested.

'It isn't as dramatic as you think, before you imagine an episode of *New Tricks*. I don't regret my actions although I'm ashamed I lost control.'

He told her how his niece had babysat for a neighbour during his sister's last visit. The next day his niece had stayed in her bedroom all day; her worried mother had demanded an explanation. Her frightened daughter had confessed how the husband of the family she'd babysat for had kissed her when he had escorted her home.

'She's a sixteen-year-old kid and that pervert … I lost my temper. I went to his house and punched his lights out, as you say. His wife called the police. He called the unfortunate situation a misunderstanding and dropped the charges.'

'Good for you, I wish I'd had someone to stick up for me. I can tell you a tale or two. It's one of the reasons I hate facial hair.'

Anita told Jake the story of her predator who wore a full

beard and moustache. 'Same story: he walked me home from babysitting, as we got halfway down the jigger behind the houses he grabbed me. I gagged at the smell of his beer breath and the touch of the coarse hair around his lips wet from ale. To this day if anyone with facial hair gives me so much as a peck on the cheek, I retch.'

'Note to self: must shave when out with Nita.'

'Only if you're planning to kiss me.'

Once again Anita fretted that her lack of subtlety might've frightened Jake off when he got up and went to the bar.

Last Thursday's conversation showed promise when Jake asked Anita to name the best country concert she'd been to. Regardless of how genuine Jake's interest Anita loved talking about her two favourite things, Vegas and country music. She told Jake she'd reached the panicle of excitement when Jason Aldean had played an open-air concert in the man-made beach area of Mandalay Bay. Anita excitedly recalled how the stage had been positioned at the far side of the swimming pool.

Anita's exhilaration gushed. 'I watched the crowd remove their shoes to wade up to the front of the stage. So I put my heels in my bag and had a prime position, a few feet from the stage.'

'Imagine doing that at Weston, you'd freeze your toes off.' Jake shivered at the thought.

'So I'm stood up to my thighs in a pool of warm water with my dress tucked in my drawers. The experience felt surreal.'

'Only in America, eh?'

The auspicious part of the conversation occurred when Anita asked Jake what concerts he'd seen recently.

'I've a mate who persuaded me to go to a number of eighties revival concerts.' Jake named the bands he'd seen at Colston Hall. 'The last two were Ultravox and OMD.'

Anita felt old as she'd seen both bands in Liverpool the first time they'd toured. Had Jake's next line been an offer to introduce her to his older friend she'd have hit him hard then sulked for hours. Instead her heart fluttered when she digested the possibility of his words.

'I'll check if any country singers appear on the upcoming acts listings. Something different might be fun.'

Given the unlikelihood of a country singer on tour in the UK, Anita took Jake's offer as a nice gesture. But fate had other ideas when unbeknown to both of them one of Anita's favourite female country artists added Bristol to her UK tour dates.

That Thursday Jake and Anita socialised with the Seven Point team prior to the start of the project appraisal. Anita caught up with the latest instalment of Elise's new romance and the gossip that Raymond might be promoted. Jake chatted with Frank, whose eldest son showed a keen interest in civil engineering

Evidence of how Elliot's popularity with Raymond had gained momentum became apparent when he bounded into the boardroom absorbed in Raymond's account of the Lola Mk5 he restored in his spare time. Jake, Frank, Elise and Anita exchanged glances. Out of earshot Anita told Jake how Elliot turned up for the Christmas bevvy in a posh Jag.

'Elliot doesn't own the car, look. It's for show. I heard him tell Alan he's part of a club. He pays for the use of one of a pool of high-end sports cars twelve weekends a year.' Jake shook his head when he heard Raymond accept Elliot's offer to take him for a spin in his souped-up sports car at the weekend.

Frank kept the chocolate biscuits hidden as the project appraisals opened with regular formalities. Billy Bullshit delivered the prologue, which Anita doubted anybody around the table listened to, then Raymond hijacked the meeting to discuss proposals for the additional work he intimated Elliot should lead.

Jake whispered, 'Look what happens when Raymond asks me a question; he looks at Elliot and that prick gives him a subtle nod to confirm my answer's correct.'

Anita thought Jake had imagined the collusion until the second part of the meeting when Jake answered Raymond's question then tapped her knee with his pen. As she witnessed Elliot's nod to Raymond Jake gave her his 'told you so' look.

Later at Casey's Jake's frustration manifested. 'What's Elliot got? The guys in the office flock to him, you seem to think a lot of him. Raymond thinks the sun shines from his badonkadonk.'

Anita recognised the expression from a Trace Adkins song. 'Have you been listening to country songs without me?'

Jake couldn't muster a smile. 'I'm handing in my notice. I can't cope with being patronised by the Maserati twins, look.'

Anita tried to keep the panic out of her voice. 'If it's because of Elliot he goes back to Liverpool soon.'

Jake moved closer to whisper in her ear. 'Why will you miss me if I go?'

'Behave, soft lad; you're leaving, not dying.'

Jake looked perplexed, then confessed how maddened he felt when Elliot went into her office and shut the door. Anita decided not to mention that she guessed Elliot only did it for Jake's benefit.

'It's been a hard slog. I think Ryan will ask Elliot to stay. The boss isn't my biggest fan since the cock-up. I can do without this crap, look.'

As Anita tucked into Tess's hand-cut chips Jake unloaded, vented and whined about Elliot, Raymond, Ryan and every other injustice in the western hemisphere. Anita wrestled the urge to dissuade Jake but suggested he speak to Ryan rather than make a rash decision.

'Oh, I almost forgot.'

Anita could hardly contain her surprise when Jake waved two tickets to see Mary Chapin Carpenter at Colston Hall under her nose.

Over the weekend as frustration nibbled at Anita's core she plucked up the courage to phone Carl. She arranged to go back to Liverpool and resolve the issue of their relationship. Carl suggested the first of April. Like a death row prisoner she struck through the dates on the calendar as she counted the eight days to the execution of her marriage.

Kinder Than Goodbye

Like a visitor, Anita entered Carl's home. To clear a space to sit she gathered the pages of the Racing Posts strewn across the settee.

'Leave them, will you? I have 'em organised.' Carl tossed the papers on the armchair to cover three pairs of dirty socks.

Anita switched on the table air freshener. A puff of freesia and jasmine mixed with the sweaty sock smell; she picked up the socks and threw them in the washing machine with a selection of items from the wash basket that overflowed onto the utility room floor. The evidence in the tidy kitchen that anyone ate there belonged to the solitary plate and cutlery for one that sat in the drainer. Anita switched on the kettle. As she waited for the water to boil she scrubbed at the hardened food remnants in the microwave and emptied the crumbs from the tray beneath the toaster.

The louder Carl exhaled his despair, the more dread engulfed her.

'Are you stopping in the kitchen all night?'

Her hand shook. Anita absorbed the overspill of coffee with kitchen roll, then put the drinks on a tray with a plate of biscuits to fill the space.

Anita recognised Carl's mood so his announcement came as no surprise. 'I'm down to the last of the cash, and before you start to nag—'

Anita cut him off. 'Where does that leave us?'

Carl deflected. 'It's up to you. You're the unhappy one.'

'Why is it up to me? You're the one betting your brains out.'

The animosity elevated as each of them found the words

flowed easier if they blamed the other.

'I've had an offer on the house. It's low for a quick sale. I need the money to dig out of this hole or I take the last of the savings.'

Anita wondered what ransom she would pay for her freedom. 'Why don't you get a loan and wait for the market to improve?'

Carl looked at his feet. 'I've already got one loan secured against the house, and before you ask that's all but gone too.'

Anita had suspected when she'd read the letter from the bank that Carl was contemplating a loan against the house. She hadn't realised he'd stoop as low as to forge her signature.

He snapped as if he'd read her mind, 'Desperate times call for desperate measures.'

Anita abandoned the charade. 'Do what you want. Sell the house. Keep the money; but our marriage is over. I'll speak to a solicitor about a divorce.'

Contempt replaced the tension on Carl's face. 'You finally got what you wanted.' Carl spat out his venomous words. 'You've angled for this since the day you met him.' He flicked on the switch to fire up the PC.

'Whatever you have to tell yourself, Carl; I'm done caring.'

Anita dismissed the idea of booking into a bed and breakfast. Over the last five years she'd perfected living a separate life under the same roof as her husband.

Alone she counted the same stars she'd wished upon as a child as she wondered if her dreams, Carl's gambling, the secondment or Elliot had been the catalyst that ended her marriage. Anita reminded herself how unhappy both she and Carl had been for a long time before she'd fallen for Elliot.

At four in the morning Anita snuck downstairs. Seated at the kitchen table, she hugged a cup of coffee as she gathered her thoughts to write Carl a note. When she heard footsteps cross the landing she stayed quiet, fretful that a noise might alert Carl to her presence. The toilet flushed. Anita waited for his bedroom door to shut, then jumped when she glimpsed Carl standing in the kitchen doorway.

She avoided looking at him. 'I'll head back to Chrystalmere

now to beat the rush hour traffic; I'm in the middle of writing you a note.'

Carl looked at the blank piece of paper. 'We should talk.'

They avoided contentious issues as they ironed out the details for the sale of the house. Kinder than an angry goodbye, they agreed to discuss the future when they both felt less fraught.

Engulfed in a mixture of dread and anticipation as she drove back to Chrystalmere, Anita considered the prospect of being alone for the first time in her life until her subconscious contemplated her unspoken question: *What if my fifties are the prelude to death?* Fear crept in and seized her heart.

Elliot

Juliet lingered in the office to quiz Anita on Gerry's shenanigans. Anita diluted Ryan's version.

'One of the Big Companies, who've had a site presence for years, won't go away without a fight. They've exercised their right to object. The fraud division will investigate the client's compliance with the strict procedures.'

Juliet wasn't easily pacified. When she folded her arms Anita continued.

'They've claimed lack of compliance with the prescribed procedure and accused the client of imprecise scoring that prejudiced his bid. He's issued the thirty days' proceedings notice to challenge the result.'

As a semi-satisfied Juliet unfolded her arms, an obviously upset Abigail blocked her at the door.

'Can we go into the village from work? I'll book a taxi; as you'd say, "this conversation needs alcohol."' A tearful Abigail screwed up her nose to tell the tale that eclipsed Anita's man troubles. 'I gave Dickey the inevitable ultimatum.' Abigail stifled her tears to tell the girls how she'd told Dickey she wanted more. He wanted to have his cake and eat it. Like most men he judged the adequacy of their relationship from the amount of sex. Abigail measured her emotional fulfilment. 'He said it's best we end things before someone gets hurt. I'm already hurt.'

Juliet took a step towards Abigail.

'Don't, please.' Abigail's watery eyes looked away. 'If you hug me now I'll lose it.' Abigail wiped her eyes and shook her hair to fall over her face as she left the office with Juliet.

Anita had no sooner turned than the office door opened. 'Why does nobody knock? Barge straight in, why don't you?'

Jake ignored her sarcasm and walked to the coffee maker.

'Help yourself.'

Jake handed Anita a coffee and sat on the edge of her desk. He told her he'd discussed his future with Ryan, who had blindsided him with an offer to oversee the Marsh Moore project for the next few weeks. 'I'm off to see him and discuss terms. Wish me luck.'

Anita stood on a box of printer paper to replace the flip chart pad. Deep in concentration to update her action list, she didn't hear Elliot come into her office.

Anita wobbled on the printer paper. 'Moron, you frightened the life out of me.'

Elliot covered his mouth and chuckled. 'You avoiding me?'

'Yes, actually.'

He took an overstretched stride to tap the door shut with his heel. Anita stepped down from her podium. Elliot sat on the edge of the chair, rested his chin on his chest and massaged his fingers. As he looked up his wrinkled forehead forced his eyebrows together.

'Have you got something going on with Jake other than a work relationship?'

'Mind your own business.'

'Come for a bevvy or dinner with me tonight.' Elliot sounded like a toddler who pushed his mum's boundaries to get what he wanted.

Anita opened the door. Elliot pushed it closed.

'Can't, sorry, busy woman and …' Anita let her voice tail off.

Unsure of what else to say Anita grabbed a random document from her desk and sifted through the tabs in the alphabetised grey metal cabinet. Elliot cracked each of his fingers in quick succession.

Anita plugged her ears. 'I hate the way you do that.' She shoved the cabinet drawer, which rattled against the track then slammed shut. Anita rested her forehead on the cool metal. 'I can't do this, Elliot. Not now.'

Shielded from the prying eyes of the office by the six-foot document cabinet, Elliot stood and pulled Anita toward him.

'There's something I never told you; well, never told anyone really. My missus left me, not the other way around. She took up with some feller from work.'

Anita took a step back; she could see Juliet and Abigail watching from their respective desks. 'I don't believe you. Why tell me this now, why not then? You do me head in.'

'I kept it quiet for the kids sake, and a bit of male pride. The boys already had issues with me. I couldn't have them disappointed in their mum.' Elliot cupped his large outstretched fingers under Anita's chin and guided her to face him. Anita pulled at his hand, then curled her fingertips to burrow into his palm. She looked towards the outer office to see Jake bear witness to Elliot's overfamiliarity.

'It wasn't entirely my fault we fell out. I asked you.'

Anita pulled Elliot's hand from her face too late for Jake to see. 'You asked me lots of stuff.'

'You know what I mean.'

Anita wanted to run to Jake but she still had hold of Elliot's hand. 'Do I? Anyway, it doesn't matter now, does it?'

Elliot raised his voice. 'It matters to me.'

'You hurt me, Elliot. You made me cry.'

Elliot let go of her hand. 'What did I do? You did that random weeping.'

Here stood the same old Elliot who refused to accept responsibility. Anita stared across the office. The outer door reverberated as Jake stormed off.

'No. You cast me aside without enough respect for me or our friendship; you acted selfish, thoughtless and cruel.'

He bowed his head. 'It hurt when I read your e-mail. I'd been to hell and back. Dumped by the missus, then you gave me the bum's rush.'

'It's all about you.' Anita cringed at how like Carl she sounded.

Elliot explained his curt reply as the best way he could respond. Confused and worried he'd inflame the situation further if he said the wrong thing, he had chosen a neutral response.

Anita sighed. 'I had genuine feelings for you.' The emphasis on the 'had' part of the statement made Elliot look up. 'I respected you, cared for you; though when it mattered, you didn't give a rat's ass for me.' Elliot had been at the end of Anita's rants enough times to know to wait until she dispensed her last breath. 'I still care, more than you realise, but you made your choice, remember: the younger prettier model. I wanted to be with you, and you chose to be with someone else. Anyway, I've moved on.'

Elliot went to leave but made a sharp turn back. 'I … you don't understand, you took it the wrong way. You had no time for me. I thought you understood.'

'Oh no, Elliot, I can't go down that road.'

Elliot nervously transferred his weight from one foot to another as if he planned to Morris dance his way back into her life. Abigail went to enter. Anita caught her eye and shook her head no.

Elliot's raised voice interrupted. 'Do you think I don't know, aye, do yer? Why do you have to go on, why can't we try again now you and Carl are getting divorced? Can't we forget what happened? I made a mistake. I am human.'

Anita wondered who'd told him of her divorce as she reached for her eyebrow. An extra-hard squeeze made her wince. She'd waited too long to remain silent.

'And what?' Her disfigured expression spat the words from her mouth. 'Love you again, jump into bed this time, then you can notch up another one? Then what, wait for some bit of a kid to flash you her tits, then you can bin me like a used-up dish cloth? I suppose you've had spring chicken, now you want to try a tough old bird?'

Elliot banged the desk with his fist. 'Do you think so little of me?'

'And the threesome with Kylie and her mum; I suppose at least I'd be safe from that humiliation given you'd have to dig my mother up first.'

'I didn't have a threesome; I went to a party with Mark. I bumped into Kylie and her mum snogged me in the kitchen.'

Elliot slammed the door as he left.

Leaving Anita no time to compose herself, Juliet opened the door. 'Thought you might like to know the villagers are here to take back their idiot.'

Anita assumed Juliet directed the 'idiot' quip at her. 'It isn't like that.'

'It never is, chuck.' Juliet quickly apologised for her snide remark and left.

Anita watched Juliet shake her head as she passed the friendship baton to Abigail, who stormed through Anita's door. 'What's his problem?' She nodded towards Elliot as he stomped across the office. 'C'mon, babba, I've booked a taxi; let's go. I think we all need a drink.'

Anita grabbed her coat and followed.

In the pub Anita threatened to go home if the girls mentioned Jake or lectured her on Elliot. She'd wait for her weekly dinner date with Jake to explain the Elliot situation. She felt she owed Jake that as other than a few nice words, the occasional hand-holding and a few kisses they weren't an item. Her unease softened as she remembered how Jake had been kind, caring and twice the gentlemen Elliot had been.

When Anita got up to go to the ladies' the girls encouraged her to call Jake. Juliet ranted with fury when Anita told her she hadn't phoned him. When Anita said she'd never seen Juliet so angry Juliet reminded Anita how she'd never seen her so upset before Elliot and how she hadn't seen her so happy before Jake.

'And what if this with Jake's no more than a rebound relationship?'

Thankfully Abigail remained neutral although Anita suspected she'd side with Juliet if she weren't so distracted with her own upset.

Anita recited the textbook summation like a lecturer. 'I certainly don't want to fall into the trap of letting male attention stroke my fragile ego or play a pivotal role to soften the emotional devastation from a painful breakup.'

Juliet sat stony-faced with her arms folded. 'Oh, chuck, I get you're cautious but … oh, I give up, there's no reasoning with you when you're in this mood.'

'What if Jake's a quick fix to rebuild my self-esteem? I know I've complained for years how Carl's lack of attention made me feel empty, but I still feel horrible about the collapse of our marriage. You know better than anyone that once you connect with someone and add intimacy that's a strong bond to break.'

Juliet remained unconvinced and insisted Anita should stop trying to take the moral high ground and take a chance.

'Oh, and wasn't it you who quoted as high as ninety-five per cent of rebound relationships fail? I need to be sure that if I get serious with Jake I don't become another statistic.'

Exhausted from the emotional battles the girls ended the night with a long hug and a semi-inebriated Abigail declaring she would come to Vegas with the girls in August.

At home as she waited for the kettle to boil Anita butted her head against the kitchen wall and rationalised how if they still piped town gas, she could stick her head in the oven and end it all. She found no solace with the realisation that in the 1970s natural gas had replaced coal gas or that Anita lived in the country and used all-electric appliances, so other than singeing her hair it would be a fruitless exercise.

The next day Tammy updated Anita with the news that Jake had cleared his desk and left to work on the Marsh Moore project. She handed Anita an envelope and studied her reaction when Anita tipped two tickets for the Mary Chapin Carpenter concert onto the desk, then checked twice for a note.

The Azure Dress

The first Thursday Elliot and Anita car-pooled to Seven Point on the way home they stopped at a country pub. This gave them the opportunity to talk in private. At the end of the night Elliot asked if Anita could put the past aside. Anita said yes and over the next five days they fell into their familiar routine.

The next Thursday when they stopped for a drink on the way home Elliot asked for Anita's help to collate the quality assurance paperwork for the client. Anita said yes and over the next five days and half a Saturday Anita helped Elliot.

By the third Thursday the harder Anita tried to suppress her feelings the more Elliot occupied her thoughts. When they stopped for a drink on the way home Anita leaned into Elliot's arms when she laughed. When Anita ranted in frustration at the subcontractor's dilemma of how to accelerate work and remain compliant with the inexhaustible constraints imposed by the power station's site licence conditions, Elliot massaged the tension from her shoulders. At the end of the night Elliot asked her to represent him at Ryan's Friday progress review as he'd arranged to take his children for the weekend. Anita said yes and went into work early to prepare.

The fourth Thursday Elliot asked her to join him for dinner the next night. Anita said no. He reminded her of their fun-filled relationship. Anita remained adamant. When Elliot kissed her, he rekindled the passion she'd desperately tried to deny. The feelings Elliot aroused wavered her judgement. When Anita told him she'd sleep on it Elliot phoned the Italian restaurant down the road from the Duck and Goose and reserved a table for two. He told Anita he would eat alone if she stood him up.

*

At home Anita delved into her memory box to find the faded dusty pink envelope shrouding the collection of photos that catalogued her friendship with Elliot. Years earlier Juliet had teased how Anita had a crypt with a shrine dedicated to Elliot. Even without a basement or a secret room Anita agreed her oddness bore an uncanny resemblance to a psychopathic stalker from a Hollywood movie.

As the rocking chair creaked against the floorboards Anita dared herself to peruse each snapshot. She beamed at the picture of Elliot who held her hand as she showed off the plastic purple Christmas cracker ring he'd placed on her wedding finger. She scrutinised the evidence of how they'd skirted the periphery of an affair, then put the photos back into the envelope. Her trip down memory lane put the ghosts of the past to rest. Her desire to accept Elliot's dinner invitation overruled common sense; she deserved to see if Elliot really was her destiny. Before Anita went to bed, or gave her friends the opportunity to express a different opinion, she texted Elliot to say yes, she would meet him for dinner. Anita signed off, *Hugs and Kisses. A.xxxxx*

The occasion to wear her azure dress for Elliot finally arrived. Five past seven, Anita engaged in the usual round of hesitance, then strode into the restaurant.

As she'd recently attended a seminar on kinesics, her date with Elliot would give her a perfect opportunity to use him as her guinea pig. As she couldn't trust the words from his mouth maybe she'd glean more insight if she studied his body language.

Anita palpitated at the sight of Elliot's hazel eyes as he glimpsed her above the rim of his pint glass. Her heart melted as her lips met with the warmth of Elliot's clean-shaven complexion. A healthy glow coloured his cheeks. Elliot's body language screamed, *I want you.* Hers replied, *Take me now.*

'Wow, titch, you look stunning.' His eyes focused on her cleavage then inched up her neck.

The murmurs of dialogue from the small huddles standing at the bar faded to background noise as an array of conflicted emotions plagued Anita.

'This for me.' She picked up the Jack and Coke that waited on the bar and took a large gulp. The acne-clad pubescent who stood at the end of the bar to stack dirty glasses into the industrial dishwasher smiled as he pointed. Anita turned around to see Elliot walking to the podium. She hurried to catch up.

'I've booked. Parker, table for two.'

The waitress tucked two menus under her arm as she pencilled her seating chart. They followed her ponytail, which swayed like a pendulum, to a corner table.

As the night unfolded for them, cocooned in their own world, Anita responded to Elliot's posture, which had the hallmark of an alpha male: legs spread wide with his toes and hands pointed towards her. Anita offered him her wide child-bearing hips. As they talked Elliot focused on her mouth; Anita licked her lips to mimic his gesture. He raised his eyebrows and smiled when she made a double entendre. When they talked Elliot finished her sentences and Anita completed his. They suspended their mating ritual when the pubescent collected their empty glasses, then again when the waiter interrupted to satisfy another basic need.

As they ate the flirty mood changed. Elliot's conversation revolved around the weekend he'd taken his children to one of the family-oriented holiday parks. Anita's mummy fantasy came to mind. She'd often daydream of feeding the ducks with Elliot's young daughter as Elliot placed the boys' backpacks for goalposts and dribbled the football through the boys' legs to tease his two lads to tackle him, then he'd pretend to be outplayed and let the boys score a goal.

Elliot saddened. 'At the end of the weekend each of them cried and begged me to come home. It's the youngest, her big tearful eyes. Daughters, they're a heartbreaker.'

Anita empathised with the pain Elliot felt when he handed the children back to their mother.

'I thought I might go back, for the sake of the kids, now her feller's done a bunk. I couldn't. They know I love them but I need to move on.'

Anita squeezed his hand. As the waitress cleared the plates Elliot told her they'd have coffee in the lounge.

Snuggled in the alcove, Anita heard the words she'd longed for. 'So, titch, can there be us?'

Her reaction wasn't what she'd anticipated. 'I've got my own issues, plus I'd want to see your all-clear from the clap clinic before I went to bed with you.'

Elliot slipped his arm around her waist. 'So you think you might go to bed with me.'

Anita slapped his thigh and turned slightly. 'No. So think again.'

Elliot rested his hand on the small of her back. Anita found herself torn between thoughts of Jake and guilt from a raw yearning to feel Elliot's naked body shroud hers.

'You've no excuse this time. We're both single; well, you're almost.'

'Yes, but this time you dumped me, for a girl young enough to be my daughter, and then rubbed me nose in it. That's quite a passion killer, I can assure you.'

Elliot pulled his hand from her back and huffed. 'Do you have to drag that up? Did it occur to you I needed to lose you to realise how much I wanted you?' Elliot picked up his pint. Anita watched the pink tinge of his cheeks deepen as he huffed a second time. 'I made a mistake, titch. It won't be the last. I'm ready to give us a go if you want.'

The hurt he'd inflicted couldn't be erased. 'I think we should both take time to sort our feelings. I'm glad we're friends again; I've missed you. But—'

Elliot put a finger to Anita's lips. 'Friend it is then, at least for now.' He tugged at her elbow. 'Will that be a friend with benefits?'

'No.' Anita inched closer and rested her head against his toned bicep. 'Let's go out a few times and see what happens.'

Elliot locked Anita's lips with a passion-filled kiss, then turned the conversation to sport. Anita laughed as Elliot gave her an action replay of the rugby union game he'd seen in Gloucester with the local engineers.

'Rugby league's defiantly a man's game,' he said. 'Union's for tarts.'

The couple on the next table frowned at Elliot's comment.

Anita stroked the side of Elliot's face as he kissed her again. 'I have to ask. What happened with Chantelle?'

'That's an episode I want to forget.' Elliot let his neck relax against the back of the seat to face the ceiling, then he closed his eyes.

He told Anita how Chantelle had invited him and two other couples to dinner. The youthful conversation had consisted of an update on the weekly soap operas and MTV's hottest videos.

'One of the girls listed at least twenty songs. I pretended I hadn't heard of them.' The smile and the colour drained from Elliot's face. 'She goes on and on till finally she asks if I've heard of Timbaland.' Elliot described the horror on the quintet of faces as he replied, *Aren't they the people that make nice shoes?*

Anita cupped her mouth with her hand to contain a combined laugh and cough. As her snorts exploded the couple on the next table gave a sympathetic smile to Elliot. Anita threw her head back and cried at the sight of Elliot forlorn expression.

'You're as bad as them.' He poked her in the arm.

'Carry on. I've stopped,' Anita lied.

Elliot waited as Anita shook herself into a sensible state.

'So this spotty-faced cheese ball who's obviously had his sense of humour removed gets indignant and asks, "Bloody hell, Chantelle, how old is this dude?"'

Anita grabbed the tissue from her bra strap to dab her eyes.

'I'm kidding them. My eldest lad keeps me up to date with music or the latest gadget the kids at school must have.'

Anita contorted her face to distort the smile.

'Go on, laugh or you'll explode.'

'I need to wee.'

In the ladies' toilets Anita squeezed her fingers into the toilet roll dispenser and plucked a handful of tissue to mop up the tears. She sat for the next five minutes. Each time she thought of Elliot's story she tittered.

When she resumed her position Elliot rested his forehead on hers and curled his top lip. 'Chantelle enrolled in beauty school. It's one of them times when you look back and wonder what the bloody hell possessed you.'

Anita kissed the tip of his nose, then picked up her drink. 'And your performance with Kylie?'

'When I told her I'd be Ryan's deputy she came on heavy. I led her on a bit, mainly to wind you up.'

Anita pondered Elliot's words as he paid the bill. Outside as they waited for a taxi, the night ended with a succession of long intense kisses and her refusal to go back to the Duck and Goose. Neither of them came up for air until the taxi driver pulled up outside the chapel. As the black cab turned onto the main road Anita looked into the stars; she said her prayers and asked her parents not to be too disappointed in her, then asked the goddess Aphrodite to guide her destiny.

Content she'd resolved her issues with Elliot. Anita savoured the detail of their date, and burnt each minute of their encounter into her memory for future reference.

It took three lust-filled dates with Elliot for the issue of sex to lead to a row. Anita should have guessed when he coaxed her back to the Duck and Goose how the night would end.

Half undressed they wrestled on the bed. Anita enjoyed their heavy petting but when Elliot tugged at her knickers she reacted like a virgin on her wedding night. She crossed her legs and covered her cellulite-dimpled thighs with the bed sheet.

'What the hell's wrong with you?' Elliot's frustration was amplified around the room.

A niggle of common sense reminded Anita how Elliot's selfish behaviour had left her wounded like the runner-up in a competition, unworthy as the first choice. 'I can't. Every time you touch me I imagine you being intimate with that young girl. I've tried. I'm sorry. It won't work. A kiss and a cuddle I can do but sex I can't.'

Without caution she'd lost her heart to Elliot; she wouldn't lose her self-respect as easily. Anita thought of Merlot's expression. 'I mightn't know what I want from the future but I sure as hell know what I don't want.'

Elliot broke the silence. 'Oh, here we go again.'

'Yes. Here we go. It isn't merely sex to me, it's—'

'Spare me the sermon; I've been here before. Men want sex, women want a cuddle. Yes, I get it.'

'Yes, well, you won't be getting it tonight, not off me anyway.'

Elliot turned on the TV and flicked through the channels until he stopped at a rugby game. 'What do you want from me?'

'I'm sorry, Elliot. I think I better go.'

'And you call me immature.'

Anita slammed the bedroom door as she left.

'Trying to sleep in here,' Alan shouted from a room down the hall.

At home Anita phoned Juliet, who said no more than, 'These conversations require alcohol. You pour the drinks, I'll call in to the late shop and get the nibbles.'

Once they'd got the 'I told you so' speech out of the way they did what friends do best: they analysed her behaviour.

Juliet concluded Elliot wasn't Anita's destiny; rather than being in love with Elliot, she'd simply loved the feelings he'd aroused in her. Despite the night's events Anita remained unconvinced.

The Job Offer

For the next four weeks Elliot said hello and goodnight with no conversation in between. Anita wanted to clear the air, but her enthusiasm waned when she couldn't muster the right words. This morning Anita watched Elliot hover outside her office as she ended her phone call; right on cue Elliot came into her office and shut the door.

'So, titch, is it true you're leaving Liverpool to become a Southern softie?'

Anita looked at Elliot's hair. 'What's happened to your sideburns? You had a million grey hairs the other week.'

Elliot stroked down the coarse hair at the side of his face. 'You do exaggerate. I had six.'

'Yes, six million.'

'I plucked them.'

Anita used her hip to bump him out the way.

Elliot leaned on the door with his hands tucked in the pockets of his designer trousers, which hung better since he'd gained a few pounds 'Have you been offered another job?'

Anita busied herself as she replied, 'Raymond pitched an offer last week when he heard my secondment ended soon. I told him I'd consider his proposal.'

'I thought you'd go back to the sidings.'

Anita supposed to Elliot it seemed a logical assumption. 'Why, will you miss me?'

Elliot scowled. 'I'll plead the fifth, as the Americans say; anyway, I mightn't be at the sidings myself.'

Intrigued, Anita asked Elliot to explain. He shocked her with the news he'd submitted his resignation. 'I've given Mr M a month's notice. I plan to start afresh.'

'What? Why? Where you going? When you going? Have you got another job?'

Elliot winked and tapped his nose. Anita didn't press for details, aware Elliot liked practical jokes.

As Elliot turned to leave he looked at Anita over his shoulder. 'It's ironic. The times I asked you to leave Carl, you wouldn't in case I blamed you for the breakup of my family. So I acted like a prat and took up with, well, you know the rest. Now you're on the verge of a divorce and because I acted like a prat, you tell me it's too late. Is that irony?'

Not technically didn't seem the most appropriate thing to say. Anita maintained at a safe distance behind her desk. 'I'll love you forever, in my own way. I wouldn't swap our friendship for the world but now isn't our time.' Anita felt tears prickle her eyes. 'So I might never see you again.'

'Don't be so sure.' Elliot tapped his nose as he winked.

Jokingly she called him a tosser. Elliot gave a faint smile and left.

Juliet came in. 'Have you been offered another job?'

Before she could answer, Abigail shouted that Ryan wanted her.

In his office the greyness of Ryan's unshaven face concerned her.

'Juliet said you've been approached by the client.'

'Tell Mata Hari. Don't bother, I'll tell her myself.'

Ryan's mouth twitched. Anita eased back into the chair to brace herself.

'I've planned to speak to you for weeks. I want to offer you the position of South West principal contract manager. You can pick your own team, bigger office.'

Ryan explained how following Gerry's lucky escape from prosecution due to Mr M who had called in favours, lack of substantiated evidence and a strong ultimatum from Raymond, Mr M had banished Gerry from the company and asked Ryan to oversee the Marsh Moore project and nominate a strong team to run the Chrystalmere division. Ryan's plan hinged on Anita's agreement to be based at Chrystalmere to oversee the entire portfolio of South West projects, especially since the client's announcement of the five-year contract extension. Anita wondered if Ryan's promotion had something to do with Elliot's cryptic statements. If Ryan oversaw the Marsh Moore work, then Elliot would be the obvious successor, but Elliot had said he'd given Mr M his notice. She wondered where Jake fit in to the new set-up.

Anita wanted to ask but got distracted as she watched the colour drain from Ryan's face and beads of sweat form on his forehead. He blamed a headache. Anita should have realised Ryan wouldn't admit he felt ill.

When Anita mentioned to Juliet that Ryan looked unwell she shrugged and told her the doctor had given him a clean bill of health a week ago. He'd suggested Ryan take more exercise to reduce his stress, so Juliet had signed them both up to join the ramblers' society.

Two am Anita woke up to a frantic Juliet who screeched down the phone.

'Ryan's had a heart attack!'

Wearing Ryan's hi-vis jacket on top of her housecoat a dazed Juliet stood outside the hospital. She jumped when Anita touched her arm. Anita scrutinised Juliet's solemn expression, her eyes dry of tears.

'The nurse won't tell me how he is. I'm not a relative.' She stared at the pavement and disclosed how Ryan had struggled to get his breath. 'I think he's in trouble, he's been worried, he won't tell me. Gerry's on and off the phone all hours.'

Anita linked her arm with Juliet's. 'Ryan's got his work cut out with the Marsh Moore job. Don't worry. Tell me what happened.'

Anita suspected the dilemma of how much he should confess to Juliet and his own lucky escape from prosecution had added to the stress.

'He took an indigestion tablet. A few minutes later he complained of a pressure inside his chest.' Juliet clutched her own chest to mimic Ryan's actions. 'He massaged his jaw, next he's nauseous, light-headed.' Juliet gasped Ryan's final instruction to phone an ambulance. 'He said at first it felt like toothache.'

In reception Anita introduced herself as Ryan's sister and demanded an update on his condition.

'He's stable. Doctor diagnosed a mild attack but they'll keep him for a few days, to run tests as a precaution.'

The ward nurse consented to a five-minute visit.

A few days later Ryan went home with a restrictive activity schedule and a doctor's note that signed him off work for two weeks. Mr M asked Elliot to deputise.

Monday Elliot announced his upgraded position when he asked Tammy to clear the contents of his desk and divert his phone to Ryan's office. This irritated Abigail, who asked if Anita would be cross with her if she had sex on Elliot's temporary desk on the proviso Elliot wasn't sat there at the time.

Jake's Back

Anita ignored the commotion in the office, since the gossip of Ryan's heart attack and speculation on who'd replace him created a sense of unease that distracted the team from work and resulted in daily confabs. Instead Anita concentrated on the job profiles to accompany the advertisement for her new team.

'Pssst. Psst.'

Anita glanced towards the direction in which Abigail pointed, then stood to look past a small crowd of people congregated in the middle of the office. She recognised the back of the person who stood on the edge of the pack. He turned around. Anita waved. Jake smiled, then glanced at Elliot who looked up from conversation with Tammy.

Between scowls from Abigail and Juliet, Anita relented when the crowd dispersed. She took a deep breath and tried to sound cheery as she walked towards Jake, unsure what reaction she'd get. 'Hi, stranger, I've missed you. How'd you like Marsh Moore?'

Jake bit the inside of his lip. 'Hard work.' He rubbed his mouth with his hand.

Anita could see Elliot, Tammy, Juliet and Abigail watching from their respective desks.

'Say what's on your mind,' she said. Sorrow burned in her chest as the goodness from his soul shone in his blue eyes.

'This isn't the time or the place. Can we talk later? I'll call you.'

When Jake phoned her at home he declined Anita's offer of coffee with a suggestion to join him for dinner the next night. Jake texted ten minutes later to say he'd booked a table at the Italian and would pick her up at 7.30. Anita wondered what the odds were of sitting at the same table she'd sat at with Elliot.

Anita polled the girls to ask if her dinner with Jake might constitute a date. Juliet told her to pucker up and kiss him when he picked her up and see if he stayed or ran for his life. Donna told her not to fret and to enjoy herself. Abigail told her not to blow it with Jake, as she wouldn't get another chance.

Four fifteen she hurried from the office to get ready for her potential date with Jake. By 7.15, dressed in her emerald green Roman-style dress, Anita felt her heart exploding as every sound that resembled a car sent her darting to the window until Jake turned up at 7.25. He looked as if he'd stepped from of a magazine cover in his silver-grey Armani suit with a pale blue shirt and slate grey tie. Anita felt a flush come on.

Awkwardness filled the car as they engaged in polite conversation. Jake updated her on his mother's improved health. Anita told him the details of Ryan's job offer. In the restaurant when Jake slid Anita's coat off her shoulders a tingling sensation ran down her neck. When she'd dated Elliot her insides had felt like the Fourth of July celebrations. With Jake Anita felt alive in a different way, as if Cupid sat in her stomach and played pinball with her insides; her heart thumped and exploded like the rapid action of the metal ball bearing as it hit the high-value target and the electronic display racked up the points.

As they waited for their drinks, Jake tapped the table with the butt of his knife. He looked from under his lashes and smiled. The waiter took their food order. Jake took three gulps of water before he spoke.

'I wanted to bring this up before, in case you still want me to go with you, but, well, I'm not sure if I should … look, it's none of my business, I mean it's not like—'

'Oh, spit it out.' Jake looked stunned at Anita's tone. 'Sorry, patience has never been one of my qualities.' Anita smiled. 'Just be honest; I'm not good at reading between the lines.'

'What's happening with you and Carl?'

It was Anita's turn to be stunned. 'He's happy on his own; the sale of the house should resuscitate his depleted finances. I've contacted a solicitor to discuss a divorce—'

Jake cut her off. 'And Elliot, I heard, well, I kinda thought you two had a thing, look.'

'Well, you kinda thought wrong.' The sharpness of her tone caused the water boy to halt. Anita turned her head and listened for the ice to stop clinking as it dropped in the water glass. She looked back at Jake.

'Do you think you and him will get together?'

Anita told Jake the summed-up version of her history with Elliot. When she confessed she'd been to dinner with Elliot, Jake scraped his fork down the white linen tablecloth. Anita wondered what he'd do if she added how Elliot had brought her to the same restaurant.

'I wanted Elliot for a long time, but when he asked me to get together, I said no.'

'What about me?'

'You're too old for Elliot and your boobs are too small, he likes cleavage.'

Jake's attempted smile faded as he gripped hold of her hands. 'I mean you and me?'

'I like you a lot, Jake, but . . .'

Jake released her hands and pushed back. 'It's OK, I shouldn't have asked given the shit day I've had. You can spare me the "it isn't you" talk.'

'Excuse me. Before you rudely interrupted, I wanted to say I'd love to go out with you properly but I have to take any relationship slowly.'

'Because of Elliot?'

Anita's Scouse tone worsened as she raised her voice. 'No, but I'm ending thirty years of marriage to locate here alone. I'm scared. I don't want us to turn into a rebound relationship.'

Jake shook his head. He sat in silence and glared at her.

'What if this relationship's a flash in the pan? Juliet says there's an extremely low success rate for workplace romances.'

Jake explained his shock at the sight of Elliot touching her face. 'I pussyfooted around because I thought you might go back to your husband, look. When I watched Elliot and you I thought I'd blown my chances. I'm not ashamed to admit I was jealous. I picked the phone up every day to call you, then I heard a rumour you and Elliot were an item.'

Jake confessed he'd considered leaving when Mr M had asked him to return to Chrystalmere to help Elliot in Ryan's absence. Jake's plan had been to avoid Anita until Abigail had told him to grow a pair.

The date ended with a visit to Casey's for dessert. Tonight when they walked in Tess called them 'the lovebirds'.

Jake squeezed Anita's shoulders and kissed Tess on the cheek. 'You know you're my girl, Tess, but don't let on to Billy, look.'

Jake ordered Tess's homemade apple pie to share and two coffees. As they sat at their usual table Jake held Anita's hand. 'Mary Chapin concert; do you still want me to join you?'

Anita pulled Jake towards her and kissed him. 'Of course I do.'

They finished their pie, then bade goodnight to Tess, Billy and the three old codgers sitting by the door who made up the dominoes team. Jake searched for her hand as they walked through the car park.

At the chapel Jake left the engine running and walked his date to the front door. Anita melted like an ice cream in a baby's hands when she stretched her arms around Jake's waist. His tender kisses warmed her like summertime; she felt his firmness. Jake smiled and pushed his groin against her thigh, Anita wondered what he'd do if she did an Abigail special and whipped a tape measure from her bag.

As he kissed her again Anita inhaled his aftershave. 'Nice. Is that Gucci for Homme?'

'It took you long enough to notice. I bought a bottle ages ago when you told me you were a Gucci fan.' He squeezed her tighter for their final kiss.

Anita waved to Jake until the red taillights of his car disappeared onto the main road.

Over the next few days Juliet's texts to update Anita on Ryan's progress became infrequent as Ryan's health improved, although not quickly enough for Jake whose patience with Elliot had worn thin. He'd been especially annoyed when Elliot had redlined two grammatical errors in a thirty-page report Jake had hurried to prepare as a favour for him.

Jake deliberated for two days, then attended an interview for a civil engineer's position with a local company. When Jake returned from his interview Anita watched him pace to the window at the far end of the office and back to his desk. After the fourth lap Jake walked into Ryan's office and handed Elliot his resignation. Elliot told him to leave at the end of the week.

Mid-day Jake shut Anita's office door to update her on his phone call from Mr M. 'He's asked me to reconsider or at least postpone my plans. He said he needs my help with the Marsh Moore job until Ryan's back to full fitness and that Elliot's off in a couple of weeks.'

'What did you say? How'd you leave it?'

'I said I'd work a month's notice to give Ryan time to get back to work.'

It took all Anita's resolve not to throw her arms around Jake's neck and let out a yippee.

Despite his doctors' cautionary words a weary Ryan returned to work and evicted Elliot from his office.

Nicky

Anita posted the advertisement for the three vacancies in her new team: contract clerk, contract manager and development opportunity for contract specialist.

As she read Donna's weekly e-mail to count down the days to their fighting fifty Vegas holiday she pondered how it felt more like six weeks than six months since they'd excitedly discussed the holiday at Anita's fiftieth birthday surprise party.

Anita's mobile vibrated against the desk. Carl's name filled the screen. She suspected the house sale had fallen through.

'There's no easy way to put this: Nicky's dead.'

'I spoke to her last week; she came to my birthday party. She can't be. Who told you?' When Carl didn't answer she realised she'd dropped the phone on the floor. She checked Carl hadn't been disconnected, then repeated her question.

'Her brother's lad knocked; he didn't realise you'd moved.'

'How'd she die? She's fifty-four, how can she be dead?'

Carl recited what he'd been told; 'May came home from work; as her toddler was at nursery she thought Nicky had taken a nap. She made a cup of tea then tried to wake her mum. The ambulance man pronounced her dead.' Carl paused. 'The coroner's done an autopsy, ruled natural causes. Funeral's Tuesday afternoon.'

Carl suggested they say goodbye to Nicky together. When he added Anita's visit would be an appropriate time to clear the rest of her stuff from the house, it looked like she'd be burying more than Nicky.

Anita gave Abigail a brief update, asked her to reschedule her appointments until next Thursday, then went home.

Monday afternoon as Anita passed the coffee shop her mother's words haunted her. *You go nowhere until you've eaten breakfast, young lady.*

As the journey to Liverpool would take at least three and a half hours she went inside and ordered a toasted sandwich and a large latte. In exchange for money the till lady presented her with wooden spoon number four and instructed Anita to position the spoon in the holder at the end of the table. Anita ticked off her tasks; she'd ordered a wreath for the cemetery, a bouquet of flowers to be sent to Nicky's brother's house with a second spray sent to Cumbria for May. Anita recalled the three individual messages that accompanied her order, none of which truly expressed the depth of her sadness. A few moments later a waitress appeared and offered her customer the cheese and tomato toastie as ransom paid for the safe return of spoon number four. Anita ate out of duty rather than hunger. As she watched people pass through the coffee shop oblivious to the fact they could be snuffed from existence at any moment, Anita dwelled on the thought that Nicky wouldn't be around to answer her question from the ladies' lunch; she'd have to figure out for herself why heartache hurt as much at her age.

Distracted as she returned Jake's missed call, Anita stopped at the top of the car park ramp and scanned the line of silver four-by-fours looking for the one with the illuminated interior light. As long as the fob to her keyless Toyota Urban Cruiser came within a certain radius of the sensor, the light came on and when she touched the inside of the door handle the car unlocked.

Jake's voice crackled through the phone. 'Nita, you there, are you listening?'

Frantic, she rattled the handle as she listened for the click of the door lock. Nothing happened. 'The car door won't open. What am I going to do? I can't get the stupid door to open.' Her voice echoed panic around the hollow concrete structure.

'Where's your keys, have you checked your bag, your pockets?'

'Do yer think I'm a simpleton? Of course I've checked!' Anita plunged her hands into her coat pockets, then patted the outside for the umpteenth time.

The contents of her bag scattered onto the bonnet. 'I must've dropped them. I'll have to go back to the coffee shop.'

Three men walked up the ramp. Anita looked for the security cameras. A series of daytime rapes in a multi-storey car park in Liverpool years ago still came to mind when Anita found herself alone in a dimly lit car park. She waited for the men to pass. Tears welled up in her eyes as she whispered, 'What am I gonna do? I've gorra get to Liverpool. I can't get home and it'll cost more than the car's worth to get it out of the car park if I have to come back in a week or so.'

'Don't exaggerate; take a deep breath and think. Retrace your steps. I'll come and get you and take you to Liverpool if you can't find them.'

Anita's voice took an accuser's tone. 'Did you leave your suit jacket in the back of my car?'

'No. I wore my leather last time we went out.'

'Strange, there's a black jacket on the back seat.'

'Are you sure the car's yours?'

'Ummm, now I come to look, it's a Nissan.'

Anita made Jake stay on the phone as she scurried past the three men to the next floor where she'd actually parked. When she approached her car and the interior light came on she remembered she'd put her keys in the side pocket of her bag so as not to lose them.

Anita concluded her phone call to Jake when she told him she'd miss him too. Next she phoned Carl to tell him she'd organised the flowers and give him her estimated arrival time. Carl offered to stay in the flat he'd rented at the Albert Dock.

Weary from the frustration of the conga line of motorway traffic where instead of the three shuffle steps Anita got repetitive arm strain from the three-gear change, she arrived in Liverpool late Monday.

Unlike the home she'd been raised in, happy memories didn't rush to greet her at the door. The warmth from the oil-filled heaters left on low failed to combat the hollowness in the lounge. The abandoned workstation left no evidence of its part in Carl's extensive gambling activity. Anita picked up the redundant power lead left over from the technology that had flashed betting odds in line with the deep excitable rumble of the sports commentator's voice.

As she stood on the hearth to warm her legs in front of the log effect gas fire she touched the wall to check the fresh magnolia emulsion that decorated the discoloured lounge walls had dried. Polyfilla smoothed the scarred plaster they'd concealed with Carl's treasured Grand National 1985 limited edition print, which sat covered in bubble wrap and propped up in the corner. Anita grabbed a tissue to wipe the dust-covered ornaments displaced on the mantelpiece by Carl's clutter. She tossed discarded till receipts in the bin, scooped up the slummy and dropped it into her handbag.

As she waited for the kettle to boil she packed a few items from the kitchen cupboard into an empty box. Carl had stocked the fridge with cold meats, a bottle of Jack Daniel's and a pack of two-litre bottles of Diet Coke. Anita poured a small measure of bourbon into her coffee cup. Upstairs freshly laundered sheets, a winter quilt and two clean towels sat on top of the ottoman.

Hormones combined with grief to interrupt Anita's sleep. The quilt she'd discarded with the irregularity of her night sweats lay crumpled on the floor. As she reached for the switch on the plastic table fan the edge of the sheet that barely covered her naked body slipped away. Too exhausted to get out of bed, Anita rolled towards the breeze. With another death of someone she loved she prepared for the five stages of grief: denial, anger, bargaining, depression and acceptance. Anita reckoned at the rate she attended funerals she could have a career as a professional mourner.

Agitated she contorted her body to find a comfortable position; with a tug she gathered up the quilt and rolled onto her back to snuggle into the winter comforter. When the random symptoms returned, she kicked the quilt from her legs. Anita ripped tissues from the box next to her pillow as an unexpected wave of upset engulfed her when she thought about Nicky's mum's ring-stained teak oval coffee table with a print of the Taj Mahal under a glass centre.

Thoughts of Nicky's death renewed her mortality obsession as a scroll of dead faces came to the forefront of her mind. Anita lay still in the darkened bedroom and imagined herself shut in a coffin. Her skin itched at the thought of the insect world congregating to feed on her rotting flesh. Damn the circle of life. Anita wanted to be cremated.

Creepy thoughts shot through her body like the shock of a defibrillator. Alert, she abandoned her attempt to sleep. In memory of her friend she made a cup of tea and recalled how on pay day she'd call in to Nicky's on the way home from work with a chippy supper and a bag of scallops. As Nicky's mum rushed out of the house to make the early session of bingo, the friends fell into their well-rehearsed routine: Nicky turned up the gas on the stove, warmed the plates and buttered a heap of bread. As Anita laid the kitchen table she'd wait for the kettle to whistle, then replace the centrepiece vase of plastic flowers with a teapot kept warm by the cosy Nicky's brother made in needlecraft. Then they'd eat chip butties, drink gallons of tea and natter well into the early hours.

Tuesday the weatherman talked of the wettest June since time began or some equally useless statistic. In the afternoon, as she and Carl stood at the churchyard, the summer sun struggled through the gloomy clouds to shine on a handful of mourners who waited for Nicky's remains to arrive.

Carl grumbled how he'd been awake most of the night with toothache. He'd lost count of the number of tablets he'd taken to numb the pain long enough to fall asleep. In thirty years, Anita couldn't remember Carl ill apart from his annual bout of man flu. She mentioned how Ryan had fobbed off his heart attach as toothache. Carl dismissed her concern until Anita reminded him that he could die in his chair and nobody would know until the stench of decomposition reached a neighbour's nostrils or his betting provider rushed to his aid as their profits were down. He relented and let her phone the dentist for an emergency appointment. The receptionist pencilled Carl in for the next day.

*

A lone piper played *Amazing Grace* as the congregation followed Nicky's oldest son, who held the urn of his mother's ashes like a bridal bouquet until he passed them to the vicar who laid Nicky to rest in her parents' grave.

Anita had a vision of Nicky bumping into their mums in heaven. Her first words would be, 'Come on, Greta, pass us a fag. Mam, get the kettle on.'

The service concluded with an invitation from Nicky's brother to join them for drinks to toast Nicky's life. Carl offered his condolences to the children and left.

As mourners sat in the small lounge to swap stories, Anita wondered when she looked at May all grown up where the time had gone. Watching babies play on the floor as toddlers ran in and out of the garden to remind how precious a gift life could be. Anita had sat with Nicky through each of her three pregnancies; she knew it wasn't right but May was always her favourite.

One of the tots slobbered the word 'Grandma' as he kissed a picture of his nan. Although Anita had umpteen pictures of the children she had none of Nicky. Clearer than any photograph her mind pictured her friend, legs dangled over the armchair to hold a small mirror between her knees so she could pluck her eyebrows as she shared her pearls of wisdom. Anita curled up on the couch to listen as her confidante reinforced how the melodramatic experiences, regardless of how unique they felt, were merely part of growing up. Nicky would stop talking long enough to swig her tea, take a drag of her ciggy or use the butt to light up the next. Before her mum got home from bingo, she'd spray the can of cheap lavender air freshener she kept at the side of her chair to mask the odour of stale tobacco and stop her mum from nagging.

The mourners dispersed when babies needed a bottle and the younger children whinged as they grabbed their favourite toy to curl up on their mother's knee. May, who needed a cuddle of her own, rested her head on Anita's lap.

An hour later as Anita said goodbye to Nicky's family, she accepted she wouldn't see them again despite the promises to keep in touch.

Standing in the hall Anita faced the sober realisation that the six boxes piled up by the front door were the coffins that buried her marriage. She checked the time and phoned to check on Carl to coincide with the end of the afternoon race meeting. She panicked as his slurred words sounded as if he'd had a stroke. Anita stood in the porch to get a strong signal on her mobile. 'What is it, what's up? Are you OK?'

Carl stuttered his garbled words: 'I've won the tote jackpot.'

'What does that mean?'

'I've picked six winners.'

'Check your bet to be sure; you're doped up to the eyeballs.'

'I thought the bet had gone down. I did a few combinations, as it was a rollover. I checked the printout a million times. I know I've been out of it with these painkillers but I included the winner of the last race by mistake.'

'Have they paid you?'

'I've got just short of £300,000 in my account. That's why I left the funeral early; I wanted to put a few bets on. You know what it's like and Nicky'd understand.'

Anita felt genuinely pleased for Carl. Although their marriage had ended Anita would save a special place in her heart for the best friend she'd ever had.

'I'll pay up what I owe you with a bit extra. That should stop you nagging.'

Her goodbye to Carl seemed less affectionate than the one to Elliot as he hung up for the start of the night racing.

The next day Carl told her the dentist had diagnosed the cause of the toothache, which had been instrumental in Carl's change of fortune, as an abscess. Anita thought how her father often said blessings came wearing different disguises.

It's Not the Leaving
of Liverpool

The artificial flames from the log effect fire glowed in the unadorned lounge. Jets of gas-powered heat warmed her grief in a way the June sunset couldn't as she sat amongst bubble wrap cut into strips to safeguard her collection of authentic Navaho white stoneware, lined up across the glass display case like front-line defence soldiers.

Anita sipped a large Jack Daniel's diluted with an equal measure of Diet Coke as she wrapped each piece and placed it in a box padded with discarded copies of the *Racing Post*. To delay the task of packing the last of her personal effects Anita poured another large Jack with a disproportionate volume of mixer, then another, then another.

By midnight impending doom devoured her essence. She surrendered to the urge to barricade herself in the house that had been her dream home. As she stood in her self-imposed tomb the thud of her heart penetrated the solitude. Alcohol combined with a flush to choke her from inside. Anita tore at her neck as if she wore a noose. Claustrophobia seized her as the curtains she'd hung with pride confined her to the prison she'd exiled herself to. Anita pushed open the top window. A breeze parted the fabric bars to tempt her escape; frantic, she opened all the windows and gasped to fill her lungs with fresh air. When she turned to allow the breeze to dry her drenched neck she became transfixed by the three feathers of the dream catcher that hung off an old picture hook. Her symbol of hope took the form of a coyote that howled to the heavens jailed within a turquoise leather circle. Anita harmonised to the rhythm of the tassels that swayed in the breeze, then laughed at the irony of how hard she'd tried to catch her dreams. She couldn't comprehend why the reflection in the window cried.

The aroma of freesia and jasmine from the table air freshener filled the air to resurrect the memory of an innocent young girl who played in her Wendy house one long-forgotten summer's day. Anita stared into the night sky, which glistened with a million stars and trapped the memory of her father tending his colourful assortment of flowers; she longed to be the child who'd chosen wild poppy seeds as the picture on the packet looked pretty when Mummy chose pink and white trailing plants. Carl never planted a seed; he hated gardening; he'd mow the lawn and spread weed killer, then leave the dehydrated clumps of brown foliage to disintegrate.

As Anita yearned for a pretty garden to sit in, the sadness of reality rose up to be set free in a tearful exit. Anita muffled her sobs as she clasped her mouth with a fresh tissue from her bra strap. Calmed by her childhood memories, Anita tried to rationalise what had induced this meltdown: her current tribulations, the realisation that life passed too rapidly or the grief for the loss of her friend, Carl and her childhood.

The intrusion to the stillness of the atmosphere came from each heartbeat that incarcerated her pain. Like a death row inmate on execution day she had come to the time to purge her past, make restitution and unshackle the emotions that held her hostage.

Thirty years of marriage concluded as she placed the last ornament in a sheet of bubble wrap, placed it in the box and taped down the lid.

Mid-afternoon Anita awoke in a delicate state, took two tablets and a hot shower. In the bathroom mirror Anita investigated her face from an alternative perspective. She no longer recognised the tracks of the fine lines she traced with her fingertip as a definition of age; instead they chronicled the excitement of the journey life had taken her on. The laughter lines stood as a memento from years of happiness. Stored behind her grey eyebrows lived a mind full of experiences that had made her strong, confident, accomplished, to emerge as a vibrant woman who looked damned good for fifty.

As she packed the boxes in the back of her car she embraced the future; she had a great job, sincere friends, despite the dissolution of her marriage her relationship with Carl remained cordial, she'd said an amicable farewell to Elliot and her professional and personal relationship with Jake had possibilities.

A final check of the house completed, like the star of a long-running Broadway play Anita rose with dignity for her farewell performance, Carl's Grand National print destined to be the audience for her curtain call. Anita bowed to the invisible crowd. Aware her life had been punctuated rather than extinguished she stood at the door, took one final glance, picked up her suitcase, tossed her house keys on the table, whispered goodbye to her past and slammed the front door.

The Concert

En route to the concert they strolled past private boats lined up along the harbour and Friday night revellers spilling out of the bars, which blurred similar versions of heavy-beat dance hits. With half an hour to kill they stopped at a trendy coffee house preparing to close on the hour.

Anita slipped off her heels and scrunched up with Jake on the soft leather settee. She wriggled her hand under Jake's lamb's wool sweater, then pushed two fingers between the buttons she'd opened on his shirt. As she combed her nails through his navel hair, her hand roamed the warmth of his flesh. A deeper arousal tingled within her.

Jake wriggled. 'What I can expect from this concert?'

'Did you know Mary Chapin Carpenter's *Come On Come On* album is the first country CD I bought? And seven of the songs made the *Billboard* hot country single charts.'

'Can't we stay here and snuggle?' Jake nuzzled her neck.

Anita undid two more buttons on his shirt and let her hand roam his stomach. Her finger glided across his hard nipple. Jake wriggled again, then kissed the tip of her nose.

'She sings folk and country.'

Jake leaned his head on the back of the settee and murmured. As her hand rested below his belly button she tucked her pinkie finger in the band of his jeans.

The young girl eager to join the Friday night fun crowd shouted a ten-minute warning to closing time.

Disinclined to move, Anita rubbed her face into the softness of Jake's sweater. Like a bunting feline she released pheromones to mark her territory. 'Let's go before I ravish your body.'

Jake glanced around to check nobody could hear. 'They had a name for girls like you in school.'

Anita laughed. Jake kissed her nose, then headed to the gents'.

At the concert Mary Chapin Carpenter sang Anita's favourite songs: *Passionate Kisses, He Thinks He'll Keep Her, I Feel Lucky* and *The Hard Way*. She entertained her audience with witty anecdotes as her roadies swapped her guitar between each number. Anita laughed at the political quips although the American satire appeared lost on Jake and most of the Bristol audience. The singer touched on personal experiences and how much she loved her dogs. Anita thought how much she missed Tara.

On the walk back to the car park they tangoed like ballroom dancers as Jake swung Anita's hand then pulled her close to slip his arm around her waist. She gasped in anticipation of a kiss. Jake stopped, pivoted Anita, then serenaded his partner with his Bristolian version of his favourite song of the concert: *Shut Up and Kiss Me, Look.*

When Jake pulled into the driveway of the chapel he left the engine running as they kissed goodnight.

She could hardly breathe when his urgency for her taste reached a crescendo.

'I had a great night,' Jake gasped as he poised himself inches from her face.

'Actually the night isn't over yet.'

Jake turned off the engine and followed her inside.

New Beginnings

When Juliet invited Jake and Anita to their first social event as a couple Jake repeatedly asked if he had to go; Anita repeatedly told him yes.

Saturday night the warmth of Juliet's hospitality and the smell of Lancashire hotpot welcomed them into her country cottage. Unlike Anita's home Juliet had antique furniture that complemented the olde-worlde style of exposed wooden beams and original stone floor.

Juliet placed a tray of nibbles on the hand-carved thick oak occasional table. 'Dinner won't be long.' She dealt out coasters like a blackjack dealer.

Ryan passed the drinks to their guests, then settled into his favourite chair as Anita updated Jake and Juliet on the applicants for her new team.

'Tammy beat the competition for the contract clerk position by a mile. She actually aided her application with a clear statement of her career aspirations and a short summary of the work she'd managed for Elliot.' Anita looked at Ryan. 'Tell them who *you* made me pick for contract manager.'

Ryan embellished the tale of the one application from Bitchy Beryl and how Anita had frantically double-checked the other piles to see if an application had been misfiled.

Juliet laughed.

Anita pulled a face of displeasure. 'He convinced me to consider Beryl given, what did you call it, oh yes, her "improved conduct".'

Juliet threw a cushion at Ryan. 'You're mean.'

Ryan tucked the cushion behind his back.

Jake winked at Anita. 'Beryl did a good job when she worked for me.'

Juliet threw a second cushion at Jake, then got up to check on dinner.

'Oh yes, when exactly: when she hid documents from me or when she screwed up the electronic contract files?' Anita spoke louder so Juliet could hear from the kitchen. 'Anyway, I relented and agreed to give her a six-month probation period.'

The smell of scorched potatoes sent them scurrying to the dinner table. Juliet dished out the hearty meal. Ryan placed chunks of crusty bread in the middle of the table. A nervous Jake held Anita's hand.

Anita asked, 'Did you tell Juliet who we selected for contract specialist?'

He replied no so Anita summarised how she'd rejected the four applications as none of them demonstrated experience. 'Then Ryan tossed an application pack on the desk: Donna's.'

Juliet and Anita shared a look that didn't require words. They both knew how hard Donna had worked and what a wonderful opportunity it was for their friend.

As the guys couldn't keep track of the multiple conversations that covered the cookery shows Juliet found herself addicted to and Anita's summary of the plots for the must-watch American TV programmes, the dinner conversation turned to football despite Juliet's objections. Bored of sport, Juliet updated Anita with the latest instalment of gossip from the ramblers' society's hotbed of seniors who enjoyed a mid-day tipple and occasional romp.

Juliet served cheese then tapped her port glass with a fork. 'Ryan and I have an announcement.'

'Bloody hell, you're getting married or you're pregnant?'

'If you'd shut your gob for a minute, chuck, I'll tell you.' Juliet took hold of Ryan's hand. 'May I introduce the new South West director, to be based in Marsh Moore?'

Anita recognised Ryan's promotion as a shrewd play from Mr M in response to the rumours that touted Raymond as the client's next director of projects for the southern region. Ryan deserved the promotion, although Jake despaired at the news.

'I thought it would be like old times when Donna got here. You know I'll miss you both.'

Juliet grabbed the laptop. 'It's, what, a few hours down the road?' She clicked the link to the dream property they wanted to rent.

Ryan cleared his throat. 'I've been asked to recommend someone to replace me when I go to Essex.'

Jake nodded and spoke curtly. 'When's Elliot back?'

Anita refused to look at Jake's 'told you so' expression.

Ryan's mouth twitched. 'Actually I'm asking you.'

Anita gave Jake her own 'told you so' gesture and stuck out her tongue

Ryan offered to make coffee; he asked Jake to help. The kitchen door ajar, Juliet and Anita listened in on the conversation. Jake expressed his opinion that he had expected Elliot to be Ryan's first choice. Ryan explained Elliot had declined a prestigious role as engineering manager; he had said he wanted a new challenge.

As the girls cleared the table Anita joked how the sight of the men retiring to a different room to talk of important issues while the women cleaned up resembled Victorian times. Except instead of a scullery maid Juliet had a dishwasher.

When they agreed not to listen any more Juliet shouted in her best Yorkshire accent, 'Put wood in t'oil, will you?'

The menfolk closed the door to carry on their discussion in private.

''Ey, chuck, looks like we'll both be sleeping with our bosses.'

Jake asked for the weekend to consider Ryan's proposal.

Shai, the God of Fate and Destiny

Anita glanced at the clock through bleary eyes and realised she'd slept through the alarm. She dragged herself from her cosy bed and switched on the hair straighteners. As Anita stood in the shower it occurred to her she'd switched off the alarm, as she would be heading to Gatwick later that afternoon to meet the girls for pre-holiday fun. The 'fighting your fifties' flight to Vegas departed Tuesday but they'd booked Monday night at an airport hotel to catch up and unwind.

Anita opened the suitcase she'd wheeled into the hall to check the contents of her luggage. In between striking items from the list Anita checked her mobile for a text from Jake to say he'd left Manchester. Jake, who'd taken the reins of the Chrystalmere division from Ryan, had spent four of the last five weekends in Manchester. Anita accepted he needed to submerge himself into his new role but this afternoon was the last opportunity for a cuddle before she left for Vegas.

The introduction to Sara Evans's *A Real Fine Place to Start* stirred Anita's mobile. A picture of Jake's smile lit up the screen.

Anita looked at her watch. 'You're late; the traffic will be murder this time of day.'

'Sorry, hun, I have to stay in Manchester.'

The warmth of the August sun burst through grey clouds to remind Anita to find her sunglasses; she added them to the bottom of her list. 'So I won't see you before I leave.'

'The strategy threw up more questions than solutions. I have a consultation this afternoon and a ton of work to prep for Tuesday.'

Anita rushed into the kitchen to get the aloe vera from the fridge. 'Face-time me later; I'll show you what you've missed.' She tossed the half-empty sunburn gel into her case.

'Actually, I need a favour.' Jake paused. 'The client's rescheduled the meeting to introduce the new head honcho who's replacing Raymond to today at eleven. Will you go for me?'

'I'm on holiday.'

'Go on, it's important. I'll be indebted to you forever.'

'You'll owe me big time, buster.'

'When you get back from Vegas we can book a weekend break, anywhere you want, then I can show you my appreciation.'

Anita's heart palpitated, exhilarated at the thought of Jake and a romantic location.

'This new head honcho will be the main liaison for the current portfolio of work and the five-year extension plus the Marsh Moore job. No doubt we'll have to pander to his idiosyncrasies and pre-conceived ideas of how the project should be delivered, as he stamps his authority to impress his peers.'

Anita laughed. 'Portfolio, peers, and idiosyncrasies: we might have to play bullshit bingo if you keep talking in management speak.'

Despite her unsettled feeling she agreed to represent Jake.

She lined up the products for her anti-aging routine, which had escalated since she had slept with a man seven years her junior, then removed the polythene wrapper that protected her crepe skirt suit, cut off the price tag and hung a black and pink spotted scarf to check it would complement the black piping around the pale pink jacket to give the outfit a mature look. Her stomach growled in annoyance when the kitchen clock confirmed no time for breakfast.

Edginess knotted Anita's stomach to a point where she considered phoning Raymond to see if he'd postpone the unveiling of the new head honcho until Jake came back from Manchester. She reminded herself she'd be in work long enough to collect her file and check she had no urgent messages, then she would meet the client in Bristol. By one o'clock she'd be home and in holiday mode and Jake would be appreciative of her help.

Abigail greeted Anita with an update. 'Time's changed. They asked if you could make 1.30, I said yes.'

With time on the clock Anita grabbed a coffee.

'You OK? You look washed out.'

'I could do without this today. I feel odd. My head's muzzy, I can't for the life of me organise my thoughts.' Anita picked a handful of crisps from an open packet on Abigail's desk.

'When we're in the hotel bar tonight you can forget work. What time we meeting everyone?'

To check her logic Anita closed her eyes to run through the schedule. 'I pick you and Juliet up at four. Donna, Libby and Merlot got an afternoon flight from Liverpool.' Anita looked at her watch. 'They'll be in the bar by three.'

'I can't believe tomorrow we're off on holiday; for the next ten days we can bask in a hundred degrees of heat.' Abigail picked up the empty coffee cups and looked at the sky. 'You better get a move on, the rain's about to lash down. Typical British summer.'

Abigail waved from the office window as Anita quickened her pace to cross the car park, the moisture-packed grey clouds dashing from the horizon to engulf the sky. The wind picked up a paper bag which scurried across the asphalt, stuck to Anita's leg then scuttled away to cling to a wheel hub.

Entombed in her car Anita came under fire from the wet bullets that pelleted from every direction. She rubbed her temples, as the wrath of the gods echoed through her head to form a migraine behind her eyes.

The slow journey into Bristol intensified her headache. She squinted between the paces of the erratic wipers, then judged whether to stop or move by the brightness from the brake lights of the car in front.

As Anita sheltered in the multi-storey car park exit doorway, to wait for a break in the miserable day, she phoned Jake to reassure him she'd arrived fully prepared, with time to spare. Their five minutes' conversation added to her woe.

'I spoke to Raymond. I explained I'd delegated to you. He said he'd tell me the name of his replacement but then he'd have to kill me.'

'Maybe he thinks you should come back from Manchester.'

'No. I asked him. There's something going on.' Anita heard a mumble of voices as Jake's colleagues came back into the room. 'Maybe I should drive back?'

'Don't worry, I'll show a bit of cleavage and thigh to cover my bases.'

Anita heard Mr M's dulcet tone. Jake lowered his voice. 'You keep your boobs and legs for my eyes only.'

'Honestly, I'll be fine. I'll phone as soon as the meeting's ended.'

'I'm still surprised I haven't heard who the replacement is, given the grapevine in this industry.'

Anita looked at the sky. The large dark cloud hung overhead. 'I'm gonna make a dash for cover; the sky's black. I'll call you when I get back to the car.'

Anita's irritation squished in her stomach. Jake was right; in this industry the gossip mill kept the projects running. Ten yards down the high street the heavens opened.

Anita shielded her face from the rain as she peered between the spokes of her handbag-sized umbrella. She sidestepped a large pool of water, then stumbled into a café sign tied to a drainpipe. The picture of hot food and a vapour-rich coffee encapsulated behind the plastic cover stirred Anita's tummy to gurgle. Through a clearing in the steamed-up window Anita spied an empty table in the far corner. She paused on the doormat to close her umbrella as a woman in supersized tan spandex pants with an arse like a vandalised bus seat, as Mark from the sidings would say, bent in front of the counter to shake her hair like an Afghan hound.

'You know, Doris, my old mum used to say without the rain there'd be no rainbow.'

Anita took her place in line as Doris wiped the Formica

surface with a coffee-stained dish cloth and dried her hands on the tea towel tucked in her apron.

'That'll be £3. Take your tea, dearie, I'll bring your food.'

The hound panted to the table nearest the counter.

Doris turned her attention to Anita. 'What can I get you, dearie?'

Doris rang up the hot dog and large coffee order as Anita answered yes to onions, mustard and tomato sauce.

'Fully loaded dog, Bernie; take your coffee, dearie. I'll bring your food when it's ready.'

Doris and the Afghan exchanged weather predictions they'd heard on the news and how the inclement weather for early August had given the police a chance to regain control of the protestors who'd recently taken part in the countrywide riots. Anita checked the white plastic clock above the counter; with forty-five minutes until the meeting she asked for a caffeine refill when Doris delivered her fully loaded hot dog.

As Doris returned with a fresh cup, she pulled the tea towel from her apron. 'Oh, dearie, your lovely jacket!'

The orange dribble from a clump of onion mixed with yellow and red condiments had left a Morse-code message down the lapel of her expensive suit, then added a full stop in the bow on her black leather court shoe. Doris pointed to the toilets. Anita grabbed the tea towel. Instead of blotting out the stain she managed to leave herself with a miniature version of the Japanese flag on her lapel. She wished she'd stayed in bed as she held her head under the hair dryer and gave her damp hair a sharp brush. She held her breath to lacquer her hair, then applied a generous spray of Gucci to her neck, wrists and cleavage and a quick spray up her skirt. She rolled gloss over a fresh coat of pink lippy, then positioned the handles of her shoulder bag to mask the stain. Anita dropped the tea towel on the counter, thanked Doris and tossed a pound in the plastic tip cup.

Anita presented herself to the new head honcho's PA with five minutes to spare.

'Miss Richardson, this way.'

Obedient, Anita sat in one of three chairs outside an office labelled *Senior Project Development Manager*. She presumed the discoloured area below came from the predecessor's nameplate.

As Anita contorted her head to peek under the slats of the part-closed blinds she jumped when the door opened and a rounded man with cherry-red cheeks bustled from the office. He took a large handkerchief from his top pocket and wiped his brow.

As he approached the PA he muttered, 'He's a hard one to please.'

Anita's nerves jittered. 'Just what I need: the meeting from hell with an arrogant idiot.'

The expressionless PA glared in Anita's direction. Embarrassed she'd been caught talking to herself, Anita asked a question: 'Do I have time to visit the ladies'?'

With her elbow balanced on the desk the PA let her wrist flop to the right; with her finger pointed, she reluctantly replied, 'End of the corridor.'

Anita checked her appearance as she practiced her hello in the mirror. Distracted by the stain, she ripped a length of loo roll from the dispenser, smeared liquid soap on it then added water. As she rubbed the infected spot of her lapel the damp patch became encrusted with flaky white tissue paper. As only a piece of Beryl's oversized costume jewellery could obscure the papier-mâché stain Anita adjusted her scarf to fall like a clergyman's stole.

The PA knocked on the outer door. 'They're ready for you.'

Raymond greeted Anita in the hallway, then manoeuvred her into the office as the new head honcho barked his instructions into the phone. Anita recognised the shirt stretched across his broad shoulders. Raymond stood by the window, unable to conceal a smirk. Transfixed on the familiar torso, she felt for the chair. Like she'd been hit by an assassin's bullet, the full weight of her body dropped onto the seat; her bag and file hit the floor a few seconds later.

Her mouth agape she glanced at Raymond.

The new head honcho made his authority clear. He continued his telephone conversation without acknowledging her presence. He ended his conversation, swivelled the chair then replaced the receiver.

Raymond stood behind the new head honcho, with both hands resting on the back of the same beige luxury recliner chair she'd asked Abigail to order for Jake's office. 'May I introduce you to our new senior project development manager?'

Anita pushed her tongue against the roof of her mouth to generate saliva, then swallowed. 'Elliot. What you doing here?'

'I accepted a generous offer from the client to join them. Shall we get down to business?'

Although she'd interpreted the dreams and nightmares that featured Elliot as premonitions, not in her wildest fantasies had she foreseen this encounter.

Anita shook Raymond's hand and wished him every success in his new career when he offered to leave them to it.

Elliot grinned. 'I'm unhappy with your subcontract submissions; they're erroneous.'

Anita adjusted her posture to sit tall in response to his challenge on the accuracy of her work.

Elliot nodded to the three subcontracts she'd submitted for approval, which sat on the edge of his desk. 'I'd like a comprehensive explanation, to convince me how, contractually, I won't be vulnerable.'

Anita wanted to slap him. Her heart raced. 'I can work on the report this afternoon and e-mail you a revision tonight.'

Elliot strummed his fingers on the desk, then reclined with both hands clasped behind his head; he cracked his fingers. 'I've marked up my areas of concern. I'd prefer to debate this now. Do I have to remind you of the implications if I accept your proposals willy-nilly? You can claim contractual inclusion later.'

Anita hoped for a meteorite to strike the Earth and obliterate her from existence as Elliot sought payback for her outburst at the sidings. She knew Elliot's status forced her to be agreeable regardless of her personal feelings; like a breaking news alert on the TV, the department motto ran through her head: *Whatever you can do to keep the client happy.* Jake would be livid when she told him.

For the next hour they battled. Elliot failed to hide the pleasure he took as he watched her squirm. As her agitation elevated Anita squeezed her eyebrow.

Elliot smirked. 'I'm still to be convinced. And before you get tempted I suggest you don't throw the papers in the air.'

The banter as Elliot imposed his authority made the tedious fun. She flirted a little when a speckled rash formed on Elliot's neck, was satisfied she'd made him nervous when the rash deepened. At the end of the meeting she'd won the battle but not the war.

'Have a good holiday. I look forward to next time; make sure Jake attends.'

'Will do, Mr Parker.' She mimed a tug of her forelock.

As Anita left the office the PA gave her a quizzical look. 'You're the first person to come from his office with a smile.'

Anita felt happy at the prospect of working with Elliot. She kept that snippet of news to herself when she phoned Jake. At least the day's events would stimulate an interesting topic of conversation with the girls on the ten and a half hour flight to Vegas.

10 Tips for Fighting Fifty

1. Look forward; life's measured in new experiences, not missed opportunities.
2. Count a year as 365 full days, not twelve short months to tick off the next birthday.
3. Allow yourself to dream without limits.
4. Pick goals that inspire you to smile.
5. For every negative think of a positive.
6. Adopt a good anti-aging routine for your face as that's the face you see each day in the mirror.
7. Allow yourself indulgences.
8. Forgive yourself for the mistakes you've made, even if you make them again; hindsight is a wonderful thing.
9. When you arrive at a crossroad in the broken road of life, take a new route; if it leads nowhere, then move in a different direction; just don't ever stop your journey.
10. It's the individual mixtures of qualities and idiosyncrasies that distinguish us. Appreciate the uniqueness of the woman you've become and don't let stereotypical ideas force you into conforming to other people's ideals. Be the person you want to be, embrace your freedom to think for yourself and don't constrain your mind to limit what you wish for.

Lightning Source UK Ltd.
Milton Keynes UK
UKOW04f1827281115

263699UK00001B/13/P